THE TEACHERS' ROOM

LYDIA STRYK

Bywater BOOKS

2022

For the teachers
and in memory of Esther Bauer and Wesley Gibson

PART
ONE

THE
CLASSROOM

·

FALL 1963

1

"I don't think you're an Indian, Lydie."

The girls titter, the boys let out war whoops.

"I am, too," she says, and defiance flashes in her dark brown eyes, those flaming orbs. There's enough fire in those eyes to burn the school down, but you fall into them, just the same.

She's starting a new game. It appears to be called Staring at Miss Murphy. I am trying very hard to ignore her scrutiny, but it's impossible to look away. She's making me self-conscious, and I'm at her mercy. I feel tears welling up, which I'm fighting to contain. And there she sits, dead center in the classroom, like the earth's molten core, her tangled auburn hair lit devil red by the sun.

"The Illini were force-marched out West from Illinois more than a hundred years before you were born," I say, and I write FORCE-MARCHED in big letters on the board.

But she's not impressed. She's drumming on her desk. She's very good, as it happens, very rhythmic. If you close your eyes, you might be on the plains. "Close your eyes, class. Let's listen to Lydie beat the drum," I hear myself saying.

She stops, astonished, hands in midair, and then she carries on. We listen, eyes closed. The beats rise up to the high ceiling and fall back down, reverberating through the body. The children join in, at first slowly, in ones and twos, until they're all at it. The scuffed wood floor buckles under us and the walls give way. We're transported somewhere, I don't know where. But the hour's up. The children toss their battered American history books in their desks and scurry off homeward.

"Don't forget your gym bags!" I call out. "Or your homework!" And "Have a happy weekend, children!"

"You, too, Miss Murphy!" most cry out, but not Lydie. She's among the first to dash away.

She's got an important job as school patrol, on the corner of my block, wouldn't you know, where she directs the children over leafy South Tenth like a New York City policeman at a busy intersection. From up the road on my way home, I'm stopped by her wild gesturing and fierce commands. As I approach, she looks right through me as if we've never met and blows her whistle. The whistle's shrill cry pierces the air, sending shivers through me. *What have I done to you, Lydie?* I ask her, under my breath. *Give me a chance at least.* But she's already turned her back on me.

I walk on, fighting feelings of antipathy toward her, even ill will, feelings a teacher must avoid at all costs, I know. *Poor Lydie*, I say, without conviction. To look at her, you'd swear she's been neglected. Those scruffy jumpers, straps permanently falling off her shoulders, socks around her ankles, that hair. But nothing I've heard about her home life—her father teaches art up at the college, her mother is apparently devoted—comes close to explaining her behavior, which feels calculated to upend all my lesson plans. With all the sympathy in the world, life under Lydie Kaminski's rule is proving exasperating.

2

"Drink this," Esther Jonas says, placing a steaming cup in my hands. "It'll give you strength."

She sits down across the table from me in the tidy teachers' room, with its lone window looking out at the school gym, its dog-eared reference books and teaching manuals sorted with care on the shelves, its kitchen a mere sideboard with kettle, its rickety table, chairs—and in the corner, its lumpy couch, where Irene Bachmeier, third-grade teacher, is currently dozing, head back against the pillow. The coffee is good, strong, and sweet. Esther is watching me with a look of pity, but there's something else in her look, something like surprise at what she sees, and I find myself blushing. She notices and looks down at her lap. *Don't look away*, I want to say. *I like your eyes on me.*

She's looking up at me again.

"It's tough being new, Karen," she says, gently.

"Well, I feel old already," I tell her.

She laughs in response, and suddenly I'm feeling better, able to admit that some of the children have their own ideas as to what should happen over the course of a lesson. I can't bring myself to mention Lydie, however. It would be like salting a wound.

"They're testing you, that's all. That's what they do, I'm afraid. It's practically the rule by fifth grade. You mustn't take it personally. Repeat that to yourself at least twice a day. They're children; they're ten years old; never forget that. And we're adults."

Esther Jonas is in her mid-thirties, I'd guess. She's been teaching fourth grade here for *twelve long years*, as she puts it. I have so many questions, and she's always ready with an answer: where the school supplies are kept, for example, or how to use the library. But then, everyone's been lovely. From Will Lindquist the jovial principal on down to all the teachers and Dorothy Hughes, the school secretary who pretty much runs things here, I'm quickly discovering, and who doubles as our school nurse. Even the janitor, Cliff Johnson, has gone out of his way to make me feel at home, fixing my wobbly desk and the stubborn window at the front of the class. And generally speaking, I'm content. It was a kind of joy I felt climbing the stairs of the old red brick school building for the first time up to the top floor and stepping into my very own large sunlit classroom.

And it's joy I'm feeling now with Esther. My uncertainty has vanished just like that. It'll all work out, like Esther says. She's here to guide me.

"You're right," I tell her, grinning from ear to ear. "I'm the adult. I seem to have forgotten that."

"You're new to teaching and the school," Esther says, observing me with some amusement. "The children sense that instinctively. And as if that isn't enough, you're young." She stops and sighs with yearning. "But that will pass in time. Much too quickly, in fact. It happens to us all, doesn't it, Irene?"

Irene Bachmeier opens one eye, then two, and struggles up from the couch to join us at the teachers' table. "Discipline and boundaries. That's what the children need," she says, and I realize she's been listening the whole time. "You must establish order, Karen. Only then can learning take place."

4

That learning took place in Miss Bachmeier's third-grade classroom was legendary. The children of workers who canned corn and peas, operated the wire and cable machines, bagged seed, built pianos or small motors on the edge of town *learned*. As did the children of seamstresses at Brody's coat factory and the sleepy-eyed sons and daughters of farmers bused in early from surrounding corn, wheat and dairy farms. Irene's children learned by rote and recitation, drilling and quizzing, methods newly under question at the teacher's college, but that didn't stop the children from learning. And without exception, they were held to the highest standards and expectations.

"And learning is the goal, is it not, after all?"

She stops short, chin held high, waiting for an answer. I nod my consent under her stern gaze and struggle to find words. Irene was also widely feared, famous for bouts of temper in which she might hurl a chalk eraser or turn a student's desk over, spilling its contents across the floor. If you were stood in the corner in Miss Bachmeier's room, you were unlikely to misbehave again. Even Principal Lindquist cowered in her presence. She was fifty if she was a day, sturdy, with a rare shock of snow-white hair; wild eyebrows; bloodshot, bluish eyes; and a bulbous nose that in anyone else would indicate a predilection for drink or prize-fighting. Her family were members of the Baha'i faith who fled Germany to escape persecution, I'd been told. But you'd be hard put to detect any religion in her, not unlike a nun or two who'd taught me in grade school.

Esther is speaking up, relieving me. She's not afraid of anyone, it seems.

"Well, generally speaking, we want to widen the children's horizons, turn them into good and useful citizens, don't we? Isn't that the teacher's role? Not to shut them down."

Irene's brow furrows. Esther winks at me. We're having gentle fun at Irene's expense, it turns out.

Though Irene was, by all accounts, the most accomplished teacher in the school, she was rivaled by the much younger Esther. They were spoken of in the same breath as a wellspring of pedagogical knowledge. *Ask Esther or Irene* was a constant refrain. I felt lucky to share my free period with them both. In any case, their rivalry may have gone far to explain the tension evident between them. Though they were the same height, a good head taller than me, they didn't see eye to eye on anything. And though they were both German, they addressed each other stiffly and never in their native tongue.

"There's nothing wrong with a little disorder and the occasional detour," Esther says, addressing me. "That's how discoveries are made."

Esther likes a good argument. I could listen to her for hours, I'm sure of it. Her voice is melodious, with a lilt from the old country. But there is something decidedly exotic about her that I can't quite place. Her hazel hooded eyes, fine prominent nose, and full lips. Her dark brown hair bound in a French twist at the nape of her long neck.

Today she's wearing a knit suit with three-quarter sleeves; it's camel, the color of the desert, with a small collar and a belted waist. The suit clings to her body, which is thin, but her arms are muscular and covered in bracelets that slide up and down like musical instruments. Her manicured hands, almost outsized in appearance, are adorned with rings and there's a delicate gold chain around her neck, but its pendant is tucked in, hidden from sight, as is so much about her. She pulls you in with her warmth, and there is attentiveness and humor in her eyes, and yet there's something private, even guarded, in how she carries herself, how she chooses her words. I'm dying to find out more about her and, if truth be told, to have her to myself. *I could ask her over for dinner* runs through my mind. Well, one day. I've got much to learn before I can even think of socializing.

As dusk falls, schoolbooks unopened on my desk, I stop staring at the old elm outside the window and find Esther Jonas in the telephone book. I take the liberty of giving her a call.

"Hello?" she says.

Her voice is softer than I remember, and warm with sleep. I

must have woken her from a well-deserved nap.

"It's Karen. Karen Murphy."

"Karen, what a lovely surprise," she says, but she doesn't sound surprised to hear from me.

"I was wondering if I could see you this weekend." My voice sounds anxious, more earnest than I intend, as if I've dialed emergency. Well, it *is* a matter of life and death, in a way.

"Is everything all right, Karen?"

She sounds less concerned than amused, I think.

It turns out she has plans already, but she's inviting me along. She was thinking of asking me anyway, she says. Esther is taking me to Chicago! She has friends there, also teachers. We'll take a walk along the lake and then meet them for dinner. I put the phone down and float back to my desk, set to work on the Founding Fathers with new purpose, find myself humming.

3

I'm starting the lesson on Our Founding Fathers when little Alan Simpson raises his hand. He wants to know what *force-marched* means. It's my own fault, I tell myself, for putting it up on the board last week. I don't have a lesson prepared. It's not in our history book. But I do know a thing or two on the subject. Black Hawk had been born in my home town and a statue stands in his honor on the bluff above the Rock River. The great stone warrior, as tall as a building, arms crossed, thick hair in braids, robe flowing, looks out over the wide river and beyond with an expression as mysterious as it is knowing. This giant figure of the Eternal Indian, as it was called, held me in awe. Surely, the Holy Father looked like him, I decided, not like Santa Claus. I devoured everything I could find in the library on Black Hawk's life and the Indians of Illinois, which didn't amount to much. With these slim pickings, I put two and two together and imagined the rest. I wrote my first school paper on the Black Hawk War of 1832, which caused quite a stir among the nuns.

"That's a very good question, Alan," I tell him. "Our

Founding Fathers forced the Indians off their land."

But it's not enough. He's confused. I can see it in his eyes, flickers of doubt. I look around the room and it's the same story. They need convincing.

"America was *their* home, children. The Illini tribe lived right here where you are sitting. The land all around us and beneath our school was Indian Territory."

I've got their interest now. No one is fidgeting. With big eyes, they look over their shoulders and under their desks. Even Lydie, who's been staring out the window, appears thoughtful.

"They'd lived here a very long time, boys and girls, ten thousand years or even more, we can't be sure. Whereas Christopher Columbus arrived here from Europe less than five hundred years ago, in 1492. We talked about that. And the Pilgrims arrived in 1620. We learned that, too."

I'm scribbling dates on the board as I speak. From out of the corner of my eye, I can see them grappling with the onslaught of numbers. I'm about to lose them if I'm not careful, but how else to describe the passage of time?

"Today we learned about the Declaration of Independence. Signed in 1776. Which seems like a very long time ago. But, is it? Everything is relative, children."

They're skeptical, at best, raising their eyebrows.

"Let's figure it out, shall we? How long ago is 1776? Who can tell us?"

They shrink back in their seats, cross their arms. They're looking anywhere but up at me.

"Well, in what year are we living now? Children? Anyone?"

They're stymied, eyes up to the ceiling, shoulders shrugging.

"It's 1963, for heaven's sake!"

There's an intake of air and nodding heads. A single hand shoots up and waves. It's Joanne, coming to my rescue. Tossing her yellow pigtails, she tells the class 1776 was one hundred and eighty-seven years ago.

"Thank you, Joanne," I say, nodding my approval. "The United States is only one hundred and eighty-seven years old!

9

Your grandma and grandpa's grandma and grandpa were alive back then. That's nothing in the scheme of things, is it? It's a drop in the bucket compared to the ten thousand years the Indians lived here!"

I hardly wait for them to take it in. I'm on a roll. Esther's words are spurring me on. I'll expand their horizons, like she says. Turn them into good and useful citizens if it's the last thing I do. It's time they knew their country's history.

"Our American forebears were greedy for land, I'm afraid. They wanted more and more. They didn't want to share with the Indians. They wrote a law signed by President Andrew Jackson. They called it the *Indian Removal Act*. This was in 1830, children. It called for the removal of all Indian peoples to west of the Mississippi River."

I pull down our yellowing map of America and trace the mighty river with my finger.

"Here's the Mississippi. Look how long it is. It cuts our country right in two, into east and west."

It's just a line on a map, I know that. I'd like to take them there, to my childhood haunt, with its wide banks and mighty bridges conjuring adventure and escape. The freighters and giant barges with their cargoes of grain, logs, coal, on their way to far-off shores, the tugboat's moan.

"We've got a river right here in town," I remind them.

Some nod, others look surprised and frown. It's news to them. It seems they've never heard of the river. Their world is the walk to school, their block, the backyards and alleyways, the shops.

"The Indians named our river the Kishwaukee. It runs right across the state of Illinois." I take up my pointer with relish and turn back to the map. "Look closely. The Kishwaukee flows into the Rock River and joins the Mississippi right here."

I place the pointer squarely on a tiny dot where the rivers meet. "This, children, is where I was born." They sit forward, taking notice. I hear giggles, chuckling. They're finding it amusing that I was born. "The rivers connect us!" I shout, arms in the air like a circus ringmaster, and now they're laughing for no reason at all. I give them time to calm.

"Rivers bring us together, but they can also divide us," I say, growing serious. "There are two sides to every river, children."

They know that. They're in on this particular secret of rivers, and knowing makes them proud. Their heads are nodding.

"Now, the warrior chief Black Hawk led his people in the fight to defend their land. They refused to cross the Mississippi and leave their home. But brave as he was, Black Hawk and the Indian nation were defeated. The United States had big guns, you see, whereas the Indians had bows and arrows. That's not a very fair fight, is it?"

The children shake their heads like little experts. They know the story of the Cowboys and Indians. They know the white man always wins.

"The Indians were forced to surrender. They were marched off their land at gunpoint. And that is what we mean by *force-marched*, Alan."

"They took the Indians' land," he says, his sweet face clouding.

"I'm afraid they did. They also lied to them. Our forefathers promised to pay the Indians money for the land. They promised them a new country. But they never intended to keep their promises. The laws were crooked. You must always read the fine print, children."

The children appear confused. I watch their brows furrow and their mouths turn down. They're scratching their heads, biting their thumbs. They seem to be troubled by their country's history. Esther would be proud of me, I'm thinking, when Joanne raises her hand.

"What's *the fine print*, Miss Murphy?"

So, it's the fine print that's troubling them, not history. But I won't give up.

"The fine print is part of a document, Joanne, like a contract, for example, or a receipt you get when you buy something at the store. It's the writing that comes at the bottom of the page. The thing about fine print is that it's so small you can't read it without

11

a magnifying glass, but it contains exceptions and contradictions to what is written above it."

I've overwhelmed them with big words, I know. They're weighing up whether to ask me to explain the big words or not, and I'm doing the same.

"I'll bring in an example of fine print tomorrow, how's that?"

Joanne, nods, contented. Thank God for tomorrow. Tomorrow is a teacher's friend. I dust myself off and start again. I've got more to tell them.

"The road the Indians were forced to march is known as the *Trail of Tears*. I think you can guess why."

Their little heads bob. Their mouths turn down.

"The forced march ended west of the Mississippi river on godforsaken land that nobody wanted. The earth was dry and lifeless. No corn would grow. No buffalo roamed. The white men called these desert places *reservations*, but they were prisons, surrounded by barbed wire, which tears your flesh if you get too near it. There was no escaping, once you were inside. The Indians called barbed wire *the devil's rope*. Which sounds just about right, don't you think? Barbed wire was invented right here in town, as you all know. It was never intended for humans, though."

I should get back to the Founding Fathers, but something is compelling me onward. I spring from my desk and wander among the children, taking them in, one by one. They look up at me and into my eyes, surprised by what they see there, whatever that is. As they turn their heads to follow me, I have the feeling I was born for this moment. Here and now, I have become a teacher. Esther appears in my mind's eye, cheering me on at the door. This lesson is by no means over.

"The Indians had done nothing wrong!" I cry out, like a courtroom lawyer. "They weren't the guilty party here. Their colorful clothes were taken away. Their long hair was cut short. Even their language and the games the children played were forbidden, just like that. They were forced to eat white men's food, which upset their stomachs, and worst of all, they caught the white men's diseases which made them very sick, indeed.

Many, many died. And something else—they were made to pray to *our* god, a strange old man in their eyes, and his son, Jesus, whereas they had many gods and goddesses. Their prayers were songs and dances. They didn't fall onto their knees and bow their heads. No one forced them to be quiet in a church. Their church was the great outdoors."

They're open-mouthed, spellbound.

"But do you know what? The Indians *never* forgot where they came from. They never forgot their gods and goddesses. They perform their songs and dances *to this day*. Do you remember any of those gods and goddesses, Lydie?"

She's preoccupied, harmlessly enough, carving her desk with a pen, but her ears prick up.

"We mentioned a few last week when we talked about the Pilgrims."

"The corn god!" a voice shouts from the back.

"Yes, Karl," I say, "But not out of turn! The Corn *Goddess* is very important."

"Lydie?" I ask again.

She's rising majestically out of her seat. I should have seen it coming.

"I am the Corn Goddess," she intones, her hands crossed above her head, fingers fluttering, in a fairly convincing imitation of a husk and tassels, her eyes rolling heavenward. The children shriek with hilarity.

"That's enough, Lydie," I say too sharply. "And please stay in your seat."

She collapses dramatically into her chair, setting off another bout of laughter, but I won't let that stop me. I turn quickly to the others. "The Indians worship all that nature has to offer, the elements and animals, the seasons, everything that grows. Things you can see or touch or eat. Let's imagine what some of our own gods and goddesses might be."

In short succession, the children propose gods and goddesses of all their favorite foods and animals, including hot dogs, popsicles, hamsters, and worms. I propose mountains, at their prodding. These children of the Midwest have never seen a mountain in real life. Everyone is taking part, except for Lydie who sits arms crossed in a display of resistance and appears to be weighing her options and deliberating her next move and is currently whispering demonstratively in the new girl Janie Dolan's ear. But the rest of the children are bursting with exuberance, half in their seats, hands flying, gods and goddesses tumbling out of them. My voice takes on the timbre of a tent revival preacher, mesmerizing and very somber, and I remind them of the sky, the sun, rain, snow, wind, the Earth itself. A hush settles over the room.

"And fire!" Lydie shouts, stealing my thunder.

"Yes, fire, too!" I answer, welcoming her. "The goddess of fire keeps us warm and cooks our food. That's worth singing and dancing about, isn't it?"

We've exhausted ourselves. But I find I'm not done.

"Let's dance to the Fire Goddess!" I cry out. I grab Alan by one hand and Lydie by the other. It happens so fast she can't resist, and we pull the rest of the children up with us and merge into a line and dance to the goddess of fire, and all the gods and goddesses we can remember, snaking our way around the room. Our movements are clumsy and silly by turns, but we call some sort of joyful spirits down. For a split second, I swear I see my Aunt Helene, my mother's youngest sister, long dead, in a shaft of light. My favorite aunt, who'd gone off to New York, attended the famous Hunter College for women, and become a math teacher at a private girls school in the city; who, during the war, joined the Women's Army Corps, at first as a switchboard operator and then as a cryptographer sworn to secrecy, in the Signal Intelligence Service. My beloved Aunt Helene, who I visited in New York one summer, where she and her best friend, Bea, lived their whole lives together until they were killed in a small plane crash on one of their many adventures, and it's a ghost dance now, I shouldn't wonder. And then the bell rings, and the day is done, and I send the children packing.

I'd won them over, I'm sure of it. They're dancing out of the room, even Lydie.

But as I'm tidying up, the room begins to spin. I'm overcome by queasiness, accompanied by sudden exhaustion and a heaviness of heart. I'm forced to sit and bury my head in my arms. It's deathly still after all the merriment. It occurs to me I may have gone too far. A Ghost Dance is sacred, after all, and not for the taking. I'll be more careful from now on, I promise myself, and stick to the lesson plan.

4

I change my outfit three times, ending up in my usual pleated skirt and blouse out of sheer desperation. I sit at the mirror determined to do something with my unruly hair, but instead of my reflection I see Esther's eyes, fixed on me, surprised. I give up, lie back on the bed in my jacket and shoes, heart pounding, and wait for her.

She pulls up in a beat-up black convertible with red leather interior. Though a storm is threatening, the top is down. She's got a head scarf on and a trench coat with the collar up. Underneath her open coat I can't help noticing her slim skirt is pulled up above her knees to free her legs. I want to tell her how magnificent she looks and how relaxed, away from the confines of the teachers' room, but I don't dare. She's still a perfect stranger. Besides which, if I let go now, I'll be swept down the river. I've never seen such a beautiful car, I say instead as I climb in, and she says I can drive if I like.

"I can't drive," I confess.

Esther looks startled, and her disapproval shows. "Why ever not?"

"I flunked my test."

"How on earth did you manage that?"

"I backed into a telephone pole." And a mailbox, too, in actual fact, but I don't tell her that.

"Well, you must try again, Karen. Driving is freedom. Especially for a woman."

"I value freedom, believe me, Esther." This seems to impress her, so I carry on. "I make my own rules, go my own way."

"Well, then," she says, starting the car with a roar, "let's go enjoy some freedom."

We're off to Chicago, talking of this and that related to the classroom, mundane things that colleagues share. But the nearness to her is distracting me, and I struggle to follow our conversation. Happily, Esther doesn't seem to notice. She's on to one of her favorite topics, Will Lindquist. The principal, it turns out, is fairly new at the school, and Esther has little in the way of praise for him.

"We'd all been teaching for years, but he would stand at the back of the classroom and watch us teach. I think he called it *observation*, some newfangled program the Board of Ed dreamed up. Well, we quickly put an end to that."

"How?"

"We teachers are unstoppable when we want something. We held a meeting. We came up with a plan. We would observe each other from now on, we told him."

"And did you?"

"What do you think?"

I'd observe you night and day if you let me, is what I'm thinking.

"I think you didn't," is what I say.

"A teacher's classroom is sacred territory," she tells me fiercely, in answer. "Anyway, the whole thing was quickly forgotten."

Esther talks with her hands, I realize, hardly touching the wheel. At any moment we might be veering off the road, now right, now left. I reconcile myself to an early death, but at least I'll die happy, and when I'm sure she's not looking, I make the

17

sign of the cross.

"Has he called you in for a meeting yet?"

"No," I say.

"You should watch out for Mr. Lindquist. He has trouble keeping his hands to himself."

"Isn't he married?"

"Of course he is."

"Thank you for the warning."

"I'm surprised he hasn't made a pass at you yet."

"Well, if he does, he'll learn quickly not to do it again."

Something is happening in this small automobile. I feel charged with energy. Esther glances over at me.

"Do you have anyone in your life, Karen?"

"No, not really. Teaching is my passion now."

"As it should be," she says, smiling, eyes fixed back on the road.

"Besides, I'm not terribly interested in men at present," I can't help adding.

"Oh!" she says, and this seems to make her happy.

We hurtle down the highway in silence. Esther drives fast. I feel myself flying over every cornfield we pass. Chicago appears before us out of the nothingness with its skyscrapers and neon signs, its grittiness.

On our walk along Lake Michigan we battle to hear each other over the choppy waves lapping and crashing against the shore. The lake is silver under heavy clouds and there's a chill in the misty air. Esther walks briskly, holding the collar of her light jacket up against the wind, and I find myself running to keep up with her.

"I know so little about you," I offer, shouting.

"And I about you, don't forget," she says, making everything easier all at once.

"I went to Catholic school through grade eight," I start, in answer to nothing, confessional, perhaps. "My brother, Thomas, is a priest. I thought of joining an order myself."

"Really!" Esther says, stopping in her tracks, looking me up and down in amazement.

"Yes, it's true," I say, buoyed on. "That's really all I knew as a child. Our lives were centered around St. Anthony's, our church."

Esther is studying me. She shivers and smiles. I do the same.

"For you then, sin is easily expiated."

There's a question in her eyes. She brushes the hair, which has come loose in the wind, from my face.

"Well, if we do penance, yes."

We are standing so close our bodies are touching. I hear a dog barking and a seagull's cry; then all sound stops. Esther is all that exists in the world. I close my eyes.

"We'd better get going," I hear her say, and she's walking swiftly ahead again. "So why didn't you join the nuns?" she's calling back to me.

"Well, after thinking it through, I decided to become a teacher instead," I answer. Which is half true, in a manner of speaking.

Esther bursts out laughing. She has a dark and hearty laugh, which her thin frame seems hardly able to contain and yet it fits to her exactly. She's wiping tears from her eyes, and I realize that if nothing else I've succeeded in amusing her no end.

What I don't tell her is that I'd have followed Sister Maria, my Bible studies teacher, into the fires of hell. It was she who accounted for my ardor for the convent. "Love knows no limits," she read to us from Corinthians, her piercing eyes settling on mine. Boundless love was her constant theme, in fact, and her yearning was palpable. I opened my heart to the novice nun. I became her star pupil. Her voice was husky, her gait almost mannish, but she was quick to blush. I studied her hands, the only exposed part of her, which she kept tightly clasped at her chest, and the small window of her freckled face. I dreamed about what lay beneath her habit. Even her ears were off limits. There was something incongruous about her that fed my imagination and quickened my heart.

At home, around the dinner table, my father spoke in one breath of the communists and homosexuals. The McCarthy hearings were in full swing and he followed them religiously. The communists had infiltrated the state department and were setting out to destroy the country, and it seemed that homosexuals, whoever they might be, were right behind them. The word *homosexual*, which I had not heard before, had a pleasing ring, despite my father's obvious revulsion. As strange as it seems, I sensed it had something to do with me. How I knew this was anyone's guess. Was it instinct? Self-preservation? More mysterious still, I knew what it meant. I was twelve years old. I didn't dare ask my father for an explanation. My sisters insisted it was something I'd learn when I was good and ready, an adult like them, as they saw their teenage selves. I drew the obvious conclusion that I had stumbled upon something taboo, but also a word that was all mine.

I turned to the Standard College Dictionary, where the sparse definition of homosexual confirmed my suspicion. It wasn't exactly clear to me what sexual relations entailed, but I'd kissed enough girls by then to have an inkling. In other words, I knew the feeling. I knew what happened when Sister Maria leaned over to look at my work, her trembling hand on mine. It started in my heart, which began to beat rapidly and made me lightheaded, and spread down into the pit of my stomach, but the pulsing didn't stop there. It continued its downward trajectory. Did that qualify as homosexual? Had I mistaken it for boundless love? Were they one and the same?

I looked up communism while I was at it and discovered, to my surprise, that it was very like the teachings of Jesus. The communists, apparently, shared their wealth equally. Didn't Jesus share his seven loaves and fish? If Jesus was a communist, was he also a homosexual? I shared my musings in class with Sister Maria who turned as red as a beetroot and let us go home early. It was not so long after this exchange that she and Sister Theresa, our science teacher and Maria's constant companion, were rushed off to separate parishes. The religious calling left me just as quickly.

Esther, meanwhile, has recovered her composure, but I'm

not done with her. I want to hear her laugh again.

"A convent and a school are not that different, Esther."

"How's that?" she says.

"Well, they're both chock full of women, aren't they?"

"That's true," she says, chuckling. "I never thought of it like that."

"With men at the very top, of course."

"Yes, there's that," she says and sighs.

The waves are roaring now against the shore. The effort to keep up with Esther is leaving me breathless. I'm practically gasping. We stumble forward through the sand.

"And your family, Karen?" Esther asks. "Tell me about them."

"Are you sure you want to hear?"

"I'm dying to hear."

I don't know if she's joking or not, but I oblige her. "My father was an engineer for the Chicago, Rock Island and Pacific Railroad Company."

"Oh!" she exclaims, and she looks impressed.

"He was gone more than he was home. Until my mother put her foot down. He moved over to Logistics, then. When he was home, he made his presence felt. I think my mother regretted her insistence."

"And your mother?"

"There was the church and family. She had eight children in all. The first child died in childbirth, the second, Paul, at three of meningitis. But six of us survived. Besides Thomas, the priest, who's the oldest, there's Joseph Junior. And then my sisters, Maureen and Patricia. Then Billy, he's the youngest boy. He's on a secret mission in Vietnam. That little troublemaker is a non-commissioned officer. My family's very proud of him, but I think getting into another war would be wrongheaded, don't you?"

"It would be a terrible mistake. But we're talking about you. Tell me more."

"There's not much to tell. I arrived late. I'm the baby of the family. An accident."

"Ah! Well, that explains everything," she says.

And the way she says it makes me laugh and spurs me on.

"As for Mother, the church came first, always. She hardly seems to have raised us. My siblings looked out for me and for each other. We received little in the way of guidance from her. She left that to the nuns. I don't know that she liked us very much. She wasn't cut out to be a mother, or a wife, for that matter, if you ask me. It's your turn now," I say.

"Not yet."

"When, then?"

"Another time, Karen."

"But that's not fair. I've talked too much."

But Esther's looking at her watch, alarmed. "Oh, God, we're late," she's says, and she's running off ahead again, body bowed against the wind.

5

Her friends, Bettie and Liz, have reserved a booth at the back, she says, as we reach the restaurant out of breath. The Berghoff is a favorite haunt of theirs, she explains, which never fails to amaze her, because Bettie is Black, and it's a very white crowd. *Very German*, she warns.

But you're German yourself, I want to say, as we enter the foyer, but it's so loud you have to shout to be heard. It's cavernous, with handsome paneled walls, stained glass windows, and checkered floors, and I'm quite sure I've never seen as many people laughing and talking and drinking in one place. If they're German or not, I couldn't tell, but there's something worldly about them. You see it in the way they hold themselves, which is to say, barely. They're leaning on their elbows, hanging over the tables. They've clearly seen it all before and aren't impressed, certainly not by this small-town schoolteacher struggling to make her way through the crowded room. Cigar fumes rising to the ceiling mingle with the smell of roast pork and beer, sauerkraut and strong perfume.

"Where's Lee-Anne?" the friends exclaim as we approach.

"Working overtime. I've brought someone else to meet you. Karen's our new fifth-grade teacher."

Introductions are made, first Bettie then Liz, and we shake hands. They mean to be welcoming, to put me at ease, but I find myself troubled.

"Who's Lee-Anne?" I ask Esther, as we take our seats.

"She's my roommate, darling."

She's not called me darling before. I want to faint. But I need to know more.

"I'm sorry she couldn't join us."

"She's assistant principal at the junior high. They're in a crisis yet again. Anyway, they've scheduled some kind of emergency meeting for today. Please don't ask me to explain," she pleads, and I'm sure I see her wink at Bettie.

"That's a lot of responsibility," I offer.

"She loves it," Liz says, "all that power."

"You can say that again," Esther says, draping her arm along the back of the booth. I decide to put Lee-Anne, the roommate, out of my mind, which isn't as hard as it might seem. Esther's hand is floating along my spine, resting occasionally with a quick caress, so that I'm drained of all capacity to think, and struggle to maintain my composure.

I take in Bettie and Liz for the first time and immediately feel out of place in my buttoned-up blouse and pleated skirt. Liz Duncan could have walked in from the country club. She's suited and coiffed, pearled and manicured. But despite her feminine accoutrements, handsome is the word that comes to mind. Her blue eyes are as cool as ice and seem to look right through you. Bettie Washington is just her opposite, exuding warmth and womanliness. She's wearing a green satin cocktail dress, the color of fern, which accents her voluptuous figure. Like Esther, her arms are covered in bracelets that jingle when she moves, which happens frequently as she is very animated, and there's a storm of jangling now. They are all inordinately fond of rings, I notice. My own hands, unadorned, with their bitten nails, feel quite naked beside them, and I place them on my lap.

24

They turn their attention to me, and Liz asks me how I'm liking teaching, and I'm about to confess to a rough start thanks to Lydie, whose antics grow more audacious, not less, daily. But before I can say a word, Liz and Bettie are remembering back to their own first days on the job, amid much merriment. Liz had a case of nerves so bad she broke out in hives up to her ears. Bettie was so scared of her principal she hid in the supply closet to avoid him. Then the memories are exhausted and the ugly present rears its head. Bettie tells us the Chicago city schools are crumbling. Classrooms are overcrowded to breaking point. Black children all over this country are segregated and left behind, not just in the South. But the teachers have had enough and are planning a citywide strike.

"Girls, this will be one for the history books. Thousands of teachers on the streets. Marching right down to City Hall, to the Board of Ed. We're calling it Freedom Day."

The superintendent's days are numbered, Bettie assures us, nodding with conviction.

I'll keep my struggles with Lydie to myself, I decide. An unruly child is nothing compared to what Bettie endures. They've moved on, in any case, to the upcoming World Series. Bettie is a diehard Yankees fan. Liz and Esther are rooting for the Dodgers. The relative merits of Sandy Koufax and Whitey Ford are hotly debated, pitches gone over with a fine-toothed comb. The German beer is working on me. I find I'm not the least bit self-conscious anymore. I sink back in my seat, tune out the baseball chatter, and thrill to the nearness of Esther. We're joined at the hip. Our thighs are bumping up against each other. I observe the easy manner between Bettie and Liz. So easy, in fact, that their hands are resting on each other's knee under the table. This is how the world should be, I tell myself. I've found my place. I could stay here all night, but it's time to go. I feel a tad giddy as I try to stand. Esther has to hold me up, and I realize just how drunk I am. As we head out into the street, everything is spinning. Esther puts her arm around my waist to steady me.

25

"Can you make it to the car? It's just up the block."

"Oh, yes," I tell her. I could make it from here to eternity. Her grip is strong. She's practically carrying me.

On the drive home, I let my head fall back against the seat.

"Did you like my friends, Karen?" Esther says.

"Very much," I say.

"That's good."

"Are they married?"

"To men, you mean?" she asks, then catches herself. "Bettie *was*," she says.

"They seem to be very close."

"Oh, they are that."

She looks at me, and I can see she's weighing how much to tell me.

What she tells me is that Bettie has two teenage sons and how they had taken the boys to the March on Washington this past summer and what it felt like to be present at a turning point in history. Because she's sure that's what it was. The movement had caught fire. Dr. King's electrifying speech would transform the country. Not immediately. The resistance was fierce, and lives would continue to be sacrificed. Perhaps King's, God forbid. Like Medgar Evers in Mississippi, shot in the back outside his front door by a Klansman. Perhaps there would be a second civil war. If we're not in one already. Young bodies bloodied by police batons. Dogs set on children. Peaceful protesters hosed by water cannons. George Wallace will not give up without tearing the country apart.

She stops herself and looks over at me. "I'm upsetting you."

"It angers me," I say. What I don't say is how my father cheered George Wallace on in front of the TV. How my mother sat silent in her chair. How I vowed never to be like them.

"There *will* be equality and justice in this country. Segregation will end. Discrimination will end."

I nod, sit up, and find I'm sober.

"And there will come a time," she says, almost serenely, "when women's voices will be heard and even lead the country."

We're stopped at a light, and she's studying me. "You never thought of marrying, Karen?"

"I've been engaged," I tell her, as if the idea is preposterous, even to me.

"What happened?"

"I wasn't ready. And you, Esther?" I ask, changing the subject.

"One day I'll tell you *my story*." Her tone is strangely ironic, both dark and offhanded. Then we're outside my door and she sees me in and quickly leaves, and that's the last thing I remember until morning.

6

Lydie has brought a bright blue feather in for show-and-tell.

"I'm about to tell you something no one knows and you can't tell a soul," she announces to the class. "If you do, you'll drop dead."

The children are to place their right hand on their heart and swear to secrecy, which they do, most obediently.

"This is the true story of my life."

It turns out she was abducted from her tribe by white men while she was out hunting buffalo. At some point, I realize I've stopped listening. I'm not myself today. I should be grateful that Lydie is preoccupied and not staring. She'd be sure to notice a change in me. My mind keeps wandering to Esther and her fingers lightly stroking my back in the restaurant booth and the feel of her thigh up against mine and her arm firm around my waist as we walked to her car and what we might do next weekend.

Lydie's story, meanwhile, is growing more complex by the minute. There's a shoot-out with the United States army. The children turn to me for confirmation or denial, but I just shrug my shoulders. There are guards who force her to drink a potion meant to make her forget her Indian family, but she holds it in her mouth and spits it out when the guards aren't looking. She demonstrates this in some detail before moving on. The army, apparently, stole everything from her except the shirt on her back and this feather, which she managed to hide in her sleeve. She turns her back on the class for a split second, then turns to face them, and the feather has disappeared. The children are beside themselves. Then she pulls it out of her sleeve like a magician, and they applaud and hoot.

"Thank you, Lydie, for showing and telling," I say. "Very impressive."

"I'm not finished," she says to no one in particular. "I have to tell you about Sitting Bull, my father."

"I believe your father is Mr. Kaminski, Lydie."

"He's not my real father," she corrects me, over her shoulder. "I'm adopted."

It comes out so matter-of-factly, I'm ready to believe her. Either way, I've reached my limit. "You may take a seat, Lydie," I tell her, solemnly.

"Now I'm going to pass the feather around," she tells the children, ignoring me.

But before she has a chance to pass it anywhere, I've jumped up from my desk and snatched the feather out of her hand, startling both of us.

"It's true that feathers play a large role in Indian life," I say, turning to the class. "Feathers are said to be *gifts from the sky*. I think you can guess why, girls and boys. They're used as decoration on headdresses, on drums and rattles and dolls. They represent birds in ceremonial dances."

Then turning to Lydie and examining the feather, I say, "This feather is very pretty, Lydie, but it's been painted blue. Indians don't paint their feathers as a rule."

I hand the feather back. It's cruel, I know. But I don't care and I'm feeling no mercy. I've decided to crush this child's fantasy.

"If you would like to read about Sitting Bull, children, there's a biography of his life in the library. I believe there are several copies. He was a very brave leader. He seems to have inspired your imagination, Lydie. I suggest you write a play about him for the class. We can perform it in next month's talent show."

Lydie stands defeated in front of her classmates. It had to be done, I tell myself, for her own good. But it could just as easily be an act of revenge, a tit for tat, for the havoc she wreaks. I turn my back on her. I don't want to view her public shaming. But then I do look. I can't help myself, and her head's not hanging. There she stands, proud hunter of buffalo, straight-backed, chin up, looking out over our heads, unvanquished, feather gripped like a lance.

"But now we're moving on to the next chapter in our history," I say, firmly. "And what an eventful history it is."

I'm returning to my desk and about to ask Lydie to take a seat for the second time when a voice calls out "Pass the feather around, Lydie," echoed by a boisterous chorus, and they're all rushing to the front of the room, surrounding Lydie and begging her to let them be the first to hold the feather.

"Well, let her believe she was abducted from an Indian tribe. I don't see the harm in it," Joan says, too loudly.

"But it's a fantasy," I say, getting up to close the door to the teachers' room.

"Fantasy is a coping mechanism," she says.

Joan Smith taught fifth grade like me. She'd minored in psychology in college and dispersed insights she gained from her classes every chance she got. She was the school's go-to person for all things psychological, and I had to admit she had some good ideas occasionally, though the truth was I didn't much care for her. She was petite, even smaller than me, but she found a way of looking down on the rest of us. Her voice was clipped and nasal and grated on me no end, and her tone was superior. Her thick hair, which she wore in a bob, was dirty blonde, her round eyes which often expressed astonishment at our ignorance were blue, and she was quite pretty objectively speaking. But everything about her made me want to keep my distance.

Irene is sitting on her own, half reading, half eavesdropping, while Esther works quietly with Louise, whose voluptuous body leans in closely to her mentor. Louise D'Amato and I were hired at the same time, and she's teaching fourth grade like Esther. Esther has taken her under her wing, for the sake of the children, she says, and Louise is nothing if not enthusiastic under her tutelage. Her large black eyes follow Esther's every word, her dark curls flying as she nods in agreement. The truth is, she's fast becoming an appendage to Esther, and it's a rare moment when I have her to myself at the school. Still, Louise has the makings of a fine teacher who takes her calling very seriously, and we're on our way to becoming good friends. She's had me over to her rooming house already. We meant to talk shop, but ended up listening to albums on her roommate's record player.

"Lydie's a Jew if I'm not mistaken," Joan blurts out.

"Is she?" This was news to me.

"They're practically all Jews up at the college," Joan says in answer.

Across the room, I see Esther's body tense as she looks sharply over at Joan, and in that instant, I understand that my special friend, my confidante, is Jewish herself. A rush of a discovery courses through my body. I'm embarrassed by my ignorance and excited at the same time. I feel myself blushing and take to busying myself with my schoolbag on the floor to hide my feelings.

"No offense to anyone intended," Joan says, eyeing Esther. "I'm just suggesting the girl may feel different, like an outsider in the town, and she's connected her feelings to the Indians. It makes perfect sense to me. Freud called it *identification*."

"Are you sure it isn't penis envy, Joan?" Esther says dryly.

I can't tell if she means it or not until she winks at me. We smile widely at each other.

Irene is not amused, however.

"Very clever, Esther, but not much help to Karen."

"I don't know," says Joan. "Penis envy isn't out of the question. When it comes to certain girls."

I won't give Joan the satisfaction of agreeing. Louise, meanwhile, looks nothing if not baffled.

"Penis envy?" she asks slowly.

"You haven't read Sigmund Freud, Louise?" Joan takes Louise in with an expression of horror.

Poor Louise looks crushed.

"I'll explain later, Louise," I tell her. "It's not a crime that you haven't read Freud."

And that should be the end of it, but Irene is stewing. "Freud here, Freud there," she says, and she's turned bright red from the neck up. "Children don't have such things on their minds. They're innocent. They're certainly not envying each other's private parts."

Irene can be very naive, I'm thinking. I always took the boy's part in our make-believes. I wanted what they had, whatever it was. I wanted Becky McCann underneath me, most of all. Rocking back and forth on top of her, I instructed her in the art of French kissing, my first teaching job. I was eight if I was a day.

"It's very naive, Irene," Esther says, echoing my thoughts out loud, "to imagine children aren't sexual beings."

"Children are children," Irene cries out, pounding the table with her fist this time. "What is the world coming to, I ask you. I put it down to that music, if you can call it music, that *rock and roll*," she says with distaste, as if rocks were rolling around in her mouth. "That fellow with the hips."

"Elvis?" I ask.

"Terrible influence," she says, shaking her head.

Louise and I share a roll of the eyes. We don't tell Irene that music has moved on. Louise loves the Beach Boys. I've been smitten by Lesley Gore. Then there are the Beatles from England, the new band everyone is talking about.

We've had our say and retreat to our corners. Out of the silence, Joan takes the opportunity to explain to us that penis envy is a condition that persists into adulthood in some women, and I'm sure her button eyes are settling on me. I decide to change the subject.

"Lydie's not adopted, is she?"

"I think we'd have been informed," Joan says, a pained little smile crossing her lips.

On my short walk home along Prospect Street, I conceive a lesson plan on the origins of man. I'll take the children back further than the plains Indians who hunted and fished on the banks of Illinois's many rivers. Back to the ocean, to our first breath on land, to the primates, the Homo sapiens standing on two legs. I want Lydie to identify with all of humankind, to understand that we are all one, that the differences are minimal between us; draw her back into the fold. I look up, and there she is across the street, on patrol duty. I call out her name and wave, expecting nothing. But lo and behold, she's waving back at me. It's a short wave, more a toss of the hand, but it so startles me, I check to see if anyone's behind me. There's not a soul on the street but us. I take this as a sign of progress and look forward to seeing her in class in the morning.

7

What made the town so charmless? My heart sank the moment I stepped off the train to join the teaching program at the college. It was late summer. The air was insufferably humid. I felt my chest tighten and struggled to breathe. I had the distinct sensation of being trapped here with no escape, and yet I'd just arrived. This intuition was quickly borne out. Great pride, I learned, was taken by the locals in the invention of barbed wire. Barb City was the town's apt nickname. Fans rooted for their team, the Barbs, at football games. Barbed wire, which had been designed to rein in cattle, had fast been adopted for more nefarious purposes. It shut humans out and penned them in. Was it any wonder I felt constricted? The town's prosperity had been built on this most menacing means of confinement.

But it was corn that brought the town its fame. Nowhere was the soil so fertile. The production of hybrid maize by the Agricultural Association, or *Ag*, as it was called, with its trademark flying ear of corn, was known the country over. In August, the annual Corn Boil drew the townsfolk together to honor the golden vegetable, with tubs of free corn dripping with hot butter. And though the freshly picked sweet corn was just that, its fat kernels bursting with sugar, my enthusiasm was tempered by a pervading lack of nature. I craved forests and wide rivers like my beloved Mississippi. I ached for the heights of Black Hawk bluff. Here it was all fields as far as the eye could see and row upon row of corn.

The Kishwaukee River, or the Kish as it was fondly known, wound its way through the town practically unnoticed. The one sizable park—Hopkins Park, by name—with its bandshell smack in the middle, an overcrowded swimming pool, and a pair of unused tennis courts, provided a green oasis of sorts and a somewhat forlorn picnic area. A scrap of woods, where I took to walking, lay to one side along the river where wild things were free to bloom, a remnant of the woodlands of Illinois in bygone days. The local merchants and professional men never set foot in the place. They played tennis and golf behind the barbed wire fencing of the Country Club that abutted the park; their wives lunched and drank too much in the club bar, and their children swam in the club pool.

There were other divisions in the town, I soon discovered. The main street, Lincoln Highway, split the grid of numbered streets into north and south, a divide as real as that in our great country. The far south side was where the poor folks lived, and from out near the cannery, where our school stands, you could smell corn, peas, and beans being readied for the can when the wind blew in.

There was, in any case, rarely an occasion to head either north or south beyond downtown, which bustled and teemed with commercial enterprise. The array of things to spend your money on was overwhelming for those like me who hated shopping. There were four department stores, no less, and as if that wasn't enough, five dress shops, one with a bridal floor, another full of dreaded hats, as well as a couple of menswear establishments, a shoe store, and a children's shop. There was a Woolworth's with a sizable lunch counter, a couple of diners, an ice cream parlor, four drug stores, three jewelers, two record stores, and the Farmer's Bureau. Imposing banks graced either end of downtown, along with gift shops and smoke shops, a hardware store and a Buttons and Yarns. There was a Singer's Sewing Machine, and further down the highway a steak house, a pizza place, takeout fried chicken, and a skating rink. On the corner of Seventh and Lincoln, a newsstand lovingly referred to as Dirty Bert's sold candy and girlie magazines, placed willy-nilly alongside *Archie* comic books, from overstuffed shelves, and even dirtier fare, so the rumor went, as well as guns and ammunition from a room in the back. Despite its reputation, the whole town stopped in for the Sunday papers after church and a chat with Bert about the weather. I stopped in there, too, as did the children, despite the risk to their moral development. Nowhere to be found downtown was a bookstore. There were, however, bars galore and a couple of paint stores, a Chinese restaurant and a shoe repair, and down a side street, the town's crowning glory, the truly fantastic Egyptian Theatre, rumored to be haunted, with its golden Pharaohs on the wall. Across from the Trust and Savings, where the train tracks crossed the highway near the station, a genuine tank from WWII served as the town's memorial.

In short and viewed from above, it might have been any Midwest town, but for the college. The Teacher's College opened its doors in 1895, sending its young women out like a small army across the state and even further afield to educate the masses. Practically all of the town's schoolteachers had trained there at one time or another. Bettie and Liz had trained there, too, and Esther's classmates remained her closest friends.

By the time I arrived, however, the college had extended its reach beyond the training of teachers and become a bona fide university with a hodgepodge of ugly buildings. Young men were to be found in equal numbers in its classrooms. It had sprawled westward, like its own island, and was now quite separate from the factory and farming town in which it found itself. The town locals and the college transplants might have been living on separate planets.

They did come together once a year, for Homecoming, when the student twirlers and marching band, the Queen and King and the football team, paraded along Lincoln Highway. But when calls for civil rights and an end to the nuclear arms race led to demonstrations on campus, the townsfolk called out the police and raised their flags high against the communists. The truth is I didn't fit in either camp. I was no patriot but I was no rebel either. Put another way, my big love was anthropology. The origin of mankind was a favorite subject of mine, but all peoples of the Earth were of interest to me. I was an observer, like the great Margaret Mead. I did join one student meeting against the atom bomb. The speakers were loud and combative. You had to shout to be heard and no one listened. The girls in attendance served coffee and didn't get a word in. Suffice it to say, I never went again.

I studied dutifully in the library, made few friends, went home on weekends, and when it all got too much, made my way to St. Mary's downtown where the rituals offered comfort and an escape of sorts. I sat in the cool, dark church, looking up into the rafters, and prayed with all my might. *Heavenly Father, let my teaching career take me far away from here.*

And then, as fate would have it, a teaching place fell into my lap. My predecessor, Paula Presley, and her husband were leaving town suddenly under a cloud of suspicion. Don Presley, the husband, longtime council member, and college administrator, had been implicated in a case of missing funds used in the purchase of luxury items, including a fur coat and a diamond ring, found in the possession of his young secretary. Rather than face trial, Don Presley had agreed to early retirement and had taken his wife off to North Carolina where he could repent his sins and perfect his golf game. Poor Paula Presley, who had returned to teaching when her kids were grown, was well-liked and would be sorely missed. Her life experiences as a wife and mother had brought a breath of fresh air into the stale confines of a school full of spinsters, it was said. All this was reported to me later, of course, by the school's resident gossip, kindergarten teacher Marilyn Nowack. All I knew then was that someone at the college had recommended me for an immediate opening. I wasn't sure whether to thank or curse my mysterious benefactor for keeping me in town. I'll only stay a year or two, I told myself, and learn the ropes and then move on.

But thanks to Esther, the town had become my destiny. No amount of wishful thinking would change its nature, but it appeared before me as a blank page upon which a story of biblical proportions was sure to be written. I woke up early, flung the curtains open, hardly able to contain my excitement for the new day, watched with awe the dawn blaze across an endless horizon where before I had seen only flatness and emptiness.

Esther lives here, after all. She walks these plain streets under these old trees, looks out across the cornfields. She buys her outfits here, her stockings and toiletries, and stops off for lunch at the five-and-dime. She walks the aisles of the Piggly Wiggly, waits at the guard rail for the trains to pass. She stands in line at the bank, stops in at the shoe repair. Her head rests on a pillow somewhere in this town, in a house she shares with her roommate, Lee-Anne—but I put that out of my mind.

I'll learn more about the Jewish faith, I decide. I know too little. My encounters with Jews being limited to the Three Patriarchs of the Old Testament, and the Katz's who owned the dry goods store in my hometown. To hear my father tell it, the Jews were behind all the world's ills, pulling the strings and plotting world domination. They were as bad as the communists and homosexuals. This alone was enough to win them favor with me. If most of the professors in our large classrooms were Jewish, as Joan claims, I couldn't have told you which they were. They didn't announce it. But I have Esther now. Maybe one day we'll travel to the Holy Land together!

But first things first. I've come downtown to open a bank account. There is so much to look forward to, but I'll need to save and save some more. Dave Palmquist (nicknamed Swede by half the town) at the Trust and Savings is happy to oblige me. He tells me that we schoolteachers are the only women with our own accounts, apart from the widows and the divorcees. He admires our fortitude and respects our independence. A healthy, growing town (and town economy) needs good, dedicated teachers. It was surely a shame, though, when it came to some, that they'd had the marriage ban, but thank God those days were over. In any case, he wonders out loud how long it would take before the pretty girl sitting in front of him would be swept off her feet and leave the profession.

"I'd propose to you, myself, if I wasn't married," he tells me.

As I'm leaving the bank, I observe two women getting into a car across the street, and one of them is Esther. Esther sees me rooted to the spot and calls me over. I'm introduced to Lee-Anne, her roommate, through the car window. She's a strong Nordic type, tall, fair-headed. As she leans towards me from the driver's seat, stretching out a freckled, muscular arm to shake my hand, she places her right arm around Esther. It's easy and possessive at once. *They're lovers, not roommates,* I tell myself as they drive off.

8

I spend free period cleaning out my desk drawers and erasing the blackboard very thoroughly, anything to stay out of the teachers' room. I can't face Esther this morning. I'd convinced myself I'd be seeing her this weekend. We'd take a drive to Russell Woods outside town, walk under a canopy of turning leaves, gaze up in wonder at blood red maples, the gold of birches and poplars, and stop for a picnic, which I'd have lovingly packed with a bottle of wine. We'd spread a blanket on the edge of the fields, lie back, let come what may. Now the weekend opens like a gaping wound.

Louise stops by my room, and we make plans to see *Cleopatra* at the Egyptian on Saturday, our first date, she says, laughing. Richard Burton is second only to Gregory Peck in the dreamboat department as far as she's concerned. I don't tell her about my childhood crush on Liz Taylor, which began with her Rebecca in *Ivanhoe*. I'm grateful to have made a friend and to have something to do this weekend, but my heart isn't in it. At lunch, I sit with Marilyn Nowack who has new gossip to share. I try my best to listen, but I'm having trouble concentrating or caring. I've lost all interest in the human race. As I'm leaving school, I see Esther gesturing to me from down the hallway, but I rush down the steps and out the door.

"Karen!" She's calling out to me.

I pretend not to hear her, but she catches up with me.

"I'll be out of town this weekend," she says, sighing.

"Oh," I say. I know what that means. She and Lee-Anne are going away.

"Do you have plans?"

"Yes," I say, but I won't say more. I won't give her the satisfaction of thinking the world carries on without her.

We're stopped in the school parking lot. She's blocking the sun from her eyes with her hand.

"I'll call you when I get back."

Why bother? I think. She's getting into her car, but I refuse to look at her. I keep my head down where I can't help but see her beautifully shaped legs in their seamless stockings.

"Are you okay?" she says.

I nod without looking up.

"Let me give you a ride."

"No. I want to walk."

She's studying me with a show of concern. As if she's at a loss to understand what's wrong. I feel her eyes on me until I turn the corner. Then she's driving slowly alongside me and rolling down the window of the passenger seat. The car veers sharply over the curb. I don't want to smile but I can't help myself.

"Can I come over for dinner next week?"

"Okay," I say, without stopping to think.

And with that she speeds away.

Prospect Street comes instantly to life, like a TV switched to color from black and white. Lee-Anne's her roommate after all.

Esther and I are having dinner at my place. I've got her here in my clapboard house just where I've wanted her. We're sitting at the kitchen table, just as I imagined it. Dusk enters through the open door. It's unusually warm. Esther slips off her cardigan and smiles at me. She fans herself and laughs. She's biting the nail of her thumb and watching me. I grip the sides of my chair to stop myself from climbing over the table. *I'll kiss her at the first opportunity*, I'm thinking. I'm in love, and I'll tell her as much when the moment is right.

These are my thoughts, but what I say is, "I've created a lesson plan on the origins of man."

"Oh," she says, surprised, and she's her old self again, confident, in charge. "Don't mention evolution, whatever you do."

"Why not?"

"Well, it's not against the law in this state, but you'll spare yourself a lot of bother if you avoid the subject."

What she means is there are church groups in town who refuse to accept that we come from the apes, including some parents in the PTA. They've been fighting evolution all the way to the statehouse. But I won't let their ignorance stop me.

"No one can stop you," Esther says, reading my mind, and not for the first time. She's one step ahead of me in everything. "Teach what you want to teach. Just don't use the word *evolution*. Call it something else."

She wipes her mouth daintily, then pushes her plate away. She looks down at her hands, which are now clasped in her lap, and then up at me. She seems to be expecting something, dessert perhaps, and I'm kicking myself that I didn't stop at Davison's for a cake on the way home.

"Shall I begin in the sea or on land? What do you think, Esther?" I ask, as if words have any meaning at all.

Esther smiles and frowns at the same time. "I don't want to talk about work, dear Karen. Is that all right?"

"Of course," I say, too quickly.

"Or anything outside this room."

"No," I say, shaking my head vehemently.

I get up and close the door and sit back down. We sit in silence, watching each other.

"I'd just like to look at you if you don't mind."

"No. I don't mind."

The only sound is our breathing, which is heavy. I feel her chest rise and fall in sync with mine. Esther places her strong, jeweled hands on the table. I do the same. Two sets of hands reach furtively for each other. Yes, I am awake, and Esther and I are holding hands across a vast expanse of time and place and a clutter of dishes, wine glasses, and cutlery.

"You've hardly touched your spaghetti," I manage to say.

"No."

Our hands are clenched now. We'll fall off the Earth if we let go.

"Didn't you like it? The spaghetti?"

"I'll have it in the morning," she says, barely above a whisper. It's settled then, and didn't the nuns teach us patience was a virtue?

We push our chairs away from the table and get up in slow motion, holding back for an instant from the inevitable. But then we're in each other's arms, and we stay there, clasped together in my kitchen as our bodies discover each other. Climbing the stairs up to my bed would separate us too violently. I take in her scent, which is for all the world like fresh snow, and kiss her neck and full lips, and then her mouth opens. It's thrilling inside her mouth; her tongue is soft and firm at once, achingly sweeter than I could have imagined, and God knows I've been imagining her tongue in my mouth for weeks. I release her hair and as it falls thick and wild around her face I have to gasp because she is so beautiful. And as our breathing turns to moaning, I *do* lead her upstairs.

The night sky turns golden and trumpets blare, and I understand that what is happening was written from the first moment in the teachers' room. Nothing will ever be the same. We drift off to sleep near dawn, but she wakes quickly with a start. She has to leave, she says, but I won't hear of it. I pull her close under me and hold her with my thighs.

"It's time," I say. "You're going to tell me that story of yours."

She turns her head away. But I'm determined. The fact is I

know next to nothing about this schoolteacher whom I love. I take her face in my hands. "Speak," I order. But her mouth finds mine and offers not words but Dionysian wine. As she dresses and readies to leave, she tells me she prefers to live in the present.

"Let me be a mystery for now, Karen," she begs me, half joking, half serious.

9

We have to take things slowly, she says, so as not to lose our heads. She'll call as soon as she can. Days pass in which she greets me in the hallway or the teachers' room like a friendly, distant colleague. I invite her to dinner but she politely declines and hopes she can take a *raincheck*, she says. And then the charade becomes too much for me. I stop outside the door to her classroom, which is always open—she has nothing to hide, she says—and peer in. The children are lined along the windows, carrying clipboards and pencils, straining for a view, some on chairs, the others on tiptoes. Esther is standing behind them. "Look up at the sky, children. What do you observe this morning?" There's authority and ease in her stance, her voice exacting and yielding at once. "Clouds, Miss Jonas," they call out. "Cirrus, stratus, or cumulus?" "Cumulus!" "Will it rain?" "No." "Why not?" "The clouds are white!" The children respond as one, well-mannered, content with themselves. "Take your time with your sketches," she tells them.

She turns to look up at the clock and notices me. I've caught her by surprise. She bows her head and makes her way purposefully to where I'm standing in the doorway.

"I'm longing for you," I tell her, under my breath.

There's a flash of irritation in her eyes, which are scanning the hallway. "It will all work out," she says, with a breezy air, like a nurse calming a patient. She steps back into her room, glances back at me with a sigh, and closes the door gently, but firmly, behind her.

I stand like a naughty child outside Esther's door, unsure where to turn. I've committed a cardinal sin by intruding on her lesson. Her classroom is sacred territory after all. Thankfully, the hall is empty. I circle the length of it, make my way back up to my room and wait for the children to come up from gym. I realize, with a sinking feeling, she may not want to see me again, that what I've done may be unforgivable.

I stay after school, preparing next week's lessons, an exercise in futility with Lydie in the room, but it keeps me busy. I take the long way home and spend what's left of the day mopping the floors, anything to take my mind off my serious folly. I'm about to collapse into bed when the phone rings, and it's Esther calling to ask if she can come over, right away, within the hour—if I'm not busy, that is.

Two hours later, two hours I spend motionless on my couch, rendered helpless by anticipation, ears pricked for the slightest sign of her, for the screech of her tires, the click of her heels on the front path, the jangle of her bracelets, there's a soft tapping at my door, seemingly out of nowhere. She's panting, catching her breath. The look in her eyes is that of a hungry beggar. If she had an empty bowl, I would fill it to heaping.

She's parked on the next block, she says, closing the door quickly behind her, and walked over so as not to draw attention. She insists we close the windows, lower the blinds. She arranges her books on the table as if we're getting down to work and turns up the volume on the radio. Okay, she says, undressing me, we're safe. Safe from what? I want to ask. What is there to fear? But

I can't form words. I can barely stand. "You're safe with me," I manage to say, as I lead her up to my bed. But safe is the last thing I'm feeling. My desire for Esther is wrought with danger, the danger of losing control. In fact, I have abandoned reason and every other faculty that holds a schoolteacher together. I go ape in her arms. I babble and shriek. Below my bedroom window, a car pulls into the driveway. Esther jolts up in the bed.

"Esther, it's okay." I'm laughing, delirious with loving. "It's only Bill, my neighbor, coming home from the late shift at Wurlitzer's."

I reach for her, but she resists and pulls the covers tight around her.

"It's a very small town. People here notice everything, even things they don't understand and can't explain."

"It's nobody's business how we lead our lives," I assure her. I'm desperate to have her back in my arms. My body is bereft. But she's not convinced and keeps her distance. She seems startled, in fact. She's looking at me as if I'd said the world was flat.

"Your life is not your own, Karen. Surely you know that. You're a schoolteacher, a pillar of the community, a moral authority, whether you like it or not."

I'm panting, tongue hanging. I'm not in the proper state of mind. "A teacher should be judged by her behavior in the classroom," I answer, my own behavior in the classroom notwithstanding.

Esther looks up at the ceiling, then down. She clasps her hands. I can't tell if she's at a loss for words or praying. She gets up from the bed and walks to the window, glancing out from behind the curtain. Satisfied that Bill is not lurking outside, she sits on the nearby chair and takes me in with a perplexed expression.

"We're like those nuns of yours. They put us on a pedestal. We live for the children, and the children alone. One false step, Karen, and down you fall. Even the slightest deviation can compromise your standing in the town and lead to your undoing. Our present conduct is grounds for dismissal."

47

Esther's words are preposterous to me. Love is one thing, work is another. My life is my own. I refuse to care what other people think. But I don't say anything. I nod my head. I'd stand on my head if I could. Anything to get her back in my bed. Her brow is still furrowed, but she's coming round. She's in my arms.

We make love. The holiest of acts. Heart pounding against heart. A pure communion. "We are not immoral," I inform her as we calm. "Our conduct is a form of devotion."

That does it, apparently. Esther is sitting up, purposefully. "I want to tell you a story, Karen. It doesn't have a happy ending, I'm afraid. You met Liz and Bettie in the city with me. Well, they had a dear friend, Albert Sims. He'd been teaching English at Liz's school for several years when she was hired. As Liz tells it, they knew instantly they were kindred spirits and destined to be friends for life from the day their eyes met in the teachers' lounge. Al knew who was to be trusted and who not, and their friendship served a practical purpose. They quickly presented themselves to the world as a couple. They attended school and community events together, and even considered marriage. Marriage is the perfect cover for people like us. In most cases, the spouse is normal, doesn't understand what they're getting into. What a nightmare, for both parties. Liz was with a married woman for years."

"Bettie, you mean?"

"Exactly. You're very perceptive. It was an ugly divorce. Bettie and Liz had to stop seeing each other for almost a year so Bettie didn't lose her boys. We're unfit to be mothers, according to the law."

"Why did Bettie marry in the first place?"

"Because it was expected of her. She expected it of herself. She fought her nature. But nature always wins out. Still, the pressure to marry is enormous, perhaps even more so for us." Esther looks at me with a quizzical expression. "You said you'd been engaged."

"In another lifetime," I tell her, which is true. My tone is casual, dismissive. *My life is with you,* I want to say, but I hold my tongue. "Go on with your story," I say.

"Liz and Al both agreed eventually that marriage was a step too far. Liz and Bettie were already together, and though Al was single, he had an active circle of friends in the city and a steady stream of male houseguests. But they passed perfectly. They were an attractive, all-American couple, you might say. They went on theater vacations to New York City once a year. They rented a beach house in Key West, Florida. They led an enviable life to those looking in from the outside. But where teachers are, there is talk. Why aren't they married yet? the teachers asked themselves. What are you waiting for? they teased them to their faces. The truth was, you know, that Al and Liz *were* in love."

"So, it's a love story," I say. *Perhaps it won't end so badly, after all.*

Esther nods and sighs. "But desire is something else entirely. This is the story of Al's undoing. It began one evening when a couple of seniors from Al's English class turned up at a men's bar he frequented in the city. It wasn't that the boys talked or that he grew frightened—on the contrary. The fact that the boys were now in on his secret was a form of recognition of his true existence. He felt acknowledged and accepted for the first time and no longer alone. He could be himself, at last. He felt a new sense of freedom, a kind of elation, and he stopped being careful. He let his guard down. And that is the point, Karen."

"What happened?"

"A young male teacher joined the staff. Al was smitten. He couldn't stop talking about him. Something took place or didn't between them in the locker room, a reckless word, a misplaced touch, Liz never found out exactly what. But it led rather rapidly to his dismissal and, even worse if that's possible, to the revocation of his teaching certificate."

"Did the young man report him?"

Esther shrugs.

"No one knows. He must have told someone. Word got around as it is wont to do. Poor Liz was devastated. Al's 'inappropriate behavior,' by the way, was never publicly acknowledged. He was quietly *retired*. But everyone knew. Liz feigned surprise, like everyone else. What else could she do? She swallowed her anger. It was a very bad time for her. She was very afraid because the same fate might have befallen her."

"And Al?"

"He moved home to Richmond to care for his mother. That was the official story anyway. He checked into a nerve clinic and received electroshock treatment."

"That's a treatment for insanity!"

"We are mentally ill, according to the psychiatric manuals. The psychiatrists use electric shock to dull desire."

"Desire is life! That's like killing someone's soul. It's murder."

I try to imagine a life without desire. It would be like wearing a gray sack, wading through mud. I study Esther, starting with her long slender toes with their painted red nails and work my way up her thighs, which are partly open, and desire springs instantly to life. How dare anyone take that from another human being.

"But that's not the end of the story," Esther says quietly. "Six weeks later, Al took a train to San Francisco and jumped off the Golden Gate Bridge."

I see a well-dressed gentleman pacing the bridge. He's slim, tall, fair-haired with a pencil moustache, his blue eyes red from lack of sleep, and then he's climbed the rail. There's no pause, no second thought. He's half somersaulting, half flailing. It's over in an instant.

"How could this happen?" I cry out.

"But it happens all the time."

I force myself to my feet, fists clenched. I don't know what to do with my anger. Esther looks concerned by my state of mind as if, having set a fire, she's eager to put it out. She gets up and takes my hands, kisses them and pulls me to her. It's calming in her arms, but I've lost my desire. I pull away, but she grips my hand tightly.

"People like us develop a certain resilience to survive. We learn to *cover our tracks*, as you Americans say. We pretend to be something we're not. We become very good actors. There are a few examples in history of those who refused to hide, who would not live a lie on principle, but they were quietly brought down. I don't know of any personally. Since time immemorial, we've been shamed into silence. And then there are the poor souls who can't pass, no matter what they do, because nature has made it impossible for them to appear other than what they are. In earlier days, they were crucified, burned at the stake, locked up for life in insane asylums. They are our martyrs. But we don't even know their names."

I'm still standing, but barely.

"You're a little too brave, darling, is all I'm trying to say. You have to learn to be a little less brave, that's all."

But I'm not feeling brave. I'm feeling very afraid. It's not like fear of the dark or fear of failure or even dying. It seems it's possible to lose everything, because of who you love. And when you lose everything, jumping off a bridge isn't frightening at all.

"Maybe I shouldn't have told you. I'm sorry."

"No, I'm glad you did," I say, and I sit back heavily on the bed.

"Innocence is beautiful," she says, sitting down next to me, and there's regret in her voice.

"I'm not innocent," I say. "I'm just stubborn."

I lie down and turn away from Esther. I'd curl up in a ball, given half the chance. I'll wait until she's gone, I tell myself, and do just that.

"In bed, we are free to do exactly what we like," she reminds me. Her tone is cheerful, gung ho. She means to comfort me. "But we can never be too careful in school and in our daily lives."

Esther looks at the clock and sighs, gets up and gathers her clothes, which are scattered across the room. But then she turns and takes me in, and letting the clothes fall where they may, she climbs back on the bed and onto me.

"Don't be afraid," she whispers in my ear.

10

My neighbors, I admit, are a bit too friendly for my liking. They keep a careful watch on me. A woman on her own needs looking after as they see it. Either it's Mrs. Harding at my door with another batch of oatmeal cookies or her famous banana bread, to put a little flesh on those slender hips of yours, she says, or Kathleen Perkins, stopping by with a baby on her arm, to let me know she's thrilled to have a teacher as a neighbor, given she's got the three and another on the way. If it gets too loud or I want to borrow a child—just kidding—I shouldn't hesitate to let her know. She doesn't want to interfere, but she did notice I live alone, so if I ever feel like some company I should stop by anytime. Or it's Mr. Brown, retired from his job as plant manager at General Electric, peering into the window on his evening walk past the house before supper and waving when he sees me. Or Bill Soros next door, who when he's not working the late shift at Wurlitzers is busy cutting my unsightly lawn and trimming my hedges or providing me with apples from his trees and late-season vegetables from his small garden. Or Cliff Johnson, our school janitor, hailing me from his small house across the alley, to ask if anything needs fixing, Miss Karen, which is what he's taken to calling me. There are a million things in need of repair in this old furnished rental, which, delightful in its way, with its hardwood floors and bending staircase, its picture window looking out onto the great elm in the front yard, is falling down around me. "I may just take you up on that one day," I tell him.

Even Louise D'Amato worries nonstop about my well-being. She tells me as much as she walks me home, a new ritual we are both enjoying. She thinks I should come live with her in the rooming house. One of the teachers is getting married, and there's a room opening up.

"Kar," she says, shaking her head, "I don't understand how you can live all by your lonesome in this big house." She's looking it up and down from the front yard, shuddering to make her point. "I hate to bring it up, but those Career Girl murders this summer?"

"That was New York City, Louise!"

"One of the girls was about to start her first teaching job. This September. Just like us. Elementary."

"What grade?"

"I don't know. They don't tell you that in the papers."

"Well, I think it's important," I say.

"You're not taking this seriously. They were stabbed sixty-three times! The teacher grew up in Minnesota! Her intestines were on the floor!"

"That's enough, Louise," I beg her.

"It's still unsolved," she says, shrugging her round shoulders.

"But you can't honestly believe a murderer in New York City is on his way here. And anyway, there were three girls living in that apartment. More like a rooming house if you ask me."

That seems to do the trick because Louise is unusually silent.

"I like my peace and quiet," I explain. "I never had a space of my own growing up."

"Have it your way," she says.

"Anyway, I have a couple of ghosts who keep me company."

"Oh, great," she says, rolling her eyes.

The truth is, there was a time I would have liked a roommate, someone like Louise. The old house is too big for me, and as for ghosts, the floorboards creak and the attic door is always ajar no matter how often I slam it shut. There was the night I woke in a panic, swore I heard footsteps on the stairs. I would have considered moving to the rooming house, if it weren't for Esther. The old rental has become our secret refuge now.

Mrs. Harding is climbing up the back stairs to the kitchen. Esther and I are having breakfast in our slips and there's no time to hide. I invite her in and introduce her formally to Esther, explaining how Esther, *would you believe it, Mrs. Harding!* had been helping me with my lessons until early in the morning and was so groggy I'd insisted she spend the night on the couch.

"So nice to meet you," Esther says, extending her hand. Her voice is relaxed, her manner pleasant. "Forgive our attire, please."

As she takes Esther's hand, I notice Mrs. Harding glancing in at my couch, which is decidedly free of bedding. I'll make sure to have a sheet and a pillow at the ready next time. I won't be so lax again.

"I hope I'm not disturbing anything," Mrs. Harding says.

"We're just at our books. A teacher's work doesn't end when the bell rings," I say, with a pitiable sigh, grasping at the well-placed books on the table.

"Too true," Esther says, echoing me, "that's when the real work begins."

We've become actors in a play, just like Esther said.

"Won't you join us for coffee?" I manage to ask.

"Well, I'll just sit for a minute. If you're sure I'm not disturbing anything."

Mrs. Harding sits down warily on the edge of the chair. I'm quite sure she's never sat down to coffee with two half-naked women before. Esther lifts her schoolbooks with exaggerated effort, clearing a space for Mrs. Harding, while I pour a coffee at the counter. We steal a glance. Mine is helpless, but the look in

54

Esther's eyes is steadying, reassuring. I join them at the table and beg Mrs. Harding, please, to share her banana bread recipe while we've got her, and make a fuss about getting the measurements and instructions down exactly.

As her expression changes from puzzled to contented, and she starts in about how they'd bought the TV with the walnut grain finish in the end, though she wishes now they had gone for the colored set, but how Arnie says they'll be cheaper down the line and you don't want to cross him just now because of his change in diet, it's all grapefruit and cottage cheese for the poor man since the scare with his heart, I breathe a sigh of relief. Mrs. Harding accepts our story. She asks us to call her June and before you know it, we're all on a first-name basis.

"Esther. What a pretty name and so unusual." She'll have us both over for coffee soon, she promises, and we exhibit great enthusiasm.

We see her to the door, and as she clatters down the steps, we wave her off like old friends, then collapse back in our chairs. It was a close call, and we're both shaken.

"Now you understand, perhaps," Esther says, "what a risk we run."

"Even so. We handled ourselves like top-notch actresses. I'm proud of us."

"We let our guard down," she says, shaking her head. She looks set to say more, but lets her thought trail off. She's leaning on the table, her head in her hand, watching me in that way of hers.

It doesn't take long until we're in each other's arms. Our kisses are so sweet we don't stop there. But as much as I try to shut her out, June Harding is lurking in the back of my mind.

I learn to keep my distance when we're walking down the street, to keep my hands to myself, a problem I solve by putting them in my pockets. I avoid gazing into her eyes in the teachers' room, forcing myself to look anywhere but in her direction, down at a book, for example. I find I get a lot more reading done. I no longer pause a moment outside her classroom door to catch a glimpse of her and hear the melody of her voice teaching the children. I adopt a collegial formality with her at work and anywhere in public we might come across each other, the local library or the grocer's, for example. When her name comes up, I respond as I would in regard to any other teacher, as if I'm as fond of her as anyone else, perhaps a little less, as if I could take or leave her. I adopt a certain distance, an air of *nonchalance*, when Louise, who is smitten with her mentor, speculates about her life while we're walking home after work.

"Do you think she was married once? Perhaps she lost her husband in the war?"

"Maybe. She's awfully private. I don't know a lot about her."

And the truth is, I don't. Apart from the very few facts apparent to all, that she comes from Germany and trained at the teacher's college, that she's been at the school for such and such number of years and teaches fourth grade, I know next to nothing about her life. She may have lost her husband in the war for all I know. It's as if she dropped out of the sky and into my arms. It's exciting, as odd as it may seem, to love a near perfect stranger. And it's her wish. I've given up asking. I have the distinct feeling we belong together, as if I've found her again after losing her, but when and where I can't remember. Perhaps it was in another life. It's a very strong sensation and scares me sometimes. I don't even know where she lives with her roommate, Lee-Anne. An address is listed in the phone book, but I don't recognize it. She hasn't volunteered this information, and I haven't asked. She'll invite me over when the time is right, she says.

11

It's happened. I've been called in for a meeting with the principal.
Will has been waiting by the door to usher me in, and as he does
so, I note his hand sliding a little too far down my back for my
liking. But he's not made a pass at me yet, and I've begun to feel
a little left out, wondering what's stopping him or what's wrong
with me.

He seats me and takes his place behind his desk,
straightening a thin tie and staring at me from behind his thick
glasses with a conspiratorial air. Something's clearly afoot, and
he's enjoying himself immensely. To his credit, Will is jocular
and unassuming with his power, but it's a mystery how someone
with his underwhelming attributes has gotten so far. And he is
on his way up the ladder, has his eye on the superintendent's
office, according to Esther. I find myself staring at his hands,
which are the daintiest part of him, like those of a woman in fact.
It's time for lunch and I'm hungry, but I've been summoned here
anyway. Needless to say, I'm none too happy, and my stomach is
growling its discontent.

"Karen, you won't like hearing this I fear, but I have to ask a slight favor."

He sits up, then forward, arms resting on the desk. "Your fifth-grade science book contains immensely interesting and varied lessons, as well as lively experiments, which you are free to adapt to your style, but let the apes go their way and humans theirs, I beg you. Parents here, to their credit, are generally hands off, but there are some topics it's just better to avoid."

"I know better than to mention evolution, Will," I tell him, sitting up in my chair.

I don't tell him I spent an entire morning last week teaching my lesson on the origins of man, without mentioning evolution once. We wiggled from the water onto the land. We crawled on all fours and rose to our feet. We howled and roared and beat our chests like apes.

"There was that unfortunate lesson last week," he says.

I lift my eyes, pretending to think back. "Oh, *that*. That was expressive dance, Will!"

"Nice try, Karen. The fact of the matter is, Dorothy received a call from a parent on Friday."

"Okay, Will," I say, giving in. "It won't happen again."

I want to quit while I'm ahead. I want to eat my lunch.

"Good Karen, let's keep it that way."

I start to get up. But he's not done. He's straightening his tie again, and clearing his throat he gestures for me to sit back down.

"While I've got you, you might take another look at your history textbook. The syllabus is excellent. It's all very well to defend the Indians, but our job, at least in part, is to raise up patriotic citizens."

"I understand my duty, Will," I assure him quickly. "We say the pledge of allegiance first thing every morning."

Or we will from here on in, I promise myself. I've forgotten once or twice, I admit, or better put, there are days when other issues are more pressing. I'll be called in for being a communist next. I'm wondering how on earth Will's come to his information, if there's a spy in the class, and thinking how best to convince him that an honest approach to our history can only make our country stronger, but he's moved on. In fact, he's jumped out of his chair and has opened the door to Dorothy Hugh's office.

"But that's not why I've asked to see you, Miss Murphy," he says, addressing me suddenly and inexplicably with cheerful ceremony. "Will you look who I've got here. Make yourself visible, young lady."

It's Lydie. She's been waiting in the office with Dorothy.

"And why have I brought you here, Lydia, my dear?" he asks with great solemnity.

"Because I fought Brenda," she answers, looking down at her scuffed tennis shoes.

"There are witnesses aplenty," Mr. Lindquist informs me with a twinkle in his eye. "Let's have the whole story, Lydie, shall we?"

She straightens out her strong little body and sighs so loudly you could hear it down the hallway. "I was playing with Janie," she says and stops.

"And this circumstance led to which consequence?"

She sighs again.

"Well?" says Will. "We're waiting."

"Brenda butted in. So, I head-butted her in the stomach."

"And do you believe, in hindsight, that your action was justified?"

Lydie shrugs.

"Well, what was the result of your *fait accompli*?"

"My what?" says Lydie, making a face.

"Brenda was left in what condition?"

"She's a big crybaby," Lydie offers, kicking the floor with her toe.

Will turns to me. "Brenda Larson was found crying inconsolably, Miss Murphy, huddled under the monkey bars. Bear in mind, the wind was knocked out of her and she was struggling to breathe at the same time. She has asthma, poor Brenda," he adds, as an afterthought.

I'm quite aware of Brenda and her asthma. She's a grade

behind Lydie, in Esther's class. She sits out gym and helps her in the room. Esther is quite fond of her little helper, as it happens.

"Have you said you're sorry, Lydie?" I ask her.

"If I did, would you still call my mom?" she says, addressing her question to Will, not me.

"I don't think we've decided yet, have we, Mr. Lindquist?" I say. I won't let Lydie deny my existence. Not here in front of the principal. It's bad enough that I spend most of my waking hours being stared down or stared through by this child.

"Please don't tell on me," Lydie cries out, and she falls, sobbing, into Will's arms. It's quite a performance; your heart could break. At once, Will's as tough as a kitten.

"There, there, don't cry, child," he says, wiping her matted hair from her face. "You tell Brenda how sorry you feel, and we'll all go on as before and forget it ever happened, shall we?"

With exquisite timing, poor asthmatic Brenda Larson appears in the doorway. She's a chubby little girl with white-blond curls, a cherub at first glance, but there's a glint in her eyes. Lydie breaks free of Will's grasp, puffing out her chest, her fists clenched, and the girls face off. They are rivals for the new girl Janie Dolan's attention and devote considerable energy to sabotaging each other and courting Janie's favor. Brenda has won out on more than one occasion with gifts bought from her sizable allowance and invitations to swim in her family's private swimming pool. Lydie's indomitable will is powerless against such enticements. These goings-on and facts on the ground have been observed by Esther and passed on to me.

Within the week, tensions between the two sworn enemies have escalated. The reluctant truce brokered by Will threatens to give way to all-out war. Brenda comes rushing up to Esther during lunch with a noticeable set of teeth marks in her arm. She tells her Lydie has threatened her life. Lydie, red-faced and furious, eyes her from across the schoolyard, while sweet Alan Simpson, her *aide-de-camp*, stands by.

This time I'm to appear in Dorothy's office with both Lydie and Janie, and Esther is to meet us there with Brenda. Will has asked Joan Smith, as our resident psychological expert, to moderate a meeting between the children in the hopes of arriving at a long-term solution. Alan has begged me to let him come along as an objective witness, though he is anything but objective when it comes to Lydie. At the appointed hour, during recess, my little threesome marches ahead of me, up the stairs and along the corridor. We pass Mr. Lindquist standing in the hallway, instigator of today's meeting, who hails us as we go by. The children are feeling very important. Well, Lydie and Alan, that is. Janie's showing nothing of what she might be feeling and it may be nothing. Her most noticeable trait is her indifference.

I sense my beloved coming up the hall behind us. I don't need to turn around. I hear the jingle jangle of her bracelets and the click of her heels. Joan is waiting impatiently for us at the door. She's set up a circle of chairs. Lydie and Brenda rush to claim theirs, and call out for Janie. She obliges and takes her place between them. Alan takes his seat next to Lydie, who promptly turns her back on him to whisper excitedly in Janie's ear.

Esther and I stand outside the circle facing each other. When Joan gets up to close the door, we take each other in with some amusement. Esther dares to wink at me and desire floods my body. Then Lydie and Alan are flying from their chairs and into her arms. Esther was their teacher last year. Watching Lydie offer up affection to Esther so readily, perhaps a tad demonstratively, I can't help feeling a touch of envy, I admit, and she's glancing over to make sure I'm looking. Janie, meanwhile, stares blankly ahead, and this is Brenda's chance. She whispers something in her ear with great animation. Janie shrugs, then nods, and Brenda smiles triumphantly. No doubt a bribe has been offered and accepted.

"Thank you for coming to see me, children," Joan begins, as we all eye her skeptically. "We've had our third playground incident, and Mr. Lindquist has asked me to help get to the bottom of things. What happened yesterday? Who wants to start?"

The children avert their eyes and shift in their seats until little Alan volunteers. His voice, which is scratchy and low-pitched for a boy of his years, takes on an air of authority. "We were in the alley," he begins.

But he is immediately kicked by Lydie and corrected. The alley is forbidden during recess. "No, we were not, Alan."

"Where were you, then, Lydie?" I ask.

"Down by the jungle gym," she says, under her breath, to no one in particular.

"That's a lie," says Brenda. "They were in the alley, kissing."

"Who was in the alley kissing?" asks Joan.

"Them," says Brenda pointing in the direction of my three children.

"Alan and Janie?"

Brenda shakes her head emphatically. "Uh, uh. Lydie and Janie."

Janie clears her throat and seems about to speak, a startling development. All heads turn to face her and the room goes silent. "We were not kissing. We were pretending." Her voice is flat and quiet.

Lydie's face has turned bright red. It seems the kisses were real for her.

"Well, it sure looked like it," Brenda says.

"What of it?" Lydie growls.

Alan pipes in where angels dare to tread, unable to contain himself, a tiny budding defense attorney. He's sitting forward, feet dangling above the floor.

"Brenda asked Janie to meet her in the alley so she could lie on top of her and feel her down there."

Joan tries her best to contain her shock, but her eyes betray her. They're saucers.

"Who told you such a thing?" she manages to ask.

Poor Alan's inner struggle is written on his face. Torn between his innate honesty and his loyalty to Lydie, he's lost his bearings. He closes his lips tightly and shakes his head. The other children hold their breath and wait, staring up at the ceiling.

"Alan, I asked you a question."

"I don't remember," he says, and he's starting to whimper.

"Well, we'll just sit here until you do," Joan says.

She crosses her legs and crosses her arms. She stares up at the clock. We're all staring at the clock, even Esther. A minute goes by, then two, then three.

"Janie told Lydie and Lydie told me," he blurts out, in agony.

If looks could kill, Lydie's would. I breathe a sigh of relief it's not directed at me.

"Is this true, Janie?" Joan asks.

I'm not sure I understand Joan's line of questioning or where it's heading. She seems to have left psychology behind and taken up interrogation.

Janie shrugs in response.

"Lydie? Brenda? I am waiting for an explanation for . . ." Joan's struggling for words.

Suddenly, I'm ten again, lying on the grass with my quiet, thoughtful cousin Fran, who was two years older than me, but a follower.

"Come on, Fran, let's play house. You'll be the wife and I'm the husband. I'll just get on top of you, like this, and pretend I'm kissing you," I say, lifting my leg over her.

"No Karie, I don't want to," Fran says, pulling away from me, and for the rest of the afternoon we sulk in opposite corners of my grandma's farmhouse.

In the twin bed in the attic, which we share at sleepovers, I turn my back to her and hold my breath, until she's tapping me clumsily on the shoulder.

"Are you awake?" Fran asks.

"No," I say.

"We can play the game now, if you want."

I roll toward her. She's flat on her back, arms stiffly at her sides, like a dutiful bride. I can still picture it. I mount her, like a king at a banquet—that's the feeling if I had to describe it, and kiss her squarely on the mouth over and over until my tongue finds its way inside, letting my fingers wander at the same time. I can taste that kiss (an experience repeated only a handful of times as my cousin drifted away from me and discovered boys) and feel her softness *down there* as I sit here.

"Liar," Brenda is saying to Alan under her breath.

"You're the liar," Lydie mumbles, nudging Alan hard with her elbow.

"Say you never said it. Say you never said it and go to hell for lying!" Alan shouts, stabbing the air in Brenda's direction.

"Lydie keeps a dirty magazine behind the fire escape. She stole it from Bert's," Brenda cries out.

Lydie and Alan freeze in place. They hadn't expected this line of attack. This is a colossal betrayal apparently of a top-secret piece of information the children share.

"I never stole anything," Lydie says darkly.

"That's it, children," Joan says, defeated. "I've had it. We'll just call your parents in if it happens again."

12

We can't help but talk about the children. A number of mine are Esther's children, too. She had them last year and has passed them on to me, in a manner of speaking, and though she wouldn't *think* of coloring my opinion, she must admit that Lydie was delightful in every way in her class, *cute as a button.* She can't think what's happened, but perhaps I should focus my attention on her friend, Janie Dolan, who is new to the school and whose passivity is troubling. Pay more attention to the girls, she advises. Boys are loud and dominate the classroom. We favor them, just like the world does. We make excuses for their behavior, because boys are good-natured and don't take things personally and never hold grudges. But the girls need our help, too, and rarely get it. They hold things in. They take everything to heart and never forget. What they don't do, as a rule, is make their presence felt.

I don't tell her how Lydie could eclipse the sun. I don't say that Lydie makes her presence felt all right. Lydie's command of the classroom is my dirty little secret.

Esther's moved on in any case. Some things are sacred, she

says. She would *never* attempt to influence my teaching methods, God knows. Those are mine and mine alone. Still, while we're on the subject, I should bear in mind that yes, we are helping to form their world view, but they must also be allowed to think for themselves.

"But they have to *learn* to think first, don't they, Esther? How do you teach a child to think?"

"They know how to think," she says, and she sounds a tad insulted. "They're thinking all the time."

Esther's answer is meant to reassure me. But in my mind's eye, I see Lydie thinking up new plans to outwit and thwart me.

"You'll figure it out," she says cheerfully, turning out the light.

We reach for each other, make love without thinking. I'm a ship out to sea when Esther stirs beside me in the dark.

"The teaching is one thing, but first and foremost, Karen, and you must never forget this, we are the guardians of these small beings," she says.

I have twenty-one.

A good half enjoy reading very much, a handful are good at math, and a few have noticeable artistic talents and perform in our school's monthly talent show. Joanne Schultz plays the violin while Nancy Walsh turns the pages for her. Dave Butler is learning the tuba. Diane Pfister and Vicky Johnson sing duets together and model themselves on the Lennon Sisters. Three children are near perfect spellers. Susie Davis is the fastest runner in the class, boys included. A number of the children are grumpy in the morning and may be lacking sleep; a sizable portion, including Janie, rarely say a word all day. Of these, five are just getting by, while three do very poorly despite my best efforts, the worst being Terry Cook who can't read and fails every test he takes. A couple of boys are so skinny you could use them for a straw. A couple of the girls are alarmingly mature. One child is smaller than the rest, but heads above the others in thoughtfulness, that's Alan, and there's one near perfect child, Joanne, and if she *is* a goody two shoes, well that's a blessing in this class. There are three troublemakers, no less, the smart aleck, Marty Fowler; the bully, Matt Schroder; and the class clown, Lydie. And then there's Karl Fiore, who answers out of turn no matter what I do. And there's the fearsome clique, two of whom make up the singing duet; the third, Becky Morris, is their manager of sorts.

Apart from the few inseparables, enemies and best friends shift with the wind, but there are three who have no friends, at all. Richard Malikowski is a bona fide genius according to the IQ test and practically mute. He spends his days hunched over paper, drawing intricate blueprints for a town of his own invention on another planet. I've told him I'd like to move there when he gets it built. The other two are teased incessantly and vulnerable to pranks at their expense. Donna Hicks wears badly fitting hand-me-downs and comes to school with dirty hair. Kent Anderson stutters and wears thick glasses. I do my best to keep Matt from bullying Kent, while Nancy, our class caretaker and Good Samaritan, who happens to be the oldest of seven, protects Donna as best she can, but neither she nor I can shield her from every indignity. There are four Hicks children in the school, and all of them are subject to ridicule and bullying. Their mother stands in line for food at the Salvation Army, but they still come to school hungry. The cruelest children hold their noses when the Hicks children pass by. They call them hillbillies to their faces and accuse them of stealing when something goes missing.

The children's eyes are evenly divided between hazel, brown, and blue. Dan O'Malley has eyes so violet they startle you, and he's inseparable from brown-eyed Pete Coffey. Esther says they've been like that since first grade and the best thing is to let them be. Dan has the messiest desk in the class while Pete is as neat as a pin and helps me clean up at lunch sometimes. There are blondes, brunettes, a couple of redheads, and three with hair as black as jet. The hair is silky, curly, thick and thin or buzzcut to the skull so you can't tell. Some are spotty, a couple are freckled, but all of the children are white as paste, as are the teachers in

67

the school and their neighbors. The Mexican laborers arrive to harvest crops in summer, but for the most part they don't stay. There's one Black family with two boys over at the high school. The father is the newly appointed football coach out at the college where kids of every hue disappear for home on the train and buses on the weekends. No one wants to stick around here.

It occurs to me to formulate a lesson plan aligned with our study of the Civil War to talk to the children about the color of their skin. What I should teach the children is always on my mind, perhaps more than the children themselves, I admit, and I promise myself to heed Esther's warning from here on in and be a better guardian, even of Lydie.

"I'll do my best, Esther," I tell her, but she's fallen fast asleep.

13

We wake in the same instant, eye each other, and stumble down to the kitchen wrapped in each other's arms, like a two-headed creature. Esther's a woman of few words in the morning, I've discovered, but over soft-boiled eggs and toast, she surprises me with her talkativeness. She asks me if I know anything about the history of our profession.

"No," I confess. "They didn't teach us that up at the college."

"How irresponsible," she says, and she looks dismayed. She cracks her egg with one sharp whack. "But then I'm not surprised. Education has changed, and not for the better. When I was a student, we had a section devoted to the history of teaching. It was very popular, taught by a lively professor who had been *in the trenches* from the beginning. She was one of our tribe by the way, British by birth. She looked like Queen Victoria, short in stature, but her knowledge was colossal. But that was in the days of the Teacher's College, when it still meant something to train as a teacher. Things have gone quickly downhill." She shakes her head, scrapes at her yolk. "It makes me very sad. We should all know our history."

"I couldn't agree more. Teach me, Miss Jonas, please."

"All right," she says, putting down her spoon. She stops a moment to gather her thoughts. "Let's start with the fact that for most of modern human history, it was only the aristocrats and the moneyed class who served them who could afford any semblance of education for their children. They hired tutors or governesses who were themselves from the middle class, mostly from families who had fallen on hard times. When a father died or declared bankruptcy, for example, or some sort of family catastrophe occurred, the daughters were allowed to leave home and become governesses in someone else's household. It wasn't romantic like you read in novels, though. They were basically servants, except the other servants had each other for company, and the young governesses were very much alone. They were rarely considered a part of the family unless they caught the attention of the husband, which could prove fatal. The mothers were often jealous of their children's affection for these young women and could be very cruel to them. They had no official status, and there were no regulations or contracts laying down the conditions of their working life. They had no real authority over the children either, and hardly a moment to themselves."

She's sitting up in her chair, spine like a pole, but her legs are opening and closing like a concertina and her hands are in constant motion like an orchestra conductor. The history of our profession is a rousing lesson. I raise my hand.

"Yes, Karen?" she says, calling on me.

"But you can only teach so many hours a day."

"They didn't only teach, far from it. They took all their meals with their pupils, oversaw their physical activities: walks or a swim before dinner, sports, that kind of thing. They entertained them in the evening, put them to bed, read to them, sang them to sleep. They were run ragged. And yet for some girls, often girls like us, the life of a governess represented freedom. They'd escaped marriage and were earning their keep with their wits, dreadful as the pay was."

"That's no small thing, escaping marriage," I say. A feeling I know all too well I can't help thinking.

"True enough, but at what cost?"

I'm absorbed by this lesson. I want her knowledge like I want her body. "Go on," I beg her.

"Even as the first schools appeared, girls were mostly kept at home. For one thing, schools cost money. They might learn to read, and a few learned to write. They attended grade school at best. Even as free schools opened up for the poor, a complete education was denied them. Women took to the streets to fight for a girl's right to higher education. And these newly educated girls went on to become the first professional women schoolteachers. You should know that the existence of the Teachers College was the direct result of women who fought for our emancipation."

She stops and looks me in the eye.

"Have you heard of the Seneca Falls Convention, Karen?"

"No," I say.

"Shocking," she says. "Elizabeth Cady Stanton?"

"No," I admit.

"But you know who Thomas Jefferson is?"

"Of course."

"Elizabeth Cady Stanton wrote the Declaration of Sentiments. It was adopted at the Convention on Women's Rights at Seneca Falls, New York, in 1848. Does that date ring a bell?"

"No," I say, head hanging.

"It's as important a document as the Declaration of Independence. It's American history, for God's sake. But you've never heard of it. And why? Because it's not taught in the schools."

Esther gets up from her chair, as if she's had enough, and moves away from the table. She stares up at the ceiling with a sigh, turns to look at me, and shakes her head. She makes her way back to the table resolutely, and placing her hands on the back of her chair leans in toward me. This is a typical classroom position of hers, one I've observed often, and denotes her wish for complete attention.

"The Declaration states that a woman is a man's equal, nothing more or less. It demands that women be given the right to the vote, but also the right to a thorough education. The signers threatened to overthrow the government if their demands weren't met. In 1848, Karen, imagine that."

She sits back down and studies her plate. She takes a bite of toast and chews it reluctantly. "Their demands weren't met, of course. The government was not overthrown. But they refused to give up."

I'm moved and galvanized by this appreciation of my calling. I see my colleagues in a new light, as part of something larger, something heroic. I picture them marching down Lincoln Highway, battle helmets on, pointers at the ready, Irene Bachmeier at the fore. The image makes me laugh. "Here's to the teachers," I shout out, raising my cup. "I'll never forget this lesson, Miss Jonas."

"I hope not," she says, taking another bite, and she looks very serious. "May I continue?"

I realize the history of our profession is no laughing matter to Esther. In fact, many things I've skipped lightly over in my life are deadly earnest to her. It must be a German trait, I decide. It's certainly contagious. I find myself growing more serious by the minute.

"Please continue," I tell her without the flicker of a smile, and she obliges.

"As men left the schoolhouses for better paid and more respected work in the new professions opening up to them, in banking and law, as accountants, managers, engineers, the women were left to teach the children. But with serious restrictions. Married women were banned from teaching. Practically speaking, they were sworn to celibacy. If they chose to marry and have a family, they were forced out of the profession. The ban is still in place in some parts of the country. Its effects linger everywhere, even in 1963, as you will be well aware. Teaching may have been the perfect escape for women wishing to avoid marriage and men altogether, but for the others who longed for a family *and* had a calling to teach, well, they had a difficult choice to make. God forbid, they became pregnant. They married quickly and left the profession or they sought help to end the pregnancy, which was dangerous and against the law. If they were lucky, they found a midwife or doctor to carry out the procedure in a back room. Others had no choice but to use coat hangers or knitting needles or drink some awful concoction in the hopes of inducing a miscarriage. Countless women have died attempting to end a pregnancy. They die of infections, perforated organs, unstoppable bleeding—teachers among them."

I push my plate away. The jubilation of some minutes before has turned to dismay.

"But it's not just history, Karen. It's happening today."

An old school friend of Lee-Anne's, a fellow teacher, became pregnant after a short affair a couple years ago. Do I want to hear about it? she asks, and I say, yes, though I'm not so sure.

"She had a backstreet abortion in the city to avoid detection by anyone connected to the school or the town. Little did she know, the procedure had gone terribly wrong. She developed a fever at the rooming house where she was sent to recover. Her body had gone into septic shock. To add to the tragedy, the police appeared in the emergency room to question her. They demanded the name of the doctor who performed the procedure. They threatened to tell her family and the school if she didn't comply, so she had no choice. This they did as she lay dying."

I see a young woman writhing on a cot in a dark hallway, flanked by policemen, one with an open notepad and a pen at the ready. Her dark hair hangs loose around her face, her eyes, already glassy, contain terror and shame.

"I'm sorry, I've spoiled our breakfast," Esther says, and lowers her eyes. She looks set to drop the subject when her eyebrows rise. "Abortion is one thing, but then there's birth itself. Think of all the women's lives cut short in the act of giving birth. Until quite recently in human history, every pregnancy brought the possibility of mortal danger for the mother."

"It hardly bears thinking about," I say.

"But you have to think about it," she corrects me. "We can never forget what it has meant to be a woman. They have suffered the worst kinds of abuse and every indignity. And yet they survive. They are so strong. They have to be. I guess that's why I love them."

She stops and looks at me, then winks.

"Especially the teachers." There it is, that dark laugh of hers, and the world is righted. "And now, darling," she says, and she's getting up. "I have to go home and prepare to teach the children in the morning."

She leans over to kiss me good-bye. Her scent and nearness awaken every cell in my body. I hold onto her arm, summon the courage to ask her the question that is always there in the back of my mind. "It's been so long since you've been over, Esther. I never know when I'll see you again. Are we a couple? Tell me, yes or no?"

"Is this a quiz?" she says, displeased, and she's won again. Yes-no questions are insufficient, both in the classroom and outside it.

But I won't give up.

"Stay," I beg her. "Spend the day with me this once."

She looks me over, bites her lip. She seems to be thinking things through, and then she nods and takes my hand and leads me up the stairs. There, on our island, we discover new treasures hidden deep inside us. When our lovemaking exhausts us, we fall asleep until desire wakes us with a start.

When Esther leaves, I have to search for my name, my body's boundaries. The sense of self that defines us, so tied up with memory and *ego*, as Freud would say, and also the bodily sensation that stops us bumping into walls, these take time to reappear. I lie down and wait it out and slowly my memories return and I feel my body on the bed and become myself again.

14

We've had lunch and recess and the children are working more or less quietly in their math books when Will pokes his head into the room and asks me to step outside. He's as pale as a ghost. "What's happened, Will?" I ask him. He tells me quietly, his voice breaking, that the president's been shot in Dallas. The reports are saying he's dead. He's been assassinated. I should send the children home and report to his office for our Friday meeting. Dorothy's informing the parents, he says.

"Oh, God," I hear myself answer.

"If you prefer, I can tell them, Karen."

"*No*, I'll do it," I say.

Will squeezes my hand and rushes off. I take a moment to draw a breath and another moment to quiet my nerves because I'm shaking, and reenter the room, which is decidedly noisier than when I left it. I float above the room and watch myself ask the children to put their books away please, and hear myself telling them I have very sad news.

"Children," I begin, "President Kennedy." I can't go on. His name evokes life itself, and all that is new and fresh, not death.

"The president," I start again, "has died today and so we have decided to stop school early and send you home. Your parents have been informed. We'll talk about what a great man he was next week."

The children are studying me with a curious expression.

"Are you crying, Miss Murphy?" our caring Nancy asks.

I realize she's right and my face is wet.

"Yes, honey. I'm very sad," I manage to say. Despite my best efforts, I'm crying openly.

I hear a sob from the back of the room and another, and the children, one by one, are joining in. Some have their heads in their arms, but most are looking at me with piteous expressions, tears rolling down their cheeks, and I realize they're crying because I'm frightening them, not because of the president. I find a tissue in my sweater pocket and quickly wipe my eyes and blow my nose.

"I see that you're sad, too, children. That's why we're all going home. Gather your things and line up, please."

I move to the door and wait, trying not to think about the terrible news or anything at all. The children gather their things in slow motion, wordlessly, and form a line in front of me. Despite my best efforts, an image of the president's smiling face floats in front of my eyes, and the tears well up again. I take a deep breath and tell myself that if I am going to be a teacher I must shape up and find some self-control immediately. This seems to do the trick because the next thing I know I'm ushering my children out of the building and sending them home. I make my way slowly back up the school steps to the principal's office. The sun beats down mercilessly.

As I reach the hallway, I hear wailing and then a stifled scream and the thump of something falling and ensuing commotion. Across from the office, Dorothy and Joan are kneeling over Marilyn, the kindergarten teacher, who appears to have fainted clean away. Esther is waiting for me in the doorway. I allow myself to fall into her arms. Then Louise comes bounding down the hall and into her arms, as well, and Esther's doing her best to hold us both. I can feel her heart beating wildly. Joan and Dorothy half carry Marilyn, who's come to and is moaning in agony, into the office, and the O'Connor sisters, Noreen and Margaret, who've rushed up from their first- and second-grade classrooms, help them get her onto the couch. We're all gathered now in the small office, red-eyed, shaking our heads, wringing our hands, covering our faces, openly crying. First-grade teacher and director of the school's Christmas play, Natalia Craddock, excuses herself with large tragic gestures, but the rest of us remain and one by one we quiet as Will adjusts his small transistor radio, and we strain to listen as the reports come in. For a time, there is no more news, and the terrible story repeats itself. Christine Olsen, third-grade teacher and sports instructor, turns her back to us, pressing her fists into the wall, her tall frame shaking. Irene is the first to speak.

"He had the makings of a very great president." Her stern tone is softened by grief. "We heard him speak at the Egyptian in '59, didn't we, Christine?"

"We knew he'd be president," Christine says, turning back toward us, her voice choked. "Everyone who saw him did. He was our great hope."

"Oh, my God," Margaret says, over and over, holding tightly to her sister.

"Too young, too young," her sister Noreen says.

Celia James, second grade, is speaking up with quiet poise. "There'll never be another like him, nor the first lady, poor woman. They brought such style, such grace to the White House."

"He was a god," Marilyn cries out, "too good for this world. That's why they had to kill him."

"Let's not rush to judgement, hon," Dorothy says. "The truth will come out soon enough. We just have to be patient and stay calm . . ." But now our school's calm and practical secretary has broken down and can't go on. I put my arm around her shaking shoulders.

More details filter in from the transistor's static. The

president's death is officially confirmed.

"No. It's not real," Marilyn shouts at the radio. "It's a lie. They made it up. It's a bad joke. It's a bad dream. It's a mistake. Turn up the radio, Will. They'll tell us, you'll see. It never happened. It can't be true. It can't be. It can't. God, let it not be true."

New details emerge. Lyndon B. Johnson will be sworn in as the thirty-sixth president of the United States. We listen in silence, covering our mouths, holding our foreheads, wringing our hands. Will speaks up, his voice just above a whisper.

"I say we head on home, ladies. Call off this week's meeting unless there is anything pressing?"

He looks around at us. We can barely shake our heads.

"How shall we explain this to the children?" It's Esther, stopping us.

The children had slipped our minds.

"We've got the weekend to think about it," Dorothy reminds us.

"Thank God," Marilyn says. "I couldn't face them tomorrow."

"Their parents will decide what to tell them," Irene says.

"But it's our duty, isn't it?" I ask. I look around at shrugging shoulders, shaking heads and lowered eyes. No one's speaking up. The only sound is a chorus of sighs.

"Not everyone had such a high opinion of him," Joan says, finally. "I hate to bring it up."

My father, for one. Despite Irish pride in our first Irish-Catholic president and my mother's quiet devotion, we all suspected he had broken ranks and voted for Nixon. His tirades in front of the nightly news confirmed this suspicion. I won't go home for Thanksgiving, I decide. I'll stay where I belong, with Esther.

We sink back into silence, and though the meeting's been adjourned, we stay where we are in the small office, numbed by shock, confused as to how to move forward, helpless to take action, waiting for some kind of instruction, but none is forthcoming. Greg Jordan, sixth-grade teacher, slips into the room, late as usual, and stands behind us.

"Sorry," he says to no one in particular, bowing his head.

"Karen's right," Will says, speaking up with sudden resolve. "It's our duty to talk to the children. We'll have an assembly first thing on Monday morning. Bring your children to the gym." He gulps back a sob and Dorothy pats him on the back like he's a baby.

The prospect of Monday's meeting gets us onto our feet. Slowly we find our balance. We make our way down the large central staircase, weary and broken, hanging onto the railing as if we've been cast about in a great storm and landed in a place of utter devastation.

We don't have an assembly on Monday. President Lyndon B. Johnson has declared Monday a day of national mourning. Louise and I join her roommates in the boarding house in front of the television set to watch the funeral. We gang up on the couch and floor, seven stunned young women, teachers, nurses, just starting our lives, unable to fathom what we are witnessing, which is the end of the world as we know it, the end of goodness. It feels like we've been robbed or worse. Our dreams are gutted. I'm grateful not to be alone. Esther's left town to visit an old college friend. I would have crawled into her arms to seek my comfort, but perhaps it's better in the end to be here with my peers. Esther's very sad, but she's not shocked like the rest of us. She's troubled, but resigned, as if it were inevitable. The world can be a very dark place, she tells me, and for now darkness has won out again.

Dorothy is waiting at the top of the stairs as we arrive at work on Tuesday to inform us the idea of an assembly's been nixed altogether. Will has decided it's best to move on and not talk to the children about the assassination of our president. She catches my eye and shrugs. I find I'm not surprised. The list of off-limit topics at the school keeps growing, in keeping with the tensions in the country at large. I'll talk to the children myself, I decide. But Tuesday morning comes and goes, and I haven't mentioned the president once. I'll wait until the time is right. The children are happy to be back at school, away from the shock and despair and the constant news.

I say nothing on Tuesday afternoon and nothing on Wednesday, either. My lesson on Thanksgiving goes out the window, too. I don't have the heart.

15

We've moved on from the terrible Middle Passage, the shackles and whips, the cruel existence on the Southern cotton plantations, to something more merciful. The Underground Railroad offers relief, and the children are spellbound. Even the troublemakers listen open-mouthed to stories of smugglers and shoot-outs, slave-catchers, and secret hideouts called safe houses run by the abolitionists.

"And this should make you very proud, children," I tell them. "The Underground Railroad ran right through our town!"

Their eyes light up, and they sit up tall.

But it's Harriet Tubman in particular who has captured Lydie's imagination. Perhaps it's the start of a new obsession, and for the first time since the start of the school year she has many questions. Yes, Harriet Tubman would have been very scared, I tell her, and no, that didn't stop her from going back nineteen times to rescue three hundred men, women and children in all. But Lydie's most insistent on knowing the exact details of Harriet Tubman's escape to freedom. I don't think she would have had a gun, I tell her, but she had her wits. No, she didn't need a map because she followed the North Star. Yes, most certainly, she would have pretended to be someone else when she was stopped on the road.

"Exactly how long did it take her to get to freedom, Miss Murphy?"

"I don't know the answer to that, Lydie."

"Why not?"

"Because it's not in the books I've read. We only know things that are written down in some form or passed on by word of mouth."

"Somebody could ask her, Miss Murphy," she says, thinking it through.

"Asking directly is indeed the best method for obtaining information, Lydie. But Harriet Tubman's not around to ask. I wish she was. She died in 1913. That's fifty years ago."

Lydie turns red. Titters erupt from the clique of three, but I choose to ignore them. I'm laying the groundwork for the Civil War and everything's going more or less smoothly.

"But I saw her," Lydie says suddenly.

This takes the cake. In an effort to save face, Lydie's raising the dead. I take a deep breath and wait. It turns out Lydie saw Harriet Tubman upstairs (off limits to the children), she swears to God, and she'll bring us up there right now if we want.

She's getting up and making for the door. The children follow suit, spilling out of their chairs.

"Sit," I order her. And she does, to my astonishment.

"Sit," she orders the children, who are huddled by the door. And they sit, too.

"You can go on with your lesson, Miss Murphy."

"Thank you, Lydie," I say, and I do go on. As if nothing untoward has happened, as if the rule book on classroom discipline has not been turned on its head.

"In the year 1860, children, the country was split right down the middle. In the North, all men and women lived in freedom. In the South, slavery was part of everyday life. Should a human have the right to own another human being? What do you think?"

The children want to shake their heads, but they're unsure. Alan raises his hand.

"It's not right," he says.

"President Abraham Lincoln thought just like you, Alan. But in the South, slavery was a part of property law."

"Slaves were niggers," Marty Fowler calls out.

There's an audible gasp, a snicker from the back. Little hands fly up to mouths. What they all feel is a change in the room. Something new has transpired beyond the bad word. Perhaps they read it in my expression. All eyes are on me, waiting for my reaction. *Take your chance*, I tell myself, *or you will live to regret it.*

"Marty," I say. My tone is very grave. "That's a terrible word you used. It's cruel and it's insulting to all of us. We're not like that. We're not hateful. You're not either, are you?"

Marty looks at me with startled eyes. His troublemaking has never brought him quite this much attention. I watch him struggle to find a proper response.

"Huh?" is all he manages.

I turn back to the class.

"Hateful words lead to hateful deeds, children. Hate led someone to kill our president. He was a good, kind man. He was working hard to make the country better for everybody in it, not just for some. A bullet took his life, but behind the trigger was hatred. Hate led men to bomb a Baptist church a couple of months back. It happened in Birmingham in the state of Alabama, but it could happen anywhere. Children were in that church for Sunday School. Four young girls—one, just eleven years old, like some of you—were killed by that blast."

I pull down our map of the Earth. A storm of dust rises. It's not been used in years, it looks like.

"Here is the planet Earth, boys and girls. This is where we live. The Earth is our home. This line around the middle? It's called the equator. The equator is the closest point on Earth to the sun. It's hotter there than anywhere else. But nature is very clever."

I write EVOLUTION across the board in giant letters. Let

Will call me to the office. I dare him.

"Evolution is nature's way of helping us survive on Earth, children. Thanks to evolution, humans who were born at the equator had dark skin to protect them from the sun's hot rays."

I point to the poles. "And here are the north and south poles. It's very cold there. Why do you think that is?"

One precious hand goes up.

"Joanne?"

"Because the poles are far from the sun."

"Very good. Humans near the poles of the Earth evolved with a pale complexion. Their whitish skin helped them absorb the sun's rays to keep them warm."

They're studying their hands, poking at their skin.

"This all happened many thousands of years ago. We've moved around a lot since then. Some of us have lighter skin and some of us have darker skin and all the shades of color in between."

I step away from the map and face the children head on.

"There is only one race, children, and that's the human race. The color of our skin is just a question of the sun's rays. We are all exactly the same. Do you understand?"

They're nodding, if barely. It's as silent as the grave.

"*We will not be judged by the color of our skin, but by the content of our character.*' A very great man named Dr Martin Luther King said that."

I gaze long and hard at Marty. *So far, so good,* I tell myself.

"Now, Marty, I'd like you to stand up and apologize to the class for what you said."

I wait, holding onto my desk. The children look from me to Marty and back.

"We're waiting."

Marty pulls himself up from his chair. His head hangs down.

"I'm sorry," he says, under his breath.

"Can't hear you, Marty."

"Sorry," he says, shrugging his shoulders.

"Stand up straight and try again."

"I'm sorry," he howls. It's plaintive, like a wolf baying at the moon.

"Okay, Marty, thank you. You can sit back down now. I never want to hear that word again."

He sits down, cradling his head in his arms on the desk, and his skinny frame begins to shake with sobs. It would take a hard heart not to feel pity for the boy. I'm sacrificing him for the sins of his fathers, I know, but the room feels cleansed somehow. We're all stopped and are watching him with a kind of fascination. And then Matt Schroder, the bully, calls him a homo and begins to imitate his sobbing. In a flash, two small bodies are one. It happens so fast I don't see it coming. Marty and Matt are rolling on the floor, in a death grip, it looks like, scratching and punching and biting and kicking, like the two tomcats on my grandma's farm, one red, one black and white, sworn enemies.

Homo, homo! other boys shout, banging on their desks. *Homo, homo,* they're chanting, urging Matt on like a mob at a boxing ring, and to my shame I say nothing.

It takes all my strength to tear the two of them apart, in any case. And then the lunch bell rings. The Civil War will have to wait.

16

Marilyn Nowack, the kindergarten teacher, has invited me for dinner at Pizza Villa, her treat, no ifs, ands, or buts. She knows she looks a state, she says. She's hardly slept a wink since JFK died. She keeps seeing the pictures of Jackie and him in the limousine in *Life* magazine. "I'm slabbing on the makeup," she says, "but as good as Avon is, it can't cover everything." Our school's own Avon lady insists on my trying a brick-red lipstick, which will bring some color to my too-pale face. Needless to say, we teachers are not her best customers, but I give in. I try to pay her, but she won't hear of it, and pushes the money back across the table.

"He had his foibles," she says, shaking her head, and it takes me a moment to realize who she means. JFK could be her lover, it's that intimate. "I know, I know, he never should have started that affair with Marilyn. But when baby Patrick died, he was on the next flight out of Moscow. He was right by Jackie's side when she left the hospital. And from that moment on, Karen, he was on the straight and narrow. We're all human, right?"

I nod, signaling my full agreement. Far be it from me to cast the first stone.

Leaning in further, her large breasts resting on the table, Marilyn's voice lowers to a whisper. "LBJ killed him, hon. In cahoots with the CIA. They all wanted him dead. The mafia, too. Lee Harvey Oswald was a stooge, honey. They paid Jack Ruby to cover it up. He was a hit man. It'll all come out. I'll be in my grave by then, but you mark my words."

My head is spinning, but she has some better news to share, she says, so I should get ready. Greg Jordan has twins on the way, and I'm sworn to secrecy. But she has something else she wants to talk to me about, something private and seemingly urgent.

"You see this figure, honey?" she says, running her hands down her bosom and waist.

"I do." It was hard to miss. Marilyn was something of a bombshell, like her namesake, for a schoolteacher, at any rate. She had the same teased blonde hair, red pouting lips, the hourglass figure, more or less.

"I'm holding up pretty good, don't you think?"

I nod with energy, my mouth full of spaghetti.

"Well, the boobs are fake. They're sponge, hon."

It spills out of her like a confession, how at twenty-four she'd been diagnosed with fast-growing breast cancer and took her one chance at survival: radical double mastectomy.

"I called off my engagement to Jimmy Miller. I couldn't bear the thought of him seeing me that way. And how could I ever have a baby? A baby needs a mother's breast."

Poor Marilyn. No one breastfeeds anymore.

"Before I went under, and I swear to you this is true so help me God, I said let me survive this, sweet Jesus, and I will devote myself to your flock. Hell, I'll become a schoolteacher."

She smiles and spreads her arms wide. "Ta-da! That was twenty years ago, little lady, and I'm still here."

"You're a walking miracle, Marilyn."

"Nah, hon," she says, brushing my words aside. "I'm just your garden variety kindergarten teacher. I know I'm no genius."

I can't contradict her, much as I'd like to.

"But the babies love me."

It was true. Marilyn's large class of kindergartners were devoted to her, without question. She mothered them no end, like they were her own.

"Life's a struggle, hon, but you dust yourself off." Her eyes tear, threatening her mascara. "*The Power of Positive Thinking* is my bible, honey."

The craze of positive thinking had spread across the country by the time I entered high school. My sisters had a copy and read from it out loud. For a while I practiced what Norman Vincent Peale preached. When a negative thought came into my head, I cast it out. But Aunt Helene's death in a small-plane crash had made me think twice. And the explosion of the hydrogen bomb confirmed my pessimism. Positive thinking was a big old scam, as far as I was concerned. *But I keep this to myself.*

"What happened to your fiancée, Marilyn?" I ask, changing the subject.

"He got over it, married Connie Sullivan. Moved out of state. Had five kids before he dropped dead, poor man." She sighs, places her hands over her heart. "As for me, I'm married to Liberace."

I have to laugh. "Don't laugh, I mean it," she says, laughing.

Then growing serious, she studies me in earnest. "But you're still young, hon, and much too pretty to waste. You should be starting a family about now, having a normal, happy life."

Beneath her cheerfulness, I sensed a wellspring of regret in Marilyn, which her story confirmed. I would have liked to tell her that I had made the life I wanted alongside strong and able women like myself, that I had chosen this path and didn't regret it for an instant, despite evidence to the contrary. But instead, I let her think her own misguided thoughts, because I didn't want to make her feel worse than she did already. Marilyn was an outsider despite her knowing more about the school's goings-on and everybody's business than anyone else. How she came to her gossip was one of life's great mysteries. Perhaps she absorbed it by osmosis. Knowing lent her a certain power, helped her get through the day with her head held high, because, generally speaking, the other teachers intimidated her. Irene made it all too obvious that she was not one of us when it came to intellectual stature. Joan had concluded she was psychologically unstable and drank too much. There *was* something decidedly childlike about Marilyn—and inappropriate—I had to admit, but I found her endearing and allowed her to take me under her wing and into her confidence.

"Now someone like Irene was born to teach. I don't think she's ever had a beau. But I know darn well that's not the case with you."

She stops and stares deeply into my eyes as if she's searching for a beau there. I don't dare look away.

"Someone broke your heart, didn't they, hon?"

"Yes," I answer, without thinking. "Someone broke my heart." I can't help but play along, she's so convinced. Far be it from me to disappoint her.

"I knew it," she says, banging the table. It occurs to me the gossip's sure to spread. The story of the beau who caused me sorrow will be all over the school tomorrow, which is not a bad thing, considering.

"You'll get over it, honey, you will," Marilyn assures me, grasping my hand in her slightly swollen one with its chipped, painted nails. "You will find your man. He's out there somewhere, just waiting for you."

Her eyes sweep Pizza Villa's ceiling as if she is seeing him up there. "I have every confidence you will not end up a spinster schoolteacher."

"I do like teaching, Marilyn."

"Of course, you do. We all love God's children. And they adore you. But you deserve better. What do you make of Esther?" she says, as if one thing followed from the other.

"How do you mean?"

"I'm not sure she's the best kind of influence."

"How so?" She's startled me. *Stay calm and don't let on,* I tell myself.

89

"I feel she's quite unnatural."

"I've never thought about it," I volunteer. My tone is light, casual.

"Be careful, that's all. Women like her, well . . ."

"I don't understand," I say, sitting back with my best puzzled expression.

Marilyn sighs as if I've twisted her arm. "Well, all right. I've observed how she looks at you. I know you enjoy her company and there's no denying she's a wonderful teacher. There's much to be learned from her in that arena. But keep a distance."

"Why?" I should change the subject, but I'm pressing her instead.

Marilyn rolls her eyes, turns red. She looks around the restaurant, gulps back her wine. "She lives with a woman," she says in a whisper, "in a farmhouse outside town. Lee-Anne Anderson, assistant principal at the junior high."

"In a farmhouse?" I manage to say.

"Route 23 out past the cannery," she says, nodding, certain.

So that's where my lover lives. I've walked alongside those fields. I can picture the very house.

"And they aren't just friends, Karen."

It's true then, what I've known all along. I have it from Marilyn. I'm sure I'm as white as a sheet. I look down to gather my thoughts, shift my knife and fork across my plate.

"Are you all right, hon? I know it's a shock."

I'm not shocked. I'm crushed, crushed by my own ignorance, by what a fool I've been. "Esther Jonas's private life is none of my concern," I say, shrugging. "Whether she has a roommate or not is none of my business."

"I have it on good authority," Marilyn says, and I have no doubt she does.

I meet her eyes. They're shining. Something monstrous has taken possession of this big-hearted woman, a venomous mix of hate and glee. She's clearly having the time of her life. A spittle of wine runs down her chin like blood.

"If Lee-Anne wasn't Lars Anderson's daughter—he's town

supervisor—she'd have been sent packing long ago. Don't think for a minute that Will Lindquist doesn't know about Esther and Lee-Anne. Money and power talk in this town."

So that's why she's brought me here. To warn me and save me. Why does it upset you, Marilyn, I want to say, a woman loving a woman? What possible harm could they pose to you? But I say nothing. Across from me sits a wolf in sheep's clothing. She doesn't know she's declared war and become my enemy.

"I just shudder to think of the children," she says, shuddering, and she looks to me for confirmation.

"I'm sure her children are in very good hands."

She shrugs. She checks her makeup, puts her lipstick on. I let her pay. We leave Pizza Villa. She links her arm in mine, wobbly in her high-heeled shoes. I'm repulsed by her, but I don't pull away. She has me tightly in her grasp.

I wish you dead, Marilyn, I really do, I tell her silently.

17

Esther is avoiding me. We nod politely in the halls, but hardly exchange a private word. She stays in her room at break, and I don't have the heart to seek her out. I'm avoiding her, too, by all appearances. I join the others in the teachers' room for our daily banter. I teach my lesson on the Civil War. Outwardly I'm soldiering on, but inside it's a very different story. I feel physical pain, a stabbing in my joints, spasms in my muscles including my heart, and my stomach aches. In a word, I am wretched. I crawl into bed when I get home from work, sleep through until morning, wake out of a murderous dream. I've torn Lee-Anne Anderson limb from limb. I spend much of the weekend with my head in my arms at the kitchen table like a drunk collapsed on a bar stool. Esther doesn't call, and I don't dare call her. Lee-Anne might answer. There's no question of my showing up at the farmhouse door. Lee-Anne's inside making love to her.

Then I hear the news. Lee-Anne has been kicked *upstairs* to a supervisory role on the Board of Ed in Chicago. She'll take up her new post at the start of the New Year, which is fast approaching. Esther will likely finish out the school year and join her there. No doubt a teaching position will be found for her.

All this I learn from Marilyn at lunch on Monday when she invites herself to sit with me. This piece of gossip confirms her story, and she shares it between bites with an air of triumph. Somehow my feet carry me into the ladies' room. Esther's there, putting her hair in place at the mirror. She catches my face in the glass and what she sees must frighten her. She grabs my arms as I begin to fall.

"What's wrong, darling? What is it?"

I sink to the floor, choking back tears. She, of all people, can't comfort me.

Marilyn comes in and stops short on seeing us.

"What's happened?" she asks, her tone accusing.

"I don't know," Esther says with genuine surprise.

"I'm getting Dorothy," Marilyn says, backing out the bathroom door. Esther takes the chance to wipe my tears and kiss my face and mouth, which only serves to make things worse. I shake my head and pull away.

Marilyn has wasted no time and is back with Dorothy, and Joan's in tow as well. The three of them are now hovering over Esther and me. They're propping me up against the bathroom wall.

Joan rushes out and brings a chair. They sit me down.

"Have you had bad news, hon?" Marilyn asks, squeezing my trembling hand. I refuse to answer and close my eyes, but the tears keep coming.

"I'll take her class to the library with mine after lunch," Esther tells Dorothy. "You need fresh air, Karen, and to get home," she says, turning back to me.

"I'll drive you, honey," Dorothy says. "Let me get her something to calm her down first," she tells Esther under her breath as they hurry off.

I'm left alone with Marilyn and Joan. They're standing by the bathroom door like a couple of sentry guards.

"If I didn't know better, I'd swear her heart's been broken," I hear Marilyn whisper to Joan.

"I don't think so," Joan says, dismissing Marilyn out of hand. "It looks like a case of nervous exhaustion. Sometimes the pressure on a new teacher is harder to bear than they let on, especially for a conscientious one like Karen."

"Rest up good, okay?" Dorothy says, as she pulls up in front of the house.

I've calmed down on the short drive here, but the kindness in her voice sets me off again, and I let out a sob.

"Oh, honey," she says, with a sigh, turning off the ignition. She's perplexed, watching me with her warm brown eyes. "Shall we just sit here awhile?" I shake my head, but I'm finding it hard to open the door. Dorothy gets out to help. She takes me firmly but gently by the arm and guides me up the path and onto my porch. We stand in front of the door while I search my pockets for my keys.

"Can I make you a coffee, Dorothy?"

Dorothy takes a step, then hesitates. "Are you sure? I don't want to intrude."

Staff didn't visit each other as a rule. I'd learned that from Esther. I'd learned everything about the school from Esther, the ins and outs, and she was leaving me.

"I've got nothing to hide. I made the bed before I left," I say, and try to smile.

But once we're inside, it's clear to us both that my making a coffee or doing anything at all is out of the question. Dorothy leads me to the couch and sits me down, and now she's right at home. She finds my kitchen and the glasses on the shelf. She comes back with water and gently opening my hand places two tiny blue pills in my palm. I swallow them, and tossing my shoes off curl up in a ball and wish myself away.

"Should I stay a little?" she asks.

I nod, and she pulls up a chair.

"Relax and let yourself go, hon," she says, in a whisper. "If you want to talk, I'm here."

I do want to talk. I want to talk very badly. I want to tell her the whole story. How I'm feeling utter devastation. How Esther's leaving town with Lee-Anne. How I love her more than life itself. How I'd jump off a bridge if there was one high enough in town. How staying on at the school without Esther is unthinkable, and I'll be preparing my resignation letter as soon as I can stand up. But I can't talk to Dorothy. No one can know about Esther and me. I'm utterly alone. I feel something like panic, but it's far away, behind the clouds forming in my brain.

To fill the silence and pass the time, Dorothy tells me about her fiancé, George, who'd gone missing in the war and was presumed dead, and how she didn't know how she got through it. It was all a blur now, but six months later he turned up on her doorstep.

"I was sure he was a ghost," she tells me, laughing. "I ran screaming out the back door."

Dorothy, you're an angel, I try to say, but no words come. So I smile instead, but my lips aren't moving either.

I wake up to familiar women's voices.

"She's been sleeping like a baby. I gave her some Valium," Dorothy's saying. "Best thing they've come up with in years. The bottle's on the kitchen counter if she needs it again."

I drift back to sleep. When I open my eyes, Esther is sitting in Dorothy's place, watching me, arms crossed.

"I have something to tell you, Karen. I had hoped to tell you under other circumstances," she begins slowly. I know what's coming but am too drugged to brace myself. I go under, hold my breath. "Lee-Anne and I have broken up."

I can't be hearing straight or else I'm dreaming.

"She's taken a position in Chicago. It's a considerable career step and one that I think will make her happy. She'll be moving out next week. She's already found a place in the city."

No, I'm awake. My body is humming and thawing.

"I needed to give it time, darling, to give her time to understand. I'm so sorry to have kept it from you. It was quite awful. She was very upset, as you can imagine. But now it's done. I've told her I'll always care for her and wish to stay the very best of friends."

18

I can't tell Esther my own secret, that I'm still engaged, officially. The fact is I've left my fiancé hanging with the promise to provide him with a final decision about our marriage after my first year of teaching.

Larry's studying medicine in Kansas now and among my nightly prayers is that he finds the girl of his dreams there. We'd been together since sophomore year in high school. We were a couple, but we were best friends, too. We did everything together, freeing me from girlish things I didn't enjoy and couldn't see the point in, like shopping and baking, sewing patterns and fashion magazines. If being a girl meant being like them, I wanted no part of it. What that made me exactly I didn't fully understand, though that mysterious word, *homosexual,* and all it implied, stayed lodged in the back of my mind. Larry freed me from all the chatter about boys and how to attract them. Because the fact remained that boys didn't interest me in the least. Not like that. They did not make me all of a tremble like Sister Maria had. I didn't seek their kisses out with hunger. But kissing Larry was fine enough and one thing led to another. We canoed and hiked, built fires and studied the night sky. We were also on the road to being married, and everybody knew it. He proposed the day we graduated, down on one knee, laughing. We were having ten children, he warned me, over my protests. The whole thing felt inevitable, and I didn't say no. I loved Larry all right, but more like a brother. It was strong affection I felt for him and my feelings confused me. They manifested as doubt and hesitation. Whatever else, I needed time, and freedom most of all, to think it through. I put our wedding plans on hold and went off to Teacher's College where I promptly fell in love, unrequited at first, with one of my professors.

Professor Adele Baxter helped me to see the nobility of teaching. We began meeting in her office to discuss the Socratic method and quickly moved on to life's purpose. The teacher's role was one of service, she explained, to be approached with great seriousness. The very day that first semester ended, she invited me to her cabin in the Dells of Wisconsin where we made passionate love the entire weekend. I told myself I was testing the waters before settling down to married life with Larry, but Professor Baxter confirmed my suspicion that there were other paths to a satisfying existence. She was physically strong and strongly opinionated concerning all the issues of the day, the Cuban Revolution, for example. She was a fan of Fidel Castro. She had traveled the world, spoke five languages. And she was lustful. I'd never met a lustful woman before and her desire drove me wild. Thanks to Adele, I became acquainted with previously unknown parts of my anatomy and discovered their capacity for ecstasy. She opened my eyes to a world where women lived and loved independently, and independent from men, but she never spoke about it. If this was my initiation, it was conducted without ceremony, behind closed doors. Discretion was a given. Any questions I may have had about the life of a female homophile went unanswered. She did provide me with a copy of *The Well of Loneliness*, but our affair was over before it began. She called to thank me for our "beautiful interlude" as she called it, and promptly stopped answering my calls or the desperate notes I left in her school mailbox. I'd been cast out, and raced back into Larry's arms. I willed myself into believing a normal life was a matter of choice and that I'd chosen him, and led him to believe our marriage was still on. We spent spring breaks and holidays together as if our future was secured.

But it was time to break off the engagement, once and for all, and as quickly as possible. I hadn't seen Larry since I'd started teaching. I wrote and asked if he could meet me at home the following weekend. I had to talk to him about a matter of some urgency. He wrote back immediately, saying yes, he needed to talk to me, too.

He's sitting on the side of the bed, the same bed we secretly shared after school and on trips home from college while his parents worked long hours running their dry-cleaning business. He's hunched over with his arms crossed.

"I've met a girl, Maureen. She's studying nursing. I can't keep on waiting," he says.

The relief I feel is so immense, putting an end to any lasting doubt or hesitation. The question of my future has been laid to rest. Marriage and children were set out for me practically at birth, but here and now I'm on another path.

"I'm in love, too, Larry," I blurt out, too cheerfully.

"I thought as much," he says, glancing up at me.

"With a teacher," I say, before I can stop myself.

He sits up. I can see his mind racing.

"His name's Greg," I tell him, quickly. Greg Jordan had the distinction of being the only male teacher in the school. "He teaches sixth grade. We're only dating, but I thought you should know."

"Greg," he says, nodding and shaking his head.

"I'll always love you, Larry."

But he's not in the mood to be humored. I join him on the bed, where he quickly turns away from me. I kiss his neck and shoulders, which are tense, resistant. I encircle him with my whole body. I want him to feel loved before we say good-bye forever. I owe him that, at least. Despite himself, he turns toward me. We undress quickly. He gives himself to me, grudgingly at first, but soon he's crying out in need and anger at the same time, and this embarrasses him and he pulls away.

"That's enough, Karen," he says, eyeing me strangely. "I shouldn't have agreed to see you again."

We gather our clothes. I study his naked body for the last time. It's a man's broad chest, covered in coarse black hair. We were children, I realize, when we first came together. I'm changed as well, coarser too, no doubt.

"I'll miss you, Larry. Can we stay friends?" I ask him as we dress.

He shrugs, his gray-blue eyes cast down. "I intend to propose to Maureen when exams are finished for the year. I'll look for an internship as far from here as I can manage and take her with me." He forces himself to look at me. "I loved you for seven long years."

His face grows hard. Larry has no tolerance for injustice. It's an expression I know so well, and now it's directed towards me. He's feeling disgust, but he doesn't know the half of it. Everything's been a lie between us, from our engagement to my true nature. I'm sick of lies, I tell myself, and all forms of deception. I take a step towards him. I want him to know the truth. But he's backing away, arms lifted as if to shield his body from a blow.

"You could have ended things sooner, you know, and put an end to my misery. But you only think of yourself and always have. You're selfish, Karen."

He turns away, suddenly modest, struggling into his underpants, pulling up his trousers. He sits on the bed to put his shoes on.

"I'd just like to know one thing."

"What's that, Larry?"

"What were you waiting for?"

He gets up from the bed and braces himself, waiting for his answer.

"To see if my feelings changed." It's a half truth. The moment for an honest reckoning has come and gone. Besides, you can't trust anyone, like Esther says, least of all a lover spurned. He's capable of reporting me to the school.

"Well, surprise, surprise, other people have feelings, too."

He's moved to the door and stands waiting to usher me out of his house, his life. I take my time putting my clothes on. I won't let him rush me. I'm not quite ready to leave him. I concentrate on the feel of hooks, buttons and cloth, pull up my stockings. But then I'm dressed, and I slip on my pumps and grab my purse. As I head out the door, I search his face for any sign of forgiveness or regret. But he's moved on; he's not even looking at me.

"Good luck with your schoolteacher. Maybe you'll treat him better," he mutters as he slams the door behind me.

19

As fate would have it, my supposed beau, Greg Jordan, peeks out of his room as I'm leaving school and, looking right and left down the hallway and finding all clear, waves me over. He needs to ask a small favor, he says. He won't beat around the bush. He's overwhelmed with recent expenditures, including a new house and large appliances, and has taken on a second job as coach in the Parks and Recreation department, and though he isn't supposed to mention it, and I should please keep it to myself, there are twins on the way. I make sure to look surprised and offer my congratulations, though I know about the twins from Marilyn who knows more about Greg than anyone, Greg included.

Greg had been entrusted with the Herculean task of teaching a combined group of sixth graders. He was ambitious and eager to prove himself, and his interview for the job had been well-nigh electrifying, according to Marilyn. He was also very handsome. The children, girls and boys alike, were smitten with him. He was youthful and burly, with a large head of silky brown hair, green eyes under heavy brows, and dimples in his cheeks and chin. His decidedly masculine presence transformed the atmosphere wherever he appeared, usually late, and I'd decided it was a good thing, all in all, to have a man among us, though I kept my opinion to myself. Irene was convinced his hiring spelled ruin, the end of the profession as we knew it, and Esther had to agree with her, and Greg *was* undeniably *laissez-faire* when it came to lessons. It was all fun and games that drifted out of his classroom.

"What do you make of the board wanting to move sixth grade over to the junior high next year, Greg?" I say, as he ushers me into his room.

I'd been meaning to ask him since hearing the news, but he's hard to pin down, dashing off after school, a stranger to the teachers' room. This news affects him most directly but he's decidedly preoccupied, and I wonder if he's even listening.

"Who knows," he says, shaking his head, closing the door behind him. He looks up at the clock and frowns.

"Are you in a rush, Greg?"

"No, no," he says, and he smiles sheepishly. "Well, I should get over to the park. We've made it to the semifinals and it's a home game."

"Congrats," I say, halfheartedly.

"Karen, I know it's a lot to ask," he says, looking down at the floor.

"What is it, Greg?"

"It's, well, listen, how would you feel about helping me out with my lesson plans? Once a week, that's all, if it's not too much to ask. Just a few notes?" He runs a hand through his shiny hair. "It would be so darn helpful."

There's that sheepish grin again. His muscular arms in his short-sleeved shirt bulge and twitch in anticipation.

"All right, Greg," I find myself answering. "We can do that."

He's about to throw his arms around me from the look of things, but then he thinks better of it and hitches up his pants instead.

"I'll need copies of your books."

"Karen, I am in your debt. Don't think I don't know it. I'll get those books to you tomorrow. And if things go as planned," his deep-set eyes are gleaming, "I may be in a position to help you out one day."

"It's all right, Greg. I don't mind, really. I need the practice. I might end up teaching sixth grade myself."

"You never know," he says, winking at me.

And before you can say Jack Robinson, he's rushing out of his room and leaving me there.

"I know what *I'd* have asked for in exchange," Louise says, licking egg roll grease from her fingers and lips.

We've ordered our usual from Heng Hoe's menu: Chicken Chop Suey, Beef Chow Mein extra spicy, and egg rolls for starters.

"What's that, Louise?" I say, leaning over my plate.

"Guess."

"Ten dollars per lesson."

"Try again," she says, shaking her curls.

"I can't imagine." Louise was fun to tease.

"His body. His hulking, gorgeous body," she says, embracing her own body like a lover.

"Louise! Greg Jordan's a married man," I say, playing shocked. "With twins on the way, but don't tell anyone, it's a secret."

"I know that. Marilyn told me. But I can dream, can't I? Don't tell me it didn't cross your mind."

"Okay, it crossed my mind."

It hadn't, to be honest. But charm is something else entirely. No one could escape Greg Jordan's charm. There's no telling to what heights he'll soar in his career in education.

20

Esther's staying in the farmhouse for now, though she's thinking of finding an apartment in town. In the country we are freer in our movements, but because I don't drive, Esther has to pick me up and bring me home, which bothers her no end. The rented farmhouse is the place of my dreams, with its wraparound porch, stands of old trees, and a red barn collapsing under its own weight across a path lined with roses and lilac. There's an attic with two comfy chairs and a standing lamp, vistas out across fields where horses graze. The only thing missing is mountains.

But I don't feel at home here. I feel Lee-Anne's presence everywhere, in the size and height of things, for example. The bathroom mirror, for one. I have to stand on my toes to see myself. Or the kitchen shelves I can't reach, or the king-size bed, which is as wide as my entire bedroom. Come live with me, I beg her. Out of the question, she says, it would draw too much attention. I know she's right. I shudder to think what Marilyn would say.

In my mind's eye, we are bound together in secret marriage. I don't need to marry in a church and take her name. We don't need to set up house. What I *would* like is to wake up with her in the morning and fling open the curtains, and walk hand in hand downtown for a pancake breakfast, and go to a matinee and kiss in the darkened theater, and head downtown for a steak dinner and stare into each other's eyes across the table, and walk slowly home with our arms wrapped around each other. That's really all I want.

"When we retire, Esther, we're going to live someplace where we're accepted and we don't have to hide. Even if it means moving to New York City!"

"We only have the present moment," she reminds me. "We have to take life as it is."

Today has been a perfect day, I admit. We've had a long, brisk walk deep into pristine woods a two-hour's drive from town, where we're safe from discovery and free to hold hands under a canopy of branches sharply bare against the winter sun and even make a kind of love against a fallen tree trunk. We've come back to the farmhouse to a bottle of wine and are stretched out on the bed in our nightgowns going over the week's homework. My children have written their responses to *The Helen Keller Story*, and shored up by the wine, I'm finding them very stimulating.

Nancy writes she'd give her own eyes to Helen Keller if she could. Alan says he used to be afraid of the dark, but after reading about Helen Keller, he's not afraid anymore. Karl says he'd like to give Helen a hug. Most of the children express similar sentiments. They love her, they write. Her story made them sad, some say. She seems happy, others note. *If she can be happy, why can't I?* Janie Dolan writes, surprising me. Joanne says she would die if she couldn't play the piano. She doesn't know what she'd do if she didn't hear music. She says Helen Keller is the bravest woman she's ever heard of. She's going to teach the deaf and the blind one day, she's decided. And Lydie? She writes that most of us have five senses, while Helen Keller has three—*touch, smell and taste*. As a postscript she adds: *Why do we have five senses? Why not seven? We should learn more about them.*

I have to laugh and put the papers down. So, it's come to

this, Lydie offering pedagogical advice! I glance over at Esther. The setting sun is reflected in her eyes, which are presently settled on me, but I'm determined to ignore her. I will continue on with Helen Keller, I decide, in the context of biology, slipping a unit on the five senses into my plan. And while I'm at it, I'll add a sixth, for good measure; that'll show Lydie. The sixth sense is my specialty.

To that end, I must prepare several sense experiments. Touch, smell, and taste, for starters. I'll need a lemon, an onion, a polished stone, a comb. I'll need a boiled egg, a bowl of water, and a blade of grass. Salt, sugar, cinnamon. A blindfold. Perhaps we'll make our own. I'm writing out my list most dutifully, but Esther's proximity is proving a distraction.

In fact, she's on top of me. My meticulous list and pen slip to the floor. She's biting her lip, something she does when she's involved in a serious undertaking, inching my nightgown up along my body and over my head. Her task completed, she lies back on the bed, content to observe me it seems.

I close my eyes and reach for her. I feel the coolness of silk slide over my arms like water as I undress her. I feel the sharpness of her pelvis, the soft hollow of her belly, now hot under my body. There's the scent of fresh snow that is Esther's alone, and as she opens for me, something else, like salted toffee, a peeled orange, an olive grove, and my mouth is watering with hunger, a hunger for her that subsumes all other desires. By now, I've tasted every surface and crevice of her body. I swallow her and beg for more. I'd lick her heart if I could, feast on her lungs, her brain. There's something cannibalistic about love, I'm finding.

Touch. Smell. Taste. These are the senses of love, I decide, until I open my eyes and find Esther watching me.

21

Irene Bachmeier has invited me over for coffee! She's baked a Christmas Stollen, a German specialty, she says, for the occasion. I'm reluctant, if truth be told, but Esther's all for it.

"Poor Irene, she's lonely," Esther says. "No one likes to be around loneliness. I suppose we're afraid it's catching. But we all experience it at some point in our lives."

She pulls me up from the couch and over to the door. "I'll be here when you get home," she assures me. "Be nice to her, Karen. We have our differences, but she means well. She has a good heart. But watch out for that Christmas Stollen. It's deadly!"

Irene welcomes me with a warm and strong handshake. Perhaps it's only me, but it feels like she's holding on a bit too long for comfort. Over her shoulder, I strain to take in the living room, which is dark and weighted down with heavy furniture and the thickest of drapes. I have the sinking feeling there's no escape. I'm Gretel, but without her Hansel. Over coffee in flower-patterned china, I learn that Irene has lived in town in this same solid red brick house most of her adult life, surrounded by large firs that remind her of home. The family had come over from

Bavaria, leaving everything behind, when she was a teenager. When her father dropped dead of a heart attack in the prime of his life, she moved back in with her mother and never left.

"We were quite a pair, really. She cooked and cleaned while I earned the money. I'm fairly hopeless at household tasks. Weekends, we'd take the train into the city, attend an opera or a ballet. She never learned English properly, so she was quite dependent on me, you see."

Then her mother's health declined and her mind began to slip away, and before long she was forgetting everything, even her own name. Irene nursed her vigilantly until the end.

"She died two years ago, *to the day*, Karen."

She stops and looks deeply into my eyes. I sense an expectation I have no desire to fill.

"I've been going a bit mad with loneliness."

I'm dumbfounded by her directness and can't think how to answer, until I remember Esther's words.

"We all experience loneliness at some point in our lives, Irene."

"I've never been kissed, Karen," she says quietly.

And now I'm speechless. Irene is staring at me in a way that is making me very self-conscious. I take a large bite of Stollen, which sticks in my throat, and begin to choke. *This can't be happening,* I tell myself. I'm going to die here in Irene Bachmeier's living room. I'm in a panic and gasping for air. Irene jumps up and whacks me on the back, sending the lodged bit of stodgy cake flying out of my mouth. Free at last, I catch my breath and try to compose myself. Things aren't going well, and I search my rattled brain for any excuse to cut my visit short.

Irene is standing over me. "How strange," she says, "I swear this very same thing happened to Esther. Perhaps it's me. Or do you think it's the Stollen?"

I look up at her and see she's smiling.

"I fear it's the Stollen. I'm sorry, Irene," I say. She begins to laugh, and this makes me laugh, too. Irene laughs like a mischievous schoolgirl, and soon we are laughing so hard that tears are streaming down our faces. Laughter offers release from the tension that has filled the room.

"Can I offer you something stronger than coffee?" she asks, wiping her eyes.

"You've read my mind," I say.

She disappears into her cellar and reappears quickly, dusting off a bottle of sherry.

"I've been saving this one for a special occasion."

She opens the glass doors of a massive mahogany cabinet with great ceremony and produces two delicate, gold-rimmed sherry glasses. We drink sherry until we're both giddy and the bottle is near to empty. Irene's nose has turned a brighter shade of red than usual and her cheeks are flushed, and I don't dare look at the state of me in the mirror. I've told her about my convent school education and she's told me about her childhood in Bavaria and how she misses the mountains, but what she misses most of all is the exacting and expressive German language. "You just don't have the words in English."

"Give me an example, Irene, please."

She thinks a moment. "*Fernweh*, for example. This means the longing to be somewhere else."

I know the feeling well, I tell her, and quickly find myself confessing that I've never liked this town. Irene listens intently.

"Me, either," she says in a pretend whisper, "I can't stand the place." For some reason this makes us roar with laughter, and I beg her to teach me another German word.

"*Weltschmerz*."

"*Weltschmerz*," I say, mimicking her.

"Very good," she says, nodding her approval.

"What does it mean?"

"How to explain it," she says, struggling. "It's as if you take on the pain of the world, something like that. You suffer for the world."

Fernweh, Weltschmerz. I can't wait to try them out on Esther!

It occurs to me that I like Irene and am enjoying her company immensely. The more she drinks, the less maudlin she becomes. She decries the destruction of her once beautiful country under Hitler's Third Reich in no uncertain terms and the tightening restrictions on the Baha'i faith that brought her family to America before it was too late.

"What do the Baha'i believe, exactly, if you don't mind my asking?"

"We believe in the power of love," she says, shrugging. "Like all believers, my dear. God's love has been expounded by many prophets over time, as the prophet Bahá'u'lláh tells us."

Sitting forward in her chair, Irene's eyes grow large. "*Love is light in whatsoever house it shines,*" she says, raising a stubby finger.

Her voice is not at all her own, and I'm wondering if Bahá'u'lláh himself is speaking through her.

"We know from example," she continues, and she's herself again, "that the absence of God's love leads to calamity."

They were ordinary Germans, those who turned against their friends, neighbors, teachers, doctors, the local shopkeepers, she tells me. Her family's dear friends, the Goldsteins, stayed in touch even after the Bachmeiers left for America. It was through their letters, which became more and more desperate and then frantic during the war years, that her family followed the sickening goings-on back home.

"You never read about it in the American papers. Nobody cared. Besides which, there were Nazis right here in town. Members of the German American Bund. They try to deny it now, but they were there in Chicago for the Nazi rally already in 1939. There were flags with swastikas waving in the breeze in Merrimac Park. Thousands of American citizens giving the Hitler salute. Shameful."

"And the Goldsteins?"

She drops her head, too overcome to speak. But then she tells me, in a rush of tears, that her parents tried everything to get them out of Germany, but when the paperwork finally came through, it was too late. They never heard from them again.

She struggles up from her chair and opens a drawer in her

massive sideboard, pulling out a pile of letters wrapped together with string. She's shaking so badly they slip out of her hands. The letters bounce along the floor and stop at my feet. I pick them up and as I do so, I feel a sting, a burning in my palm. I hand them quickly to her.

"I have the evidence of their crimes right here!" she cries, lifting the letters high in the air.

And suddenly I have to get home to see Esther right away and ask her, *no, demand,* that she tell me everything about her life in Germany.

"Oh, Irene, look how late it is," I say, pointing to the clock. "I've stayed much longer than I intended. I still have lessons to plan. But I so enjoyed our visit."

As I gather my things to take my leave, I realize that loneliness is not as frightening or as complex as it first appears.

"Tell you what, we can go to the ballet and the opera in the New Year. I've never been. We'll take the train in. Do you like Scrabble, Irene? I've had the idea of starting a Scrabble club. I belonged to one in high school and it's so much fun! Oh, and I'm thinking of making a little party on Christmas Eve. If you're free, I'd love for you to come."

The idea for a party was news to me. But as I say it, I find myself liking the idea and even looking forward to it. By the look in Irene's eyes, I've just made someone very happy. How easy it is, I realize. At the door, I let her hold me a tad too long and brush her lips against the side of my mouth. As I'm turning down the path, I see her in the window watching me and blow a kiss.

"She kissed you on the mouth!" Esther says. "Goodness me."

"Not full on the mouth."

"I've had my suspicions about her. But that is hardly appropriate."

"She's never had a lover. She's never been kissed."

"Well, before today," Esther reminds me.

I tell her about Irene's childhood in Bavaria and the mountains she loved and the words of the prophet, Bahá'u'lláh, about the Goldsteins, whose paperwork arrived too late. I tell her about the German American Bund right here in town. It all comes rushing out. Esther listens, but she doesn't say a word, and when I've finished, her eyes lower like a curtain falling. In the end, I don't ask her anything about her life in Germany. I don't mention *Weltschmerz* or *Fernweh*, either. Something stops me.

I dream of Irene. We're making love, in fact. I wake up under her sturdy, pale naked body, wet with desire. It's absurd, I know, but it stays with me. I ask myself what Freud would say. It must be my newfound freedom, I decide. I want to let everyone in. In the teachers' room, I smile widely when I see Irene and she does the same. We agree to meet once a week to go over fractions and decimals, remainders and dreaded word problems, and I'm sure I look forward to these lessons as much as she does. It feels good to be alive, I'm thinking, and in love with Esther, and to have friends like Irene.

22

The children are restless. Their feet are sliding back and forth along the floor, as if they're skating away, their minds wandering far from the story problem Joanne is solving on the board. My mind is wandering, too, and out the window I watch the first snowflakes of the year float down.

"Look out the window, children."

They don't just look; they race to the window, roaring and yelping. I'll take them out for an early recess, I decide.

"Thank you, Joanne," I say.

"But the problem isn't solved yet, Miss Murphy."

"Not to worry, the problem can wait. There's always next time. We've done more than enough math for today."

The children turn to look at me with big eyes.

"Put on your coats and line up at the door."

Cries of delight drown out any further objections from Joanne, who stomps back to her desk and may be about to cry.

"Will you teach math for us tomorrow, Joanne?"

That does the trick. Her teary eyes brighten. The truth is I'd be lost without her. Despite Irene's tutorials, the logic behind numbers continues to elude me. If I were an honest woman, I'd be paying the child.

As the children are forming their line, Nat Craddock's wide face with its squinty eyes and sagging jowls appears from behind the door. She's staging our school Christmas play and has come to beg me for extra rehearsal time with *her actors*, as she calls them. She needs to *iron out some wrinkles* in the Annunciation scene, she tells me in a very loud whisper, as if her life depended on it. The play, Nat's own version of the Nativity story, will be presented this weekend in the school gymnasium and several of my children are taking part.

Even the smallest town and perhaps every school has its eccentric. Natalia Craddock, or Nat, as she was known, was ours. Nat was partial to flowing scarves and capes, which led to the impression that she floated through the hallways, swept along by feelings she alone could understand. She talked to herself and laughed out loud in answer.

According to Irene, Nat was the daughter of Russian aristocracy who had fled from the Bolsheviks. Her mother, it was said (by Marilyn), had disgraced the family by marrying a Texas oilman. If you listened closely, you could detect a slight twang behind her British accent that seemed to confirm this sequence of events. How she ended up in town was anybody's guess. There was talk (between Louise and me) of a stormy marriage and a broken heart. She lived on Lincoln Highway, in one of the town's stone mansions that had seen better days, with a large white poodle for company.

Nat's passion was amateur dramatics. She was a founding member of the Barb Town Players, where she directed and acted in most of the plays, and she was quite an actress, according to Esther, who attended Nat's plays with loyal regularity, as did the entire staff. Her first-grade classroom was chaotic and cluttered, with runny noses and high emotions. From the outside looking in, you'd be forgiven for thinking her children suffered from neglect. And yet they came through unscathed, for the most part, and adept in the art of dramatic expression.

Joanne and Alan are to play Mary and Joseph, which doesn't surprise me in the least and is quite an honor, but Nat's casting of Lydie as God's messenger, the archangel Gabriel, gives me pause, I admit, and I can't help wondering how she was chosen for the part.

At lunch, Joan leans over to whisper that Lydie must be the first Jewish kid to play the archangel in the history of the school. I pretend not to hear her.

I'd be hard put to describe this Christmas play. Nat, dressed in a kaftan and turban, is standing off to one side with a music stand, narrating events as they unfold. I've got Esther and Irene on either side of me. Esther is struggling to keep a straight face, while Irene and I are nudging each other in the ribs to squelch our giggling. "Bite your thumb," Irene whispers, but that's not working. I focus like a laser on the words instead, a mishmash of Matthew, Luke, and Nat's own dialogue.

The Annunciation is figuring very largely, I must say. Lydie, as the Archangel Gabriel, a halo of tinsel askew on her head, covered from the neck down in a sequined bathrobe, seems to have forgotten Mary's existence and is announcing the birth of Jesus to an adoring public. Joanne's Mary, deprived of her lines, marches red-faced over to Nat and whispers something in her ear. Nat shrugs and sends her back to the manger. Little Alan as Joseph stands by in a state of utter confusion, loyal to his wife, Mary, but also to his beloved Lydie. It's mesmerizing in its way, watching Lydie sabotage the Nativity with an expression of unearthly purity. Still, things are going swimmingly enough as the three wise kings, played here by Lydie's rival, Brenda, her beloved Janie, and one of Joan's boys, arrive to offer up their gifts. The scene is barely underway when archangel Lydie intervenes to order Brenda out of Bethlehem, shooing her away when she resists. You'd think it was in the Bible, so realistic is her portrayal.

I look to Nat to gauge her reaction, but she's decidedly preoccupied. The entire cast has been herded onto the stage to sing "Hark! The Herald Angels Sing," the program's finale, and by the end of it I find I'm blubbering. I don't know what's come over me, but I look around the gym and everyone is wiping tears away, even Esther. Tears of laughter, tears of joy, it doesn't matter. We've been transported out of the gym and out of our lives. *Nat's a genius,* I'm thinking.

After praising the children, we crowd around Nat to offer our sincere congrats.

"I expect great things of Lydie Kaminski," she says, grabbing my arm. "She was quite splendid as Gabriel, don't you think?"

"How did you come to choose her for the part, Nat?" I ask, taking my chance.

"She's an angel," she says, shrugging. "The part chose her. It's a scandal that her parents aren't here," she adds, scanning the gym with her squinty eyes. "Such an angel," she says again, and sighs.

Needless to say, I don't dare to contradict her. I've heard much the same story from Esther—and Irene, for that matter. Lydie's ungodly transformation from angel to devil has taken place under my watch; there's no denying it. Her monstrous naughtiness is my own creation. I am her Dr. Frankenstein. I think back to the first days of school, searching for anything I might have said or done, but come up blank. I strove to be fair, to treat them all alike. But the more I tried to do right by Lydie, the more audacious her attempts at mutiny. Did I try too hard? Does it matter in the end? Things went downhill from day one. Perhaps we merely started off on the wrong foot. Whatever led to the current state of affairs will remain a mystery. In the New Year I'll turn over a new leaf with her if it kills me.

23

Esther has volunteered to help me prepare my Christmas Eve luncheon, and we've been at it all morning. We're nothing if not diligent and we're almost finished. I open a bottle of champagne to celebrate.

"*L'chaim*," says Esther, toasting me. The sound is strange to my ears, throaty and thrilling. "*A nous*," I answer in my high school French.

She empties her glass in long, deep gulps and goes back to peeling the eggs.

"Let's run away," I say.

Esther laughs that laugh of hers.

"I mean it."

"Well not right now. I'm busy *cooking* as you see."

She's on to the vegetables now, chopping with gusto.

"You can't just run away from your own party," she tells me, without looking up.

She's right, I concede. But I've never made a party like this, and I can't help feeling something's going to happen, something unexpected, that will lead to my undoing and the end of the world.

I invited all the teachers in a gesture of goodwill, even Marilyn, who happily has left for her sister's out of town. Joan and Greg won't be coming, either—thank goodness for small mercies. Louise has taken the train into the city to help out in her family's restaurant for the holidays. But the others are free and accepted my invitation gratefully. Christine Olsen is bringing her roommate. The more the merrier, I told her.

There was something comforting about Christine. We hit it off from the word *go*. For one thing, she knew how to make me laugh, especially in our weekly staff meetings. She was strict but fair as a teacher, according to Esther, and you could hear her sturdy, nasal voice booming from her third-grade classroom all the way down the corridor. She had the distinction of being the school's tallest teacher, rivalled only by Will Lindquist in stature, and had the largest feet I've ever seen on a woman. The only smallish things about her were her snub nose and alert, very round eyes, which looked out good humoredly from behind horn-rimmed glasses. She wore a whistle around her neck at all times and took her duties as our school's sports instructor very much to heart. I was welcome to join the town's women's softball league, she informed me early on, where she not only coached but was a fierce, unhittable pitcher. She didn't seem surprised when I declined.

"Not the sportive type, eh, Karen?" she asked, winking.

She wore baggy cardigans and plaid skirts, but her shirts were always sharply pressed with collars up, which lent her a rather handsome appearance. I knew from Esther that she roomed with a woman named Addie on the edge of town. Esther and Lee-Anne had played bridge with them on Friday nights for years.

"Are they lovers?"

"We've never discussed the subject."

"What *do* you talk about, then?"

"Everything under the sun. Apart from that."

"But you're old colleagues. Surely you trust one another."

"Some things go without saying."

Esther seems to think that's explanation enough, but I'm not having it.

"Do they share a bed, Esther?" I ask, like a courtroom prosecutor.

"They share their lives. What they do in their bedroom is none of my business."

She's answered my question most diplomatically. But my curiosity is far from sated, and the whole thing leaves me thoughtful. If old friends aren't to be trusted, who then?

But I let it go for now, swearing to uncover the nature of Christine's friendship with her companion this very afternoon. I pour us each another glass of champagne. Our party preparations are complete.

"We deserve a medal, Esther," I tell her as I remove her apron, then my own. We make our way upstairs. The guests aren't due for another hour. Our aim is instant gratification, but something happens, and we get deeply lost in each other's bodies. We've returned to the primal place, to the bottom of the sea inside us. Suffice it to say, we lose track of time, and as the doorbell rings, we're left scrambling to put our clothes on.

It should be Irene, for whom punctuality is essential as bread, but the O'Connor sisters, Margaret and Noreen, have beaten her to it. They're a good ten minutes early, bless their hearts. I picture them sitting ready for hours in their tidy living room, with its lace curtains and doilies, listening to the seconds ticking away on their massive grandfather clock, *brought all the way from County Kerry*, fearful lest they come too late. The sisters, who were getting on in years like most of the staff at school, were inseparable. The older, Noreen, was fair, the other dark, but they had a habit of finishing each other's sentences or speaking in unison so that you might be forgiven for thinking they were one organism. I struggled to tell them apart. Their first- and second-grade classrooms were impressively tidy, their children polite and well-behaved, which filled me with awe and a certain envy. They kept to themselves for the most part, but were always ready to lend a hand.

Irene arrives right on time, followed by Nat Craddock, who makes a breathless entrance in a beaded gown no less, her burgundy hair braided tightly across her head. I seat her next to Irene, who in one of life's mysteries is very fond of her. They've forged a bond over the years despite Nat's high drama and chronic disorder, which in anyone else would prove anathema to Irene. Christine Olsen and her roommate are next to appear, and there, large as life, stands my old professor, Adele Baxter. It takes me a good few seconds to register the fact. Her black hair, pulled back severely from her face, is streaked with white now, but she's as striking as I remember, her green eyes just as piercing.

Christine is introducing us in her booming voice. "This is the new teacher I've been telling you about, Adele. Our hostess, Karen Murphy. Karen, Adele Baxter."

I'm trying my best to hide my shock. Adele, meanwhile, is acting like we've never met. We exchange hellos, and she shakes my hand with great formality. Electricity shoots up my arm and down my body. I drop her hand and step back quickly.

"Thank you for letting me crash your party," she says.

"I was in your Theory of Teaching," I can't help saying.

"Well, of course, you were!" she exclaims with great delight. "I should have put two and two together. Well, I hear you've become quite a teacher, Karen. I guess all that theory didn't do you any harm."

I leave Esther to show them to the table and weave my way to the kitchen to recover my composure. It took me months to get over Adele Baxter. I pour a full glass of champagne and drain it immediately. I knew something untoward was going to happen. Didn't I have a premonition? There's a knock at the door. It's Celia James, as elegant as ever in a navy suit and pearls. She joins us, excusing her lateness.

"I'm just happy you're here," I tell Celia, which I mean with all my heart. I'm also grateful for a distraction from Adele.

Celia James had intrigued me from the moment I first saw her. But no one, not even Marilyn, seemed to know much

121

about her. She walked with a noticeable limp from childhood polio and used a cane to get around outside her second-grade classroom. Her disability had left her "unfit for marriage" it was said, and so she devoted herself to teaching. But I wasn't so sure about that. She was immensely attractive. Her light brown eyes shone forth from a face with fine, high cheekbones and perfectly applied makeup. Her dark hair (perhaps an artistic reproduction of its original color) was so well-coiffed it reminded me of Jacqueline Kennedy. I felt her gaze on me occasionally with a thrill of pleasure, I admit, and vowed to do what I could to get to know her better.

The party is complete. We're all around the table, set out with savories and sweets aplenty.

"I think it's only right we have champagne," I say. "If there aren't any objections?"

Laughter fills the room and everyone responds in affirmation. There's not a teetotaler in the house. "I say we deserve it," Esther says, drunk already. "I second Esther," Christine calls out. There are expressions of wonder over my Swedish meatballs, deviled eggs and shrimp cocktail, my stuffed celery and three Jello molds, no less. I look around the table at the women's faces and allow myself to feel a certain happiness, even a sense of accomplishment, despite Adele Baxter's presence. I refuse to let her spoil the occasion, and the champagne is helping enormously.

Irene rises with a sense of purpose, chin up, eyes twinkling, and lifts her glass. "I propose a toast to our youngest colleague!"

Christine joins her, towering above us. "Hear, hear, to Karen Murphy!"

They're all up on their feet toasting me. Even Celia struggles up from her chair and proposes a toast of her own.

"I can't recall when we last got together for the holidays. I'd like to thank Karen for inviting us."

I'm touched and don't know what to say, but speak I must.

"Thank you all for coming. Now, please eat!"

"*Brava*," Esther cries, while the others clap and cheer. Nat leans over and, grasping my arm with her passionate urgency, begs me to join the Barb Town Players. They need an ingénue desperately for their late spring production of *The Chalk Garden*.

"No, Nat. Even the thought of standing on a stage terrifies me. The one time I tried in high school, I forgot all my lines. And I didn't have many to begin with."

This seems to pacify Nat and amuse the others no end. The truth, however, is somewhat different. It's true I failed miserably in the school play, but I'm acting as I sit here at my dining room table, acting up a storm and will be for the rest of my life, it seems, playing the part of an unattached schoolteacher, whose passion is reserved for the children in her care, while my lover does the same in the seat next to me. I begin to fill plates and urge the others on. I pop the cork on another bottle of champagne.

"Merry Christmas, everybody!" I find myself shouting. Everyone, including Esther, calls out "Merry Christmas" in answer and glasses clink. The afternoon assumes a more predictable course of casual, collegial banter.

"Adele," Celia says, "are you still up at the college?"

"What are you implying, Celia? I've got fifteen more years, my dear!"

"How's Lee-Anne getting on?" Adele asks, turning to Esther.

"I believe she's fine. As of the first of the year, her new title will be Assistant Superintendent for Curriculum and Instruction in the Chicago Public School System."

"Well, that's a mouthful," Irene says.

"My, my," says Celia, shaking her head. "Well, send her my congratulations, please. We were in school together."

"I'll do that when I next see her," Esther, says, resting her hand on the back of my chair. I notice Adele observing us. "She's already moved into the city."

"If she was a man, she'd be superintendent already," Christine says, and everyone present seems to agree.

"And who'll take her job?" asks Margaret.

"I think *you* should apply, Christine," I say. "You've got just the right kind of authority."

"Not on your life," she roars. "Junior high politics are a

nightmare. No one knows where things are heading. I'll stick with my third graders, thank you very much. Besides, you can bet your bottom dollar they've got a man lined up. Lee-Anne was the great exception."

The teachers nod as one in full agreement. I open a fourth bottle of champagne with much fanfare; the cork flies off and up into the air. Irene catches it in both hands, and Christine says she exhibits real talent and should join the softball team. Champagne fountains across the table. By the time we're on our fifth, all bets are off. Esther tells a Will Lindquist story and the room grows raucous. Nat is laughing so hard she slips off her folding chair. Margaret, who studied nursing back in Ireland, checks her thoroughly to make sure nothing is broken. From out of the general commotion, intimate conversations ensue. Celia shares a recent photo of her little dachshund, Timber, with Nat and Noreen. They both agree he's exceptionally handsome. Nat, not to be outdone, demonstrates how Ophelia, her poodle, sings and dances to the radio. Noreen says she saw a dog do that in the circus back home. Nat looks a little miffed. She seems to think Ophelia's artistic talents are of a higher caliber. Across the table, Irene and Esther are debating a recently proposed social studies curriculum. The method under discussion would do away with chronological history altogether.

"If we do not study history, we are doomed to repeat it," Irene says, shaking her fist in the air. Her face is red with passion or drink, or both.

"Show me the evidence, my dear Irene," Esther challenges her. "We drown them in dates. They're bored to death."

"Dates are facts, my dear. Facts are weapons against ignorance."

It's heated, and neither is backing down. But they're both so drunk they're slurring their words. They'll have forgotten the whole thing in the morning, anyway. Christine joins in on Esther's side. I'm in Irene's camp. I've made my peace with chronology, which I now view as a signpost in our understanding of a changing world, without which we'd be lost, or I'd be lost, but it's time for coffee. I certainly need one. Adele is following me into the kitchen.

"Karen," she says, "I'm so thrilled you stayed in town."

"Are you, really?" I say, turning to face her. I'm seeing double and lean back against the counter to find my balance.

"Well, of course. I remember you very fondly."

I stifle a laugh at the absurdity of fate. Emotions are welling up in me that I'm not able to contain, at least not in my current state.

"It's funny you remember me now, Adele. You acted like I didn't exist at the time. You never answered my notes. You never once returned my calls."

"Guilty as charged," she says, and she should be turning on her heels and exiting my kitchen, but she's not. She's looking me up and down and nodding her approval.

"You're all grown up, Karen," she says, stepping toward me. "Teaching suits you I must say."

I'm backed up against the sink, and there's no escape when Noreen comes into the kitchen, shakily balancing a pile of plates. I push past Adele and move towards her.

"Oh, Noreen, you shouldn't," I say, relieving her of the plates. "Please sit down. Coffee is on its way."

I turn my back on Adele to pour the coffee at the counter, but I feel her gaze on me. I take the pot and make to pass her with it, but she stands in the way.

"Please let me pass, Adele."

"Not until you agree to have dinner with me."

"The coffee's getting cold."

"I'll call you."

I nod, looking down. I don't want to catch her eye. But she won't move, and I'm forced to brush past her so closely that I smell her perfume, Chanel No. 5, which hasn't changed, and beneath it the tangy scent of her sweat. For a split second our bodies touch and rub up against each other, and then I'm on the other side of her and back in my dining room.

It's all I can do to serve the coffee. Esther volunteers to cut the Christmas cake. Irene tells the group she almost brought a Christmas Stollen, but thought better of it, explaining the cake's near-fatal effects. The room erupts in laughter and then goes silent. We've exhausted ourselves. Out of the quiet Noreen is speaking up.

"Dears, this is as good a time as any to make an announcement. Better than over the PA system, no doubt. I'll be retiring at the end of the school year. It seems my memory isn't as good as it should be."

She pauses, shakes her head. Her sister, Margaret, offers her a hand for strength.

"Now, I forget what it was I wanted to say." She laughs, we join in. But our laughter is tinged with sadness and worry. "I'll miss everyone. I'll miss the children, most of all. They've been everything to me."

"We'll miss you terribly, Noreen dear," says Esther. We all nod and sigh in agreement.

"God bless you all," she tells us.

As Margaret helps her sister slowly up from her chair, the rest of us rise, one by one, and take leave of each other, wishing each other the best of holidays and a happy, healthy *and restful* New Year.

"Let me walk you to your car, Celia," I say.

I take Celia James's arm. She grips my hand tightly. "I'm down the street, I'm afraid."

"That's good. I get to have you to myself for a bit."

We walk in silence. Her breath grows short with effort as she drags her left leg forward, leaning heavily on her cane.

"Celia," I say, after a time, "I admire you so much. What's your secret?"

"What do you mean?"

"Your classroom positively hums! You make the children happy."

"Well, there's nothing that says learning can't be joyful."

"But you look so beautiful at the same time!"

"Well, beauty is in the eye of the beholder, isn't it? But I do, as a rule, try to look my best for the children. I like to think it makes them feel important, worthy."

She's saying things that feel exactly right. I'll seek her out, I decide, and become her disciple as soon as I can find some calm.

"Besides," she's saying with a smile, "I like nice clothes."

"I'll need a new wardrobe, a complete makeover," I say, which makes her laugh.

At the car, she stops and studies me. "I'm so glad you're at our school," she says. I help her in, and wave as she drives off. *"I want to be like you,"* I call out after her, poised and elegant, professional through and through. Life is too full of distractions.

Esther stays to help me tidy up, or so we've told the others. But we're too tired to clean, too tired even to climb the stairs to bed, and the champagne has left us both with a headache. We collapse onto the couch and surprise ourselves by making love. I find myself excited and confused by my desire. I'm in the moment here with Esther, but back too in the doorway to my kitchen with Adele Baxter.

Esther drops me off at the station just before my bus pulls off. I'm going home for Christmas with mixed feelings. Esther is spending a week in the city with Liz and Bettie. They've got tickets to see Bob Dylan, the new folk singer, plus *two* concerts at the Chicago Symphony Orchestra. How I wish I could join them, I tell her. Next year, they can count me in, for sure. But if I'm honest, what I really want is to go dancing, and Esther has promised to take me to a place she knows in the city in the New Year.

The bus is full of tired, groggy students going home for the holidays, just as I did throughout my college days. It hits me that I was one of these young people just seven short months ago. But it may as well be another lifetime. So much has changed. Years of habit, continuity of thought and action, wiped swiftly and cleanly away, like the erasing of a chalkboard. I'm a teacher with twenty-one children in my care, accepted by my peers, a professional with a home of my own and a bank account, in love with Esther. I find a seat at the back and close my eyes, wake with a start at Rock Island station. I find I'm not sorry to be home, though home is not the right word. Christmas is spent at church. Our family Christmas revolves around the Incarnation. There's Midnight Mass followed by Dawn Mass, followed by lunch and then Mass again. Christmas Mass has filled me with awe ever since I can remember, its excess of passion so unlike anything I knew from home. But this year it means leaving Esther. We've agreed to spend New Year's Eve in the city together. Liz and Bettie are having a party for which I've bought a beautiful new suit to surprise her. It's cobalt blue and, according to Louise, who chose it, matches my eyes exactly.

24

Professor Adele Baxter is on the line.

"How are you, Karen?" she asks.

I've been fearing her call since the Christmas party.

"Adele. What a surprise," I say.

I should hang up, but I'm too polite. Or so I tell myself.

"Is this an okay time?"

"Not really. I have company, I'm afraid, Adele." I'm alone, as it happens, but prefer to let her think otherwise.

"Well, I don't want to disturb you then," she says quickly. "I'll call you tomorrow."

She calls again the next day and the next, and the day after that, and each call begins with the same question, and each time, my response is a variation on the same theme.

"I'm afraid I can't talk now, Adele. I'm late for an appointment." Or "Oh, I'm sorry, Adele, but a friend just walked through the door."

Then the calls stop, just like that. I'd stuck to my guns. The fact is I knew few people less deserving of my sympathy. She used her power over me shamefully in college. I feel relieved, even proud, for controlling the situation and drawing it to a close so successfully.

Or so I thought.

There's a soft tap on the door, and it's Adele. I have a strange feeling she's been watching the house. I want to grab my keys and drive away, but I haven't got a car and I can't drive. Besides which, I'm still in my robe with nothing underneath. It's a bitter cold morning, a cold that gets in your bones. I consider throwing my coat on over my robe and dashing out the back door and down the alley, but instead I open the door and stand there saying nothing in the hope that she'll just go away.

"Hi, Karen," she says, as if it's the most natural thing in the world to appear unannounced at my door first thing Sunday morning. "I happened to be in the neighborhood and thought I'd just stop by."

"Hello, Adele," I say, and wait.

"It's cold out here," she says, shivering forlornly in the biting wind. "May I come in?"

"I'm expecting company," I say without conviction. Against my better judgment, I'm stepping aside and letting her in. "Come in for a minute. But I need to get dressed and get ready to go out."

"I thought you were expecting company," she says, coming in, hugging her body to warm up from the cold.

"Did I say that?" My voice is emotionless, my body rigid, like a soldier guarding her post.

"I had to see you," she says, her eyes searching mine.

"This isn't a good time," I say, locking the door behind her.

"Karen, I know you're angry with me. Please, just offer me a cup of hot coffee and give me a chance to explain myself."

"All right," I say, with a sigh. "Let me put something on first."

She stands at the bottom of the stairs, waiting. I feel her eyes on me. By the third step, I'm weak in the knees, and by the seventh, I'm panting for breath. By the time I reach the top stair, and there are sixteen all together, all resolve is lost.

"Karen," she calls up to me.

"What is it, Adele?" I'm stopped on the landing, in suspended animation.

"Can I come up?" she says, quietly.

"Adele," I say, turning to face her.

My robe falls open, and for all intents and purposes, I'm naked before her. Her coat drops to the floor and her clothes form a little pile, and she's slinking up the stairs like a large cat, a panther, her green eyes glinting with hunger for the kill. I stand frozen, like doomed prey, and in a flash she's pounced on me in my upstairs hallway. I'm sliding down the wall under her weight and transported back to the cabin in the Dells at the same time. Her fingers and tongue are everywhere, and all at once my body is sucked into her vortex. There's no escape, no pulling back. To my horror, I'm screaming with delight, and when she's had her way with me and satisfied herself, which doesn't take long, I pry myself loose and close my robe tightly with its sash. My body is singing with pleasure.

"Please get dressed quickly and go home," I order her. I'm lightheaded, giddy.

She shrugs, and like an obedient schoolgirl begins to dress herself. For want of anything better to do, I sit on the stairs watching her, catching my breath.

She's putting on her black capri pants, her black roll-neck sweater, her smart leather loafers—the costume that had so impressed me in college.

"Could I just have that cup of coffee?" she says, reapplying her lipstick. I feel like a waiter who's served up a meal.

"No," I say, shaking my head. "It's best you go."

"You sure know how to hold a grudge, Karen."

She's right, I think, but I just shrug.

"It would have been irresponsible for me to become involved with a student."

I have to laugh. It's a sardonic laugh, almost cruel, but I don't stop myself.

"I got you your job for Christ's sake."

So she's the one. My anonymous benefactor, Adele Baxter. It had never occurred to me. I'd assumed she'd forgotten my existence by graduation. I'll give her a cup of coffee, after all, I decide. It's in the pot anyway.

"You were an unusual student. You asked questions no one ever asked," she tells me as she follows me into the kitchen. "I knew you'd make an excellent teacher. When Will Lindquist mentioned he was looking to hire, I recommended you for the job. He and I sit on committees together. We go way back, Will and me."

"I'm grateful," I say, handing her the coffee, and back away quickly as if from a flame.

"You're not having one?"

I shake my head and watch her drink, keeping the distance of my kitchen between us. I don't offer her a seat. She drinks thirstily without pause, the way she does everything.

"Anyway, I wanted to give you time to settle in before paying you a visit."

"Please don't come again." The words fly out of my mouth before I can even consider them.

I've startled her. She takes a step back and laughs. "Have it your way," she says, shrugging.

I cross my arms and brace myself. I look her in the eye. It's time to tell her I have a lover, and my lover's name is Esther. It's time she knows beyond a shadow of a doubt that I'm unavailable and intend to stay that way, now and for eternity.

"Adele, please keep this to yourself," I begin.

"Your secrets are safe with me, Karen," she says, stopping me. "If that's what's worrying you. Secrets are my specialty."

I take a deep breath and come to my senses. I don't tell her about Esther and me. Some things go without saying after all, like Esther says. Adele sidles over, reaches for my waist, and pulls me to her. I escape from her grip and move to the door.

"I'll call you," she says, unperturbed, coming up behind me. "Maybe you'll have changed your mind."

I don't answer. I say nothing. She won't call. She's gotten what she needed. And so have I, it seems, because as she slips past me at the door, brushing up against my body, the only thing I feel is relieved she's leaving. I watch her practically run down the path to her car. She doesn't turn around to wave. She's forgotten she's been here by the looks of it, on to a new challenge, the next sensation. *That's Adele Baxter for you*, I think. Nothing changes. I wonder about her long friendship with Christine Olsen, what kind of agreement they've reached, and funnily enough, I no longer feel anger toward her. I understand that with Adele, there's no ill will, no hidden motives, no danger of betrayal.

It's over between us. I've finished with the past, with Adele, with Larry, and my future can begin in earnest, a future with Esther. Just in time for the New Year.

It's still early. I'll get dressed and go to confession, I decide. I want to be made new again, set free. I put on a freshly pressed skirt and blouse and comb my hair at the mirror. I'll hop on a train to a church in a far-off town, Rockford, Oshkosh, names I've seen on a map, where the Father will hear the confessions of a stranger.

I put on my coat and leave the house, find myself walking away from the station, out to the bare fields, where the cold winter sun offers up its absolution.

PART
TWO

SNOW DAY

•

WINTER 1964

25

Lydie has fashioned an arrowhead made of clay during art.

"It's very nice, Lydie."

I've vowed to start the New Year off on better terms, offering praise where praise is due, encouraging her better instincts.

"Almost like the real thing."

"It is real," she informs me.

"Well, Lydie, an arrow would have been carved from flint, a very hard rock," I can't help pointing out. "But what you've made is a good representation."

Truth be told, it has the look of ancient weaponry found in the Museum of Natural History.

"Is it sharp enough to kill someone?" she asks, glancing briefly up at me.

I pick it up and study it carefully. The tip has been sharpened with astonishing dexterity. It could rip through flesh and tear your heart out, I shouldn't wonder.

"Our ancestors, the hunters and gatherers, might have found it very practical," I tell her, handing it back gingerly.

"It's an *Indian* arrowhead," she corrects me.

I leave her to sharpen her weapon and am examining more peaceful objects created by the children, pipes and cigars, flowers and bowls, when Alan pulls me aside, out of Lydie's hearing.

"Lydie's gonna kill Brenda," he whispers, his breath hot against my ear. The plot involves luring her rival behind the gym after school with the promise of seeing a baby kitten or a puppy, Lydie hasn't decided which yet. I thank Alan and tell him that under no circumstance should Lydie and Brenda meet up anywhere, and I'm counting on his help. Before the bell rings, I make a point of collecting the children's work for safekeeping despite protests and placing it in a cupboard under lock and key. Lydie appears furious at this turn of events and is shouting out to Alan, who is hightailing it out the door. But I couldn't be more pleased with myself. I've headed off a murder plot. Whether confiscating their art is best practice is another question. At lunch I stop by Dorothy's office and ask her please to call Lydie's parents in as quickly as possible. They've not made it in for a meeting yet, and it's a matter of some urgency.

It's come to pass. The mother of my sorrows, the source of sleepless nights, Alice Kaminski, Lydie's mother, is sitting in front of me in Dorothy's office. She's around Esther's age, I'm guessing, but there's not a trace of time's passage on her unblemished skin. There's something familiar about her, and then it dawns on me: she looks for all the world like the *Mona Lisa* whose smile so intrigued me in first year French.

"I'm sorry my husband couldn't join us," she says with a sorry expression. "He's in his studio today. I hope I'll do?"

She's smiling playfully. *But it's not a game,* I'd like to say. *Your child's behavior is serious business, and your appearance here is long overdue.*

"Studio time is sacred," she adds, by way of explanation.

"No doubt, Mrs. Kaminski," I answer briskly. Fathers were a rare sight in the school in any case, their sudden appearance, like mushrooms sprung up overnight, at the school Christmas play something of a shock. I'm ready to move on to the subject at hand, her daughter, when she speaks up again.

"My husband's a painter, Miss Murphy. He's devoted to his students, of course. But the teaching drains him." She stops and looks me directly in the eye. "Art requires patience and time."

"Are you also in the artistic field, Mrs. Kaminski?" I can't help asking. I've never met an artist in real life.

"I'm the wife of an artist, Miss Murphy. Does that count? I was Henry's model in art school; that's how we met. I modeled nude for the figure painting courses in exchange for sitting in on classes."

I can't help picturing Alice Kaminski draped along a dais, a bunch of grapes in her lifted hand, mouth open to receive them.

"I was set on being a painter at one time. But in the end I put my own artistic dreams aside. I still dabble now and again."

I sit up, pulling myself out of my reverie. It's time to shift the conversation around to Lydie. But Alice Kaminski has other ideas. In quick succession, I learn that she's a New York City girl who hates this Midwest town. She loves city life, well, life and people in general, and she is suffocating here. Trips home are much too infrequent. Sometimes she has the feeling her life in New York was all a dream. Neighbors pop in, and colleagues of Henry's—fellow painters, poets, and students—are always welcome, but she misses her family terribly, and her world. It's crowds she misses most of all.

I know the world Alice Kaminski yearns for. I tagged along everywhere with Aunt Helene the summer I visited her and her friend, Bea, in New York. I found the city overwhelming at first, the shouting and honking, the smell of rotting garbage, the rush of bodies, the cacophony of languages. But by the end of my two-week trip, I wanted to stay on forever. Standing on the Brooklyn Bridge or walking down Fifth Avenue, I had the sensation I was a mere particle in a mass of humanity. New York was the nucleus of the universe, which was spinning around me. I had become the city. We were one. It was dizzying. I was both nothing and very important. I feel lightheaded now as I sit here thinking about it.

Alice Kaminski has taken a hanky out of her sleeve. "I'm sorry," she says, dabbing her eyes.

"No need. I understand," I say.

I straighten the papers on Dorothy's desk, line up the pens while she blows her nose and recovers her composure. I don't let on that I'm astonished by Alice Kaminski. Her outpouring is extraordinary and most unexpected and is having quite an effect on me. I've never met a parent quite like this one, though my experience is admittedly limited. Despite my open invitation, few parents have shown up for a parent-teacher meeting, and then only the mothers. I could practically count them on one hand. Those who made it in appeared out of a sense of duty. If they spoke at all, it was with a yes or a no or a shrug of the shoulders. They voiced no comment or complaint. I had the funny feeling they were afraid of me. The look in their eyes was like a deer in headlights. I tried my best to put them at ease. What I learned about their children was coaxed out slowly, and I learned little to nothing about the mothers, themselves. But I now know more about Alice Kaminski than I know about most members of my own family, and our meeting's just begun.

"Still, I would have followed Henry anywhere and would again," she says, with defiance. "Art can't fill a sandwich, but we get by. I've been wearing this old coat for as long as we've lived here. That's eleven years and counting."

She sits up thrusting her chest forward and lifts an arm to prove her point. There's a patch at the elbow, the sleeve and hem threadbare and shiny with wear.

"It suits you," I tell her helplessly. *Anything would*, I can't help thinking. Her figure is full and shapely in all the right places, in perfect proportion. No wonder they used her as a model in art school. I'd take up painting myself for the chance.

I'm beginning to see that Lydie has inherited more than her fair share of drama from her mother, but all in all I'm charmed by Alice Kaminski and moved by her sadness, which I attribute to lack of personal fulfilment. Her storytelling is entrancing, with excellent diction and facial expression, and she really knows how to build to a climax. And the stories are never-ending it seems. She tells me of her immigrant family's hardship on the Lower East Side, of the cruel hours and hazards of the garment trade.

One cold night—she remembers it like yesterday—they were sitting down to eat when the lights went out. There was no money to pay the electric bill. She can still picture her father reading *The Daily Worker* by candlelight. But despite everything, her mother, bless her, kept the place sparkling clean and never asked for handouts like people do today. She was too proud. They're both gone now. Her sisters married well, thank God, and moved to the suburbs.

She tells me confidentially, her voice a whisper, of her near death from tuberculosis and how she's never been the same since, and she hopes this explains her not showing up at the school to meet me until now and for missing Lydie's performance in the Christmas play, which she deeply regrets. All this she tells me in practically one sentence, though pausing long enough for effect when needed.

"Apropos Lydie," I jump in, taking my chance, "how does she seem to you?"

"Why?" she asks, and she's stopped by the question.

"Well, we have some concerns about her behavior. Is she getting enough sleep? Is she eating well?" The questions sound foolish even as I ask them. Lydie is the picture of health.

"You couldn't possibly think I'm starving my daughter?" She sighs and looks at me with something like pity. "She's a perfectly happy little girl, Miss Murphy, well-behaved, kind, bright. I think you'd agree? She's never caused us a moment of worry."

"There have been some playground incidents," I say, choosing my words carefully.

She shrugs, gives in. "Mr. Lindquist told me she was getting into it with the Larson girl."

"Well, yes, she threatened her life."

"Miss Murphy, are you implying that Lydie is homicidal?"

141

I'm hard put to tell her what I really think, so I change the subject.

"Did Mr. Lindquist mention the source of their conflict, Mrs. Kaminski?"

"I don't believe so. The usual childish things I assume. What do children fight about? You'd know better than I."

I'm thinking how best to describe, in the most delicate way possible, the passionate triangle behind the children's war, but Alice Kaminski has moved on.

"It's not how she's been raised. We've never laid a finger on her. The Lydie I know wouldn't hurt a flea. Besides, boys are fighting all the time. Do you call *their* parents in for a meeting?"

I'm ready to give up and send her home, but instead I say too forcefully, "We *should* call them in more often, Mrs. Kaminski, if you ask me, but right now we're discussing Lydie."

"I'm at a loss," she says and shrugs again. "She's never had a problem in school before. Ask any of her previous teachers. Ask Miss Jonas. She had her last year."

She's right. She's got me there. Sitting up, arms crossed, she looks me directly in the eye. "Miss Murphy, do you have anything positive to say about my daughter?"

I'm taken aback. I'd forgotten the golden rule. Criticism must be couched in praise.

"Of course, I do, Mrs. Kaminski," I answer effusively. "She's the most creative child in the class, and her ability to absorb subject matter and make it her own is quite remarkable."

This seems to placate her. "The neighbor girl, Janie, hasn't been a good influence," she concedes. "But that was Henry's choice, to live in town and not out by the university. Poor Janie and her sisters have absolutely no supervision. Her mother works. She's a cashier at the Piggly Wiggly. Her father's rarely home. He drives a truck if I'm not mistaken. Janie's in and out of our house, God knows. I'd never turn a child away."

Dorothy is tapping discreetly on the door, and I realize an hour has slipped by without our discussing my other concerns. At this point, I'm no longer sure that I have any or what they

142

might be, Alice Kaminski has so discombobulated me. I get up. She does the same. Suddenly I'm angry at her, out of all proportion to the crime I know, but the fact is her daughter doesn't exist for her, not really. Lydie's out of the picture. We've spent an hour talking about Alice almost exclusively. No wonder Lydie's so hungry for attention. I'm flooded with pity for the troubled little girl.

Alice Kaminski extends a hand and smiles at me. For a moment, I am lost in her eyes, which are cat-shaped, hazel. I shake her hand, which is unusually soft and covered in dimples, and as I do so, she pulls me to her and kisses my cheek. Her lips are moist and warm, her scent sweet, touched by lavender.

"You must stop by for tea," she says, her lips against my ear. "I'd love you to see some of Henry's work."

Being kissed by a parent is a first, and I step back discreetly to regain my composure. I'm not sure teachers should be visiting their pupils' homes either. Still, I find myself nodding in assent.

"One more thing concerning Lydie," I say. My voice is harsher than I intend.

She stops, lets out a little sigh, and waits.

I crack open the door, and ask Dorothy for a few more minutes. We sit back down. I won't let her off the hook so easily. There's the little matter of her daughter's fantasy.

"Mrs. Kaminski."

"Alice," she says.

"Alice," I say. "Have you noticed any particular fascination on your daughter's part with the American Indians?"

She thinks a moment and shakes her head. "No," she says. "Why?"

"She seems to identify very strongly with them."

Alice shrugs. "Well, I don't suppose that can do her any harm, can it? Their understanding of life's meaning is more profound than our own if you ask me."

"I agree wholeheartedly," I tell her. I'm surprised to discover we have something in common, even a little thrilled.

"We have nothing to do with organized religion. Is that a

crime?" she says.

"No. Not at all," I answer, and I'm electrified. I've never met anyone who's admitted such a thing. "I was just curious why she's clung to this idea."

"Idea?"

"That she's a member of an Indian tribe."

Alice lets out a pitiable sigh and raises both her hands to the heavens. "What's next? This is all news to me. I'm afraid you'll have to look elsewhere for an answer."

Alice cocks her head and looks at me a little skeptically.

"Anything else?" she asks.

"Lydie's told the class she's adopted."

It comes out of my mouth before I can stop it. But Alice doesn't seem to mind. She lets out a shriek of laughter.

"How funny," she says, shaking her head. "We hoped for a large family, Miss Murphy."

"Karen," I hear myself say.

"Karen," she says, echoing me. "But my body wasn't strong enough after the illness. I couldn't carry a baby to term. Except for Lydie. I've had four miscarriages, Karen. Two before Lydie and two after. The last one nearly killed me. I practically bled to death."

"I'm grateful for your confidence," I tell her, startled again by her lack of inhibition.

"Lydie doesn't know, of course. We've never talked about the subject in front of her." She stops, bites her lip. Her brow furrows. "But maybe she picked up on it. I hadn't thought of that. Do you think that's a possibility, Karen? Perhaps she feels she isn't enough? Would a child pick up on something like that?"

Her hazel eyes seek out mine for answers.

"I couldn't presume to know the answer to that, Alice. This is my first year of teaching." My confession comes out of nowhere and makes me blush.

But Alice doesn't seem to notice. "Children are a mystery," she says, sighing.

"They are that," I say.

We rise from our chairs and I see her out, a little giddy, promising to stop by sometime to look at those paintings and have tea. I'm left thinking that Lydie has been pulling my leg very successfully, creating an elaborate game to amuse herself and the class at my expense. There's no neglect where Lydie is concerned, no suffering, no alienation. She poses no danger to anyone or anything except my sanity. She's as happy as a clam. Her childhood is one of exemplary freedom, including the freedom to believe in what she chooses. I can't help feeling a pang of envy, in fact. With so much freedom, who might I have been? My newfound pity for her vanishes as quickly as it came.

26

We've filed down to the basement to watch a National Geographic special on the stars and planets. I seat my children, then move to the projector at the back of the small room to wait for Esther and her class who are to join us. They're late as usual, rushing in breathless, Esther behind them.

When the lights go down, we lean against the wall so close our arms and hips touch and without thinking our fingers intertwine. The projector room is pitch black; no one can stop us. But our bliss is short-lived. The door opens, casting a long shadow, and Will sidles over to warn us of the impending disaster drill. His breath is stale and reeks of tobacco.

"Duck and cover, children," we call out as the alarm bell sounds. There are protests and a couple of moans, and cries of pain as they bang their knees and heads, but they're all scrambling dutifully onto all fours and under the projector room chairs as best they can. "Hands over your heads," we remind them, an undertaking that requires considerable effort and a contortionist's talent, but eventually, they're more or less in place. Lydie's found her way under the same chair as Janie, which is quite a feat and against the rules, but I pretend not to notice.

Most of the children take Duck and Cover in their stride, whispering and giggling and generally enjoying the disruption of routine. But little Alan comes up to me after the drill with a troubled expression. He doesn't like the atom bomb, he says, and he has questions. He wants to know more about "the bright flash that is brighter than the sun, brighter than anything you've ever seen, that could knock you down, throw you against a tree or a building and burn your skin worse than a terrible sunburn," as they've learned from the Civil Defense film we showed them last week. He's been thinking about it all week, he says. He's skeptical because, even if you duck and cover, wouldn't you die anyway? Yes, Alan, you would be sure to die, I almost say, but stop myself. Instead, I promise him answers in class tomorrow and pat his soft, shaved head.

I'm standing at the bookcase in the teachers' room when Esther comes in.

"What are you looking for?" she asks, joining me.

"Inspiration. A way to talk to the children about atomic destruction."

"Oh!" she says. "You won't find it here, I'm afraid." She lets her jeweled fingers wander across the spines of teaching manuals and studies in developmental psychology from the first half of the century, and I feel my own spine tingling.

"I want them to know the truth about the bomb, Esther."

"Well, tread carefully, darling."

We're alone today, a rarity. Irene's rushed off for her dentist appointment. Louise has recess duty.

"Alan wants to know. I promised him an answer tomorrow. The children deserve an explanation."

"Of course. That's something I love about you. Your sense of dedication. The trick is to find the right words. They're afraid enough as it is. They need hope, too. We all do. But at the same time . . ."

Esther has stopped, mid-sentence, and is staring at me.

"What is it?" I manage to say, but I know what it is.

We smile widely and our breath comes heavily, and suddenly she's pinned me up against those useless books and she is kissing me, lightly, playfully, starting with my lips, my cheeks, chin, closed eyes, my neck. "Esther," I protest weakly, "not here."

Esther looks toward the door and then at the clock, and then she stumbles to the door and turns the lock, and suddenly she's not smiling anymore and neither am I. Our bodies rub up hard against each other and our mouths open with hunger. I stagger to the couch as my legs give way, pulling her down on top of me. We are chemical elements colliding in space. Explosions follow in a chain reaction. We're beyond the fear of total annihilation. Then there's a fumbling at the door, and a key turning in the lock, and we just manage to sit up and pull our skirts down when Louise bursts in, flustered and out of breath.

"Oh, Esther, you're here!" she exclaims, dropping a pile of books on the table. "I thought you were teaching!"

"Of course, I'm here, Louise," says Esther, busying herself with the pins in her hair. "Where else would I be on Tuesdays at ten?"

"Oh, God, I thought it was Wednesday!" Louise cries out, dismayed. "I missed recess duty! I was pottering around my room."

"Never mind. It happens to all of us. What's the matter? What did you want to see me about?" Esther asks, pulling herself up shakily from the couch.

Louise suddenly looks sheepish and tells us she's sorry to storm in and interrupt us like this.

"No, no, Louise, that's okay. You two go ahead," I say.

I smile at them both and pull a book at random off the shelf.

"Are you free after school?" Louise asks me.

"I have research to do at the library."

"Wait for me, and I'll walk with you."

"Okay."

Louise and Esther hunker down together at the table, and

soon enough Esther has solved the latest crisis by showing Louise how to read a map, its legend, grids and scale, in five easy steps with the use of your thumb.

The book in my hand is a dog-eared copy of *Sexual Behavior in the Human Female*. How it ended up in our teachers' library is anyone's guess. How it ended up in my hands at this moment is an even bigger riddle and gives me pause. Is anything random in the end?

Louise and I head out to the town's public library on Oak Street. She wants to stop off for a milkshake, her treat, but I tell her I don't have time. I have to prepare for class tomorrow. It's sunny but brisk as we amble down Fourth Street, arm in arm.

"Did you hear what I just said, Kar?" she says, suddenly. "I asked you a question."

"Sorry," I say. "I'm preoccupied," which is true. I'm still recovering from the close call in the teachers' room. But Louise attributes my distractedness to falling in love. "You've been glowing for weeks now," she teases. "You're on cloud nine."

I laugh out loud and vehemently deny her charge, but my heart skips a beat. Her words are more than worrying. Could she know more than she's letting on? Louise is observant and curious and obsessed with Esther.

"*Au contraire*," I say, changing the subject. "There's a mushroom cloud hanging over my head. Alan wants to know about the atom bomb."

"Better you than me," she says, "good luck."

"Thanks, I'll need it."

We've stopped in front of the library steps.

"See you," I tell her casually.

"You have to come over on Sunday. The Beatles are on *Ed Sullivan*! We're all going to watch."

"All right," I say.

We part ways with a hug, but she comes bounding back.

"I almost forgot," she says, looking over her shoulder, like a small-time crook on the make. "Have you thought about the pill?"

"Quite a bit," I lie. I'm happy to have put those worrying days behind me.

"Well, I finally got my hands on some," she whispers, excitedly. "My sister-in-law's trying to get pregnant and she gave me her supply. There's at least six months' worth! They're like gold: you can't beg, borrow or steal them unless you're married and even then you have to make up a good story. You're welcome to half if you like."

"Sure," I say, quickly. "Thanks."

Louise hasn't got a clue about Esther and me. I understand with relief that it's outside the scope of her reality. The idea is inconceivable. She could have walked in on us in the teachers' room, panting on the couch, tongues licking tongues, skirts pulled up, underpants pulled down, awash in each other's desire, and she'd still be in the dark.

"I'll bring you half a bottle tomorrow," she promises.

People here are very proud of the library, with good reason. It's one of the town's two crown jewels, along with the Egyptian. It was built with a gift from Jacob Haish, who like his archrivals, Joseph Glidden and Isaac Ellwood, grew rich on patents for barbed wire. It was barbed wire money that brought the Teacher's College to town, built streets and country roads, banks, schools and the hospital and lent them their names. The library is my favorite haunt in town. It's tranquil inside, and with its vaulted ceilings allows the mind to take flight.

I take a seat at a table in the back and stay here wrestling with the atom and fission, with the blast and shock waves, with radiating energy and complete annihilation. The atom bomb is too terrible and too enormous to take in, but I won't give up. Alan wants to know. The atomic age is our legacy to the children. They deserve the truth from us, at least. I'll teach them why the atom bomb is the most terrible bomb of all. How cities turn into shadows where it falls. How shock waves spread heat so hot everything in their path melts. How sometimes a person will look perfectly fine but they are burning on the inside.

And they need to understand that we Americans invented the atom bomb and dropped it on people in Japan, not once, but twice. No one has done it since, but they might. Next time, there won't just be one bomb or two, but hundreds. All life as we know it will end in an instant. The planet will continue spinning, but without us on it. I'll remind them we had a missile scare with Russia just last year. How President Kennedy saved us in the nick of time from atomic destruction. He knew that talking to your enemy was better than fighting. It was a good start. But then our president was shot.

We teach you to Duck and Cover, children, I'll conclude, but the truth is that getting under your desks and covering your heads will protect you from falling objects and shattering windows, in a tornado, for example, but it won't protect you from the atom bomb. You were right, Alan, I'll tell him. They tell us to build bomb shelters in the backyard. But no matter how deep you dig, you have to come up sometime!

I take a cold shower to wake myself up, dress quickly, and stumble out the door. I'm halfway to the school before I realize I haven't eaten. I've emptied my mind of all thought but the task ahead, focused like a pilot, I can't help thinking, with a bomb to drop.

The children are reciting the Pledge of Allegiance. I stand at the back of the classroom, lesson notes tucked under my arm, and look out at a sea of little heads, some scruffy, some neat. Above each one there is a halo of light, as in the depictions of the baby Jesus. The halos change color, transmuting the state of their emotions, their souls, into blues, pinks, yellows, greens.

They're all here and they're back in their seats, waiting for me to get the ball rolling. But I don't move. I watch as they grow restless, whispering and giggling and looking over their shoulders. I stay where I am, mesmerized by their innocence. I

151

find I'm having trouble getting started today.

And I don't teach the lesson I've so carefully prepared. I can't do it. I won't tell them about atomic annihilation. I don't want to be the one. Let someone else do it. Let their parents or their preachers do it. I'm sorry to let you down, Alan, I tell him silently. I'm a coward and a failure. But in any case, Lydie is whispering in his ear, and he's ecstatic.

I take attendance. We talk about the stars and planets. It's going peacefully enough, but as I'm starting in on the Milky Way, Marty waves his hand, eager to tell the class that creatures from outer space are coming down in flying saucers to attack us. "Martians!" Karl shouts out. Those are made-up stories, not news reports, I tell them.

"There's a difference between fact and fiction, children."

But they're not listening. They're debating back and forth among themselves as to which alien creatures will destroy us and in which manner. "They're green and they take over your mind, someone shouts. The Blob climbs over you and you melt into the Blob," another cries out. "The Thing eats you and makes you evil," screams a third. My lesson on the stars and planets descends into ear-piercing shrieks and monstrous renditions from the movies of everything the children fear, which in the end is fear itself, as the great FDR once said.

"If anyone is going to destroy us, it's ourselves," I shout above them, with such force I surprise myself as well as the children. They're startled into silence. The room is soundless, like an empty universe. I close my eyes and breathe in deeply. The children follow suit.

"As for Martians, Karl," my voice is calm and matter of fact, "most certainly there are intelligent forms of life on planets outside our solar system, and one day humans will come into contact with them. We can't possibly be the only living beings in the universe, can we?"

The children, following my lead, shake their heads.

"The Big Bang that created our world created an infinite number of worlds at the same time, girls and boys. We're not alone, though it sure feels like it sometimes."

They seem surprised to hear me talk like this. Their brows are raised.

"When you look up at the stars so many trillions of miles away, it's hard to imagine anyone or anything except for us."

They're weighing things up, sitting forward in their seats, heads cocked.

"But let's assume they're out there, these aliens, these life forms from elsewhere, whatever we choose to call them. Why would they want to harm us? Perhaps they are kinder than we are and gentler. I personally believe they are good and peaceful and will have much to teach us."

I'm reassuring them with stories I only half believe, with fantasy not facts, but I don't let that stop me. I'll wind up in Will's office for my pains, in any case. I've shattered the creation myth, the book of Genesis, in one fell swoop. The lesson on atomic annihilation rattling in my sweater pocket feels almost harmless by comparison.

And then Lydie raises her hand.

"Yes, Lydie?" I say.

"Don't worry about the aliens," she tells the class. "The atom bomb is going to kill us anyway."

27

Esther and I are spending more and more time together. Slowly, in passing, I'm learning more about her. How she played the piano as a child and loves to swim but dislikes dogs. I love dogs but can't swim. We're as different as chalk and cheese, I tease her. She has a passion for beautiful objects, fine china from England, for example—well, anything English for that matter. The British can do no wrong as far as Esther's concerned. She can eat a box of chocolates in one sitting. She's mad about baseball. She never met an idiom she didn't like, and despite being German, she mostly gets them right. The pendant she wears on her neck is a Star of David, and she never takes it off, not to bathe or sleep. She was born on February 24 in 1926, a fact I glean from her driver's license, a date that is fast approaching.

"We could make a little party," I tell her. "I'll bake a cake." She looks at me with something like horror. She refuses to acknowledge she was born at all. She dislikes birthdays, she says finally, and celebrating them is out of the question, apart from the children's, which she celebrates reluctantly.

"Well, I like birthdays," I insist. "Our birthdays explain a great deal about us, Esther. You and I are opposites according to the stars. You're water and I'm fire."

The look she gives me could raise the dead. It's all superstition, she says, which she can't abide. She refuses to read meaning into anything. I won't tell her I turn to the horoscopes first thing when I open the paper—just for fun, of course.

"All forms of irrationality are dangerous, including sentimentality. Reason is mankind's only hope."

Science is Esther's favorite subject, and she'll defend it to the death. She loves teaching weather the best. Her beloved cloud formations, the Gulf Stream, heat waves, cold fronts, all forms of precipitation, storms, wind, drought. The weather is an underestimated topic, she assures me, whose day will come. She learned its value from the farmers, her neighbors, whom she values highly.

And I know her contradictions. She's impatient, but is often late. If I had a dime for every minute I spend waiting for you I'd be a rich woman, I tell her. She's outspoken but concedes quickly, something I don't understand. If you believe in something you have to stand for it, I try to convince her, but she just shrugs. Though she's very particular about her possessions, she mislays everything that's not attached to her body. She can't bear a false crease in her blouses and skirts, but tosses her clothes in a heap after wearing them once. She's fastidious when it comes to personal cleanliness. I've never seen anyone scrub down like she does, but her house is very messy. In fact, she hoards things. She has twenty pairs of brand-new stockings stuffed into drawers. When will you ever wear them, Esther? I ask her. They were on sale, she says, by way of an answer. I counted fifteen jars of jam in the cupboard. Who eats that much jam? She'll be eating jam for a hundred years at this rate. She eats like a bird, in any case, apart from the chocolate. Strangely, too, despite her near obsession with privacy, she gets quite careless when her passion is aroused, a carelessness that frightens even me sometimes. There was the episode in the teachers' room, for example, and a close call in the teachers' bathroom stall. It's as if she's testing fate. She's strong as an ox, she likes to boast, and has never missed a day of school, and yet she's plagued by headaches. By now I can see it in her eyes when a headache's coming on, and I close the door and turn off the lights and let her *suffer in silence* as she says. She pops sleeping pills like candy at night and struggles to get up in the morning.

Yet her life remains a mystery. She provides not the slightest clue as to the progression of events or the makeup of her family, and I'm beginning to wonder if we'll go through life together with the curtains drawn—to the outside world, but also to her past.

"What do you like about baseball?" I ask in passing. We're in bed, but neither of us is doing much sleeping.

"I learned it from the American soldiers," she says, staring up at the ceiling. "It's because of them I ended up here." She turns purposefully on her side to face me, as if she's decided something. "You were born during the war."

"Yes," I manage to say. The war had not affected my family directly. My father was too old to enlist, my brothers too young.

"Perhaps you studied it in history?" she asks, almost gently.

"I took a course," I say, unsure where this is heading.

"After the war," she says lightly, sitting up in the bed, as if a war is the most natural thing in the world, "I made my way back to Hamburg. Hamburg's on the northern coast of Germany, Karen, a port city. It was very beautiful before the war, a wealthy merchant town with two large lakes right in the middle. Much of the city was in rubble after the fire bombings, but it had been my home. Where else could I go? If anyone survived, I figured we would find each other there."

Yes, it is happening. Esther is telling me her story. I pull the covers tight around me and shiver; it feels indecent to be naked. Esther notices and fetches my robe and helps me into it. She sits back down on her side of the bed.

"Miracles did happen. You heard stories. There were people

who found a cousin, a school friend, someone, anyone, a lover, a rival from their past. But they were a drop in the ocean, you know? Or is it a drop in a bucket?" She stops, shrugs.

"A drop in the bucket," I tell her.

"No such luck," she says. "So, I went to the next port city, Bremen, and worked for the Americans translating documents. That's where I learned proper American English, from the soldiers. I learned American baseball from them as well, to answer your question."

She stops and smiles, perhaps back with the soldiers. Don't stop, I want to say.

She doesn't, she wants to talk. She tells me she worked for the Americans until she was able to leave Germany for good and how lucky she was to get out on one of the first troop transport ships, the Marine Perch, on June 4, 1946, a date she will never forget.

"I had a visa number one, a very valuable piece of paper, which allowed me to join my aunt and uncle in Peoria."

"Peoria!"

"That's right, Peoria. We all end up somewhere. Uncle Siegfried was my mother's older brother."

Esther's not mentioned her mother before. She leaps to life from Esther's lips and tongue. Suddenly, she's in the room sitting upright at the end of the bed. She's got a brown fur coat on and a black velvet half-hat with a veil, dressed for a long trip, it seems, because she's clutching an oversized bag in her lap. I hear a train screeching to a halt and she's gone as quickly as she came.

"Uncle Siegfried's wife, my aunt Hilde, had relatives in Peoria. They got out just before emigration closed in 1941. *By the skin of their teeth*, as you say."

"Did the soldiers teach you that?" I hear myself ask.

"They did! It's still a favorite expression of mine. It makes no sense at all!"

The tone settling over us is one of easy banter. But I'm shaken by ghosts. I laugh and try not to let it show.

"I arrived in New York and two days later I was on a train to

Chicago. I sometimes wonder what my life would have been like had I missed that train, stayed on in New York City. A school friend from Hamburg was living there, I discovered later. Or if I'd gone to Israel, like so many did. I was a committed Zionist before the war. If we'd had a country, our fate would have been very different, Karen."

"If you'd missed the train, we wouldn't have met."

"There's that," she says, absently.

She looks at me and frowns and strokes my face, but the tears well up anyway.

"Don't cry. I'm here, aren't I?"

"Yes," I answer, though I'm not so sure.

"Anyhow," she says with a shrug, "I had to go to my uncle. I had no choice in the matter. I was nineteen, a young woman already, but all I had in the world was a ten-dollar bill from the refugee agency and a train ticket. And there he was on the platform, Uncle Siegfried, aged beyond recognition, carrying a sign with my name on it. That's how we found each other. He drove me back to Peoria in his Oldsmobile, and that's when it hit me: *I'm in America.* Cheerful, well-fed human beings were going about their daily lives, the ordinary business of an ordinary day, as if nothing had happened. It felt almost obscene. Well, their boys had come home from the war, or they hadn't. But nothing was broken; it was all of a piece. No rubble, no dust. It didn't look real, more like a movie set. It was too clean, too bright. I had to shield my eyes."

The woman I'm listening to is someone I've not met before. She's very young, this woman. Her voice is breathless, higher pitched than Esther's, her accent thicker, and she's speaking very quickly. Even how she holds herself is strange to me.

"Uncle Siegfried had been a reporter in Berlin, but he never mastered English. He was too old for that. It's so tragic when you think about it."

She bows her head, in honor of him, I'm guessing. And there he is at my desk, hunched over an English dictionary, wiping his brow with a handkerchief.

"In Peoria, they took over a dry goods store and lived on the floors above the shop. They worked very hard, never had children. Leaving everything behind had taken its toll on them. They joined a synagogue, but they never felt accepted. Or let's say, no one understood them. No one wanted to understand what had happened to them. They didn't want to know. But my uncle and aunt were no different. They never asked me anything. No questions asked, that's how we lived. That was the unspoken rule."

Esther stops and looks at me and waits. She's started her story after the war. I need to know what happened before. I try to ask, but my voice sticks in my throat. The unspoken rule has infected me, too.

"Whatever else," she says, and sighs, and she's practically her old self again, "I had to get out of that depressing house. I was young and hungry for life, but my uncle was a strict and unforgiving man. I wasn't allowed to stay out late or to go dancing, God forbid. I quickly found work selling watches at Block & Kuhl's department store. Selling time, I liked to say. And there I befriended a very beautiful girl who sold scarves and gloves at the next counter. She was set to take up studies at the Teacher's College here that fall. I followed her."

"Aha," I say.

"And that, dear Karen, is how I ended up here."

"Not so fast. Who was this girl you followed?" It's easy to ask a question now, I discover. The danger's past.

"Her name was Mary. Mary Roberts, at the time. She and I became 'special friends,' as we called it back then, and roomed together."

"What was she like?"

Esther thinks back. A look of amusement crosses her face. Mary is a happy memory, clearly.

"She was very sportive, a healthy, corn-fed Midwestern girl. She could walk on her hands! And she was the nicest person you could meet. Uncomplicated, caring. She was very good for me. But halfway through our studies she went home for break and took up with a fellow she met at a dance."

"What happened then?"

"They married, and she moved home. There was no question of her staying on. She left the program and she left me. It was devastating. I felt very alone in the world again. But by then I was set on becoming a teacher."

There's something more. She hesitates, looks down.

"Uncle Siegfried was determined to find me a nice Jewish husband, of German origin, of course, with good prospects, a doctor or a lawyer. I told you he died early."

She stops, shakes her head.

"Well, he hung himself; many did."

I gasp. I can't stop myself.

"Aunt Hilde found him in the cellar." Esther turns her head sharply away as if she's seeing it in front of her. "*Ich kann nicht mehr* was all he wrote her. 'I can't go on,' in English. My uncle had been so determined to survive and start a new life and he'd done it, against all odds. But he was plagued by psychological problems. Many of my people, Karen, have been left with such a legacy, which is why we dominate the field of psychology. But still it would have been my duty to marry and reproduce."

"We do have children, Esther. That's how I see it."

Esther smiles that most beautiful smile of hers and nods. "Yes, we do, my pet."

I know what she's thinking, that I don't understand and never will. That I can't understand because I'm not Jewish. She's right, of course. I can't climb inside her as much as I try.

"I'd never bring a child into this world," she says, more to herself than me.

She yawns deeply. She's finished. She's had enough. She pulls the covers over herself, snuggling in.

"The best thing of all is not to be born," she says.

And from one moment to the next she's fast asleep.

I stay where I am in the bed, replaying Esther's words, which are the saddest thing I've ever heard and the most troubling. Well, I'm very grateful you were born, I tell her, whatever you say, but she's dead to the world and snoring. I curl up next to her and try to sleep, but I can't. I'm too disturbed by Esther's story and the dark conclusion she's drawn from it. I slip out of bed, still in my robe, creep down to the kitchen and out into the yard. I hear an owl's hoot, night creatures scuttling in and out of tunnels. A coyote is howling somewhere on the plains. I even hear a winter robin sing. The night is teeming with life. Even in the dead of winter. Even in this town. Life is all there is. She doesn't really mean it. She'll feel differently after a good night's sleep, I say out loud, and I almost believe it.

28

"Did she tell you how we met?"

"No," I say.

"Has she told you anything about us?"

"Only that she hoped you'd stay the best of friends."

Lee-Anne lets out a very dark laugh.

"I've spent fifteen years waking her out of nightmares. I don't think you understand."

We're meeting at Lee-Anne's request. She's driven me to a diner on the edge of town where farmers huddle together to discuss the price of crops, the weather, the state of the world. It's ungodly early. All I want is a cup of coffee, but she orders us breakfast over my protests. Give us the works, she tells the waitress, who greets her like an old friend. I haven't informed Esther about our meeting. Sometimes you say yes to something without thinking. The truth is curiosity has gotten the better of me.

"Don't get me wrong. We had great times."

"How did you meet?" I can't help asking.

"We met at a baseball game, believe it or not. A White Sox

game at Comiskey Park, to be exact. We started talking in the bathroom line. Very romantic, isn't it?"

I shrug and try to smile. I'm finding it hard to swallow my eggs. She's nice, though, I have to admit, and down to earth—strong, stable, someone you could rely on to get things done, to be there no matter what, someone you could turn to in a crisis. If you were to lay your head on that strong, wide shoulder of hers, you'd feel all right. Part of me wants to do just that.

"She was finishing college. I was already teaching at the junior high, a real pro. But she was anything but innocent. She was worldly, you know? She spoke better English than me. I was really impressed. She'd only been here a couple of years. She'd lost her entire family over there. But she didn't talk about it. I helped her get the job at the school. She had no intention of staying on in this dinky little town. But I asked her to stay with me, and she did."

Lee-Anne sits back and throws her arms in the air, like someone who hit the jackpot and still can't believe her luck. I could draw her out. She's talkative. She knows more about Esther than anyone else. It's the chance of a lifetime, in fact. But discussing Esther in the third person is making me very uncomfortable, and I realize with a sinking feeling that I shouldn't have come.

"Why did you want to meet, Lee-Anne?" I ask, hoping to conclude our meeting as quickly as possible.

"Okay." She's shrugging those shoulders. "I thought you might want to know a few things." She's stopped buttering her bread and is pointing her knife in my direction. "Before you get hurt."

"That sounds threatening."

She shakes her head and studies me as if I'm a jigsaw puzzle.

"You bewitched her somehow. She told me you reminded her of someone. Someone from her past. I guess that's what it is."

I'm taken aback. She notices and looks at me with a guilty expression.

"I guess she never mentioned that."

"No," I say and manage a grin. I drain my cup, it's time to go. What Lee-Anne is telling me doesn't fit this diner with its cheerful yellow Formica table tops, its comforting plates of sausage and pancakes. This someone from Esther's past is too large a piece of information for me to contemplate. I need time to think it through. I need to be on my own. I need to get out of here.

"Lee-Anne, I can see that you're suffering. I'm truly sorry. I'd better get back now." I'm slipping on my jacket as I speak. "If there's anything I can do to help, let me know."

"Stop seeing her," she says, quickly, "for your own sake." Her voice is assured and smooth. She must be a good administrator, I can't help thinking, adept at giving orders and assuming control.

I look down, avoiding her eyes, which are fixed intently on me. I'm shocked and furious and on the brink of crying, but I refuse to shed a tear in front of her. Lee-Anne has no right to speak to me this way, and I'll tell her as much, I decide. I wipe my eyes with the back of my sleeve, look up prepared to meet her gaze, but Lee-Anne is looking over my shoulder and waving cheerfully to a group of farmers across the diner like a politician canvassing for votes. Her wide smile reveals perfect teeth. Then she's leaning forward, her muscular arms on the table, so that our faces are very close together.

"She'll come back to me. She always does," she says, without a flicker of doubt and something like pity, like she's sorry to be the one to break the news to me. The smile hasn't left her face.

I get up, grabbing my purse and pay the bill at the counter, not stopping for a minute to remember that Lee-Anne has driven me here. I walk, practically run, the whole way home, past the shacks and junk-strewn yards along the outskirts of town, thinking about the woman from Esther's past and Lee-Anne's parting words.

By the time I've reached my front door, I've convinced myself that we all have ghosts from our past, that we all know someone who reminds us of someone else, a school friend, a neighbor, a relative. I'm quite sure Esther would remind me of someone if I put my mind to it. As for Lee-Anne's warning, well, she's suffering and wants to put a wedge between Esther and me. Esther's left her, after all, and Lee-Anne wants her back. It's wishful thinking on her part, which is only to be expected.

29

"Put that on," Esther's calling from behind the bathroom door. She's left my cobalt dress suit on the bed, and my nicest pumps are on the floor.

"But I thought we were going dancing!" I shout to the door. The capri pants and loafers I'd planned on wearing have mysteriously vanished from sight.

"We're professional gals having a drink and a bite out."

"I don't understand."

"I'd just prefer it that way, if you don't mind."

But I *do* mind and I want to understand. We're meeting Liz and Bettie at Billie Le Roy's in the city, a women-only club. I've heard them talk about it, and after much pleading Esther has agreed to keep her promise and take me dancing. I'm about to pursue the issue further when Esther steps out of the bathroom, and I have to gasp and laugh in astonishment.

"What's so funny?" she says.

She's wearing a close-fitting mauve dress with short sleeves, pearls around her neck and in her ears and matching lipstick. Her eyes are painted too, with lilac eyeshadow and thick mascara. I've never seen her done up quite like this before. Her outfits are always impeccable, tasteful and understated. The Esther standing here in front of me is a gaudier version. The heavy makeup has the effect of making her less feminine, not more. Her large hands and muscular arms, her flat chest, create a dissonance, as if she's a man in women's clothes. After the initial shock, I must admit that I'm excited by her new look. I take her by the hand and guide her toward the bed, but we're late as it is, she says, escaping my grasp.

It's very dark inside the club, though dusk is lingering out on the street. We're here for the Sunday party, which starts early, and the place is already filling up. A stylish bartender with a pageboy haircut, dressed in a velvet smoking jacket, whistles approvingly and calls out a greeting to Esther from the bar as we enter. Esther stops to give her a kiss, but doesn't introduce me, and I want to ask her why but it's too loud. Surely, we're safe in here, safe enough for Esther to acknowledge we're together. Across the room, I'm surprised to see men in suits swigging beer out of bottles, playing pool and swapping stories loudly, their arms draped over girls in high heels and low-cut dresses.

"The butches and femmes," Esther offers under her breath, with a look of disapproval. I take a closer look, and they're women, all right. Their broad gestures and rooted stance, their legs wide open where they sit, give them the appearance of men, but their delicate features and hands, their slight builds give them away. The women, too, aren't quite as they appear. They may be dressed to kill, but they're hardly examples of feminine propriety. Their laughter is boisterous, their behavior anything but modest. One girl has her fellow pinned to the pool hall table.

I'm enthralled by this mix of woman and man. Who says we must be one thing or another? I'm finding them all quite beautiful, but I don't tell Esther. I'd join them at the pool tables if I could, but Esther's got me firmly by the arm and is guiding me toward the back of the bar where we enter a cavernous space.

It takes a while for my eyes to adjust, and when they do I see small tables surrounding a dance floor with a stage at one end. Couples are already dancing to the latest hits. "It's My Party" is playing, and before we even find a table I'm pulling Esther onto the floor. Esther is an assured and graceful dancer, I discover, but I am even better. I lead her, and as we move across the floor, women make room for us and call out encouragingly. I could dance all night. "Blue Velvet" comes on next, a favorite of mine, a slow dance for lovers, but Esther wants to find a seat.

She chooses a table near the entrance, which surprises me, and seats herself facing the door. I'd like the dark corner, where lovers are already making out with abandon. Women are sitting on each other's laps, straddling each other. They're licking each other's ears, fondling each other's breasts. It's not clear where the body of one begins and the other ends, they're so wrapped up in each other. Esther orders us Cokes without asking because she has to drive, she says. But I'm not driving and I'd like a drink, I tell her. She just shrugs and looks around.

"If anyone asks, we're out-of-towners. We happened in here by chance, you understand?"

"Sure," I answer, though I don't really understand. But I'm not in the mood for contemplation. I get up and sit on her lap. She allows me a kiss, and it's magical to be kissing Esther outside the confines of our four walls, surrounded by other women just like us. I fondle her small breasts, which she tolerates, and feel her nipples growing hard under my touch. I kiss and lick her ears, and she lets out a little moan despite herself. I'm about to straddle her, but she's lifting me back into my chair, like a naughty first-grader. "Not now, Karen," she says, "I have to watch for Bettie and Liz."

They've not shown up, and Esther seems most interested in worrying about their arrival. I give up on getting her attention and feast on the sight of bodies of women moving across the floor in all their glorious difference, moving as one. "I Saw Her Standing There" comes on. I catch the eye of an astonishing-looking Black woman dressed to the nines in a white tuxedo and tie. I'm sorely tempted to ask her to dance, but I lose sight of her in the gathering crowd. And then, from out of nowhere, she's pulling me up to dance, and she's even more beautiful up close if that's possible. She has the carved features of an Egyptian queen, the scent of sandalwood, the strut of a young man. She takes me confidently into her arms, and we dance body to body to "Can't Help Falling in Love." We're locked into each other, moving to the rhythm as one and then we discover a rhythm of our own. As the song comes to an end, she speaks into my ear, and her voice is girlish, high pitched, not at all what I'd imagined, and I'm taken aback I admit, and she's asking me if I'm going steady, and I say yes, and she says that doesn't matter, her name's Shirley and she's here every Sunday. The music stops and the drag show is about to begin. I thank Shirley for the dance and tell her I'll look for her next time. As she disappears into the crowd, I wonder if I will see her again and what would happen if I did. Meanwhile, the excitement in the room is palpable.

But Esther is on edge. I feel it, and it's starting to affect me, too.

"I shouldn't have brought you here," she says.

"Why not, for goodness' sake. I like it."

"Well, that's good," she snaps and resumes her suffering. It dawns on me that Esther can't have fun in a conventional sense, in the way that others do. She's incapable of letting her hair down.

"Why can't we have fun for once? It's not a crime."

"I'm glad you're having *fun*," she answers grimly.

But despite the gaiety, neither of us is having much fun now. She's spoiling it for me. I turn my chair away from her to face the stage and vow to ignore her. A swaggering gentleman with a moustache and fedora is removing his jacket, his tie, his suspenders, his creased trousers, to Peggy Lee's "Fever," and my temperature is definitely rising. We're all snapping our fingers in time, apart from Esther, that is. Then he's tearing off his shirt revealing large, full breasts and pulling a banana from the crotch of his boxers, and the room erupts in laughter. As he moves from table to table offering bites, Esther rolls her eyes, but I pretend not to notice. The boxers come off and the women roar. A man with a woman's body stands naked before us.

"I want to leave, Karen."

"Oh, please, let's stay just a little longer."

Suddenly, the lights go on, blinding us all, and a harsh male voice echoes through a megaphone. "Stay where you are and get some identification out. If you try to move, you'll be arrested."

We hear shouts and cries from the bar and pool hall, breaking glass, the scraping of chairs as paths are cleared, shrieks of pain and the thumps of blows. Women are being roughed up, perhaps beaten. We're frozen in place. None of us dare look the other in the eye. The naked performer scrambles to cover herself in her men's smoking jacket. An officer strolls across the room toward her. He's got a smile on his face, like he's taking a walk in the park, but his hand is on his gun.

"Let's have a look at your papers, Mister," he says. She turns away from him, shielding her breasts. "What's the matter, what are you hiding, huh? Let's see."

The policeman pulls her jacket out of her grasp, grabs at her crotch. "Where're your balls, huh? Someone chop 'em off? Or are they up your ass? And take your hat off when I'm speaking to you, fella." As he knocks the fedora off her head, thick red hair spills over her naked shoulders. The officer steps back, faking astonishment. "Well, what have we got here? A female pervert! I think you better follow me." He yanks her arm roughly. She screams out in pain. He starts to pull her across the dance floor by the hair, which quickly proves to be a wig, perhaps the final gesture of her act. "Fucking dyke," the officer says, "no dick, not even any hair." He grabs her by both arms now and she's struggling to escape, whereupon he knees her brutally, throws her to the ground, turns her onto her stomach and handcuffs her. The once-cocky fellow is now a whimpering girl. We watch in horror as he hustles her, naked, out of the room.

And the beautiful Black girl in the white tuxedo is being led away in handcuffs! "Shirley!" I cry out. She turns her head.

There's fear in her eyes and humiliation. I'm about to jump up and run after her, but Esther has reached under the table and gripped my hand so tightly it makes me wince. More officers swarm in and choose their victims. I realize it's the butches who are being singled out for especially harsh treatment.

"Stay very still and breathe normally and remember what I told you."

Esther takes a very deep breath in and out. She's attempting to appear fully at ease, but her body is rigid. I glance around the room at women breathing in and out like one organism.

A baby-faced officer with downy hair where a beard should be appears at our table. "IDs please, ladies," he says, almost politely.

"We're not sure what's going on," Esther says, looking around with a surprised expression. "We're from out of town and here on business. We just came in for a bit of supper and a drink. Our papers are back at the hotel, I'm afraid."

The officer looks us over.

"We're teachers," I volunteer.

"Well, go on and get out of here quick," he says, eyeing me, "or I'll have to book you."

Esther rises, head held high, and takes my arm. Looking straight ahead, we exit the dance hall and then the bar and walk slowly out into the cold night air. I wonder at her poise. I'm shaking so badly my teeth are rattling. There are police cars with flashing lights and sirens. The owner must have been late paying her dues to the Mafia, Esther says under her breath. All I know is women like me are being hauled away in paddy wagons. We keep walking and don't look back or at each other.

"I cannot believe you told him we were teachers," Esther says when we've gotten some distance between us and the club.

"Well, it worked, didn't it?"

"It could just as easily have gone the other way. If he hated school, for example."

"Well, I guess he liked his teachers," I say, running to keep up with her.

"Don't ever do that again."

"Where are we going?"

But Esther's not in the mood for answering.

"That was a close call," I say, catching my breath. "Thank God, you made us dress the part. I feel terrible. You wanted to leave, and if we had we—"

"Shut up," Esther says. "Shut up. Just. Shut. Up."

I'm so astonished to hear her talk this way that I do shut up.

We reach her car, having made a sizable detour, and drive the sixty miles back to town in silence. Esther drops me off without a word and speeds away. I stumble into the house and wash myself down, avoiding the mirror. I don't want to see my face.

I wake up to the phone ringing. I must have gone out like a light last night. It's Esther, just checking in, she says. I hear her soulful sigh, and the world is all right again, but different at the same time in a way I don't yet understand.

"I almost lost control, I'm afraid. If you hadn't been there I'm not sure what I would have done, Karen. I'd have been locked up last night most likely. If someone had dared to lay a hand on you, he'd be dead or I would."

I've never heard her talk like this before, so hard and unrefined. It doesn't fit to her person at all. I'm feeling something new inside of me as well. A small fissure is opening, filled with molten anger. We've been marked, branded as outcasts, as criminals. I feel shame, but also a certain shameless power of defiance.

"Come over," I order her. And she obeys.

I meet her at the door and kiss her hard. I grip her arm and force her up the stairs. My anger leaves me heartless, callous. Esther understands and plays along. The look in her eyes is knowing, ready. There's no room left for bodies gently lapping, no space here for the perfect rhythm of love. Every touch that was soft is rough, every tease now demand and seizure. The sweetness between us that made me weep and beg has been replaced by raucousness, by rampage. My body is a weapon, lawless. And

Esther? She's been to this place before with someone else it seems, which only serves to excite me more. I feel no jealousy, and I don't care. We commit crimes of passion and then some. We break laws of nature, blast safes and steal treasure, ransack and lay waste to all that remains and set ourselves on fire. When we're done, and there's not a trace of us left, we escape into each other.

Sunday we spend reading the paper and preparing our classes. It will be good to see the children's expectant faces. They haven't learned to despise us yet.

30

Louise is insisting I join her on a double date. Dating is more than a pastime for Louise; it's an odyssey to find a husband. But this date is different, she assures me. She has found her Mr. Right, and he has a brother apparently, and she's sure he's just perfect for me. Her new beau, Gary Swanson, is the manager of menswear at Penney's downtown. She'll tell me all about how they met later, she promises. The brother, Steve, who's *brainier*, is studying to be a lawyer.

"He's not just smart, though. He's adorable," she says, linking arms with me as we leave the school. "Well, they're both adorable. They're redheads. When we marry them, we'll be sisters and have redheaded babies!"

The police raid in Chicago and my near escape with Esther lends the scene an air of absurdity. I've landed on another planet. I'm in the wrong movie. I try to turn her down, but Louise won't take no for an answer. I'm single, after all, and she's giddy with excitement. Well, it wouldn't be a bad thing, I tell myself, to be seen to be dating men. I might even mention it to Marilyn in passing so she can spread the gossip.

"Okay," I say, giving in.

"You dress like a Catholic schoolgirl, Kar, no offense, with your pleated skirts and buttoned-up blouses. Or better yet, like a spinster schoolteacher. We don't have dress codes anymore you know." Louise is nothing if not direct, something I like about her. "So, let's get you dolled up."

And we're off downtown for a shopping spree. Torture is the best way to describe it. The truth is I know more about clothes than I let on. My older sisters dressed me up like a mannequin in all the fashions of the day. I had a cinched waist, Louise's favored style, at three. There are photographs to prove it. I was their guinea pig. They tried all the latest hairstyles out on me, including a bouffant. The hair spray made me gag, and I hated them for it and vowed to escape their clutches and the pressures of the fashion world as soon as I was able.

"You choose something for me, Lou," I beg her, and she obliges.

I don't look bad, I have to admit, in the tight red dress with its open neck, but it's someone else in the mirror, an imposter.

"I look like a pinup girl," I call out.

"What's wrong with that? That's what men like. Just follow their eyes. Gary goes wild for *décolleté*."

We double up laughing at her terrible French and at nothing at all, just the pleasure in each other's company. I'll buy the dress to make her happy, I decide.

"Look at you, you're gorgeous." She's standing behind me in the Charm Shop changing room, staring hard at my reflection.

"If I were a boy, I'd eat you up," she says.

The tight red dress remains in its box. I've ended up with my trusted blue suit on and sit waiting by the window. I haven't told Esther about my double date. She's in the city with Liz and Bettie, but I still feel guilty. The car pulls up right on time. Gary is driving and the brother, Steve, to my relief, is sitting in front with him. He turns to say hello and shake my hand, but I barely take him in. We head off for the Pheasant Run, an hour's drive away, famous for dinner and a band all in one.

"If we went somewhere in town, people would talk," Louise whispers, locking arms with me in the back seat.

I nod and try to smile, stare out at cornfields with their rows of grey stubble. I realize with a heavy heart that this was a bad idea. I'm wishing I wasn't here. I close my eyes and pray to God for a flat tire, a roadblock, a flash flood, an encounter with aliens, anything that might turn the car around and take me home.

The restaurant is chock full of couples who look just like us and so loud you have to shout to be heard. The tables are so close you could reach over and share a meal with your neighbor. Louise puts her arm around Gary and calls him her little tomcat, and he turns the darkest red I've ever seen a person turn. But it's clear he's smitten and they're perfectly suited. He's large and laughs heartily and has the appetite of three men, to judge by his order. Steve, who is taller and slim, hardly speaks, and in any case when Louise gets going no one can get a word in. Halfway through dinner, she taps her glass and tells us that she and Gary have an announcement to make. She hugs him tightly and they French kiss, and it goes on so long I don't know where to look, so I look over at Steve who smiles at me. His brown eyes are warm, his long face open and friendly. Their kiss concluded, Louise announces they're engaged.

"It's your turn now, Steve," Gary says, "to get yourself hitched."

Steve turns as red as a beetroot, and I'm thinking it must be a trait of redheads with their pale, translucent skin. Louise kicks me under the table, and I ignore her as best I can. Couples slowly rise to dance. The whiskey sours are going to my head. Steve wants to ask me something and because it's hard to hear he leans over, placing his arm around me.

"You smell like peppermints," I tell him. It's not unpleasant.

"I'm giving up smoking," he says, brushing my ear with his lips.

"What did you want to ask me?"

"If you want to dance."

The band is playing "Bossa Nova Baby." We get up to dance, and it's only then I realize just how tall he is. But it's easy to dance with Steve, and the bossa nova beat is hard to resist. As "Moon River" ends, and we take our seats, something has happened between us. The feel of his body up against mine has confirmed the evening's expectation. Before the night is over we will make love, like every other couple on the dance floor. Or put another way, the single girl on a double date who I've become will sleep with her date tonight, fulfilling the role that nature intended for her. It's a test of sorts, I tell myself.

Louise gestures for me to join her in the bathroom.

"What'd you think?"

"About what?" I say, though I know exactly what she means.

"Steve, of course. He's crazy about you. The way you dance together, you may as well be making love. You're made for each other."

"He's very nice," I say, and it's true.

"How would you feel if we stayed here tonight? Gary's drunk and shouldn't be driving."

"Sure," I say quickly. It's in the cards, in any case.

Louise goes to the reception desk and gets our keys, and I realize she's booked the rooms already.

"If it didn't work out, I'd have shared the room with you, and Gary and Steve would have taken the other," she whispers, very pleased with herself. "We're registered as two married couples."

All right, I tell her, but only if we're sworn to secrecy. She can't tell anyone, especially at the school, other teachers, Esther, for example. She crosses her heart and hopes to die if she breathes a word to anyone. "I've got a reputation to uphold," she says, laughing.

This is my first hotel room. It's spacious and very clean, almost clinical, a giant bed its main attraction, designed for the business at hand. It's a little disappointing, I have to admit. The hotel room of my imagination is far more elegant. But there are large photos of the Empire State Building, the Brooklyn Bridge, and New York City streets framed on the walls, which conjure up another world, a world of elegance and elegant hotels. Steve and I stand in the room's small hallway, suddenly shy, studying the room. I look up at him and shrug, which makes him laugh, and he bends down from his great height and puts his arms around me. We kiss and his large tongue fills my mouth, surprising me. He scoops me up in his arms and carries me high like a sportsman's trophy to the bed and carefully places me under his long, lean body. As he rolls his rubber on, he takes me in with a boyish grin, and there's something charming about him, about the simple happiness registered on his face. There's not the slightest complication. His caresses are well-placed, his lips and fingers eager to please, and despite his size he's gentle and makes love with a quiet, serious kind of passion.

Afterward he wants to talk and smoke "one last cigarette," and I watch amused as he inhales deeply, with guilty pleasure. He tells me he was born and raised in small-town Iowa. He and Gary are the children of dairy farmers. After his law studies he intends to move back home, live on the farm, and open a practice. His deep voice is monotonous and lulls me to sleep.

In the morning, I let him know there's someone else. I see a flash of anger in his warm brown eyes, but he nods and shrugs and says he understands.

"Are you engaged or anything?"

"No," I tell him, which is officially true. I don't tell him I live in the underworld, in hiding. I don't tell him I woke up aching for Esther. He doesn't know I've failed the test.

He's patient, he says, he'll wait for me. And because we're in bed together and the hotel room is ours until noon, we make love again. This time he's not so careful. There's longing in him, raw emotion. His body shakes with desire he can barely contain. He's crying out my name and laughing at the same time. He's never met a woman like me before, he tells me. He's fallen in love with me, he says. It's exciting to feel him come to life, and I respond in kind to his body's urgency, allowing myself to believe I've fallen in love with him, too.

On the drive home, we sit together in the back seat of Gary's car, arms wrapped around each other, holding hands. I'm newborn, nervous, someone I don't recognize. Louise is uncharacteristically quiet, which I attribute to a night of exhausting passion, and falls asleep on Gary's shoulder.

As we reach my house, a warning bell goes off in my head until it hits me that there's nothing to fear. I'm safe and free from all constraints. There's no need to check for the neighbors, imagine watchful eyes behind curtains waiting in judgment. Let them watch all they like. A man takes a woman on a date. He brings her home. It's perfectly natural. My muscles relax, my heartbeat slows. Steve opens the car door for me and walks me up the steps to my porch for all the world to see. How simple it is and carefree. I'm tempted to invite him in, but Esther's coming over later on her way home from Chicago, so I say good-bye at the door. "I love you, Karen," he says, offering his hand, bowing his tall frame like a gallant. "I love you, too, Steve," I hear myself answering. "I'll be waiting for you," he says.

I watch him stride back to the car, so full of confidence and vigor, wave as they drive off. I'll date Steve Swanson, I decide. My secret life with Esther is exhausting and taking its toll, the constant fear, the subterfuge. Despite my love for her, I know there's no happy end in sight. I'll end up spending weekends in the back rooms of dingy bars in Chicago if I'm not careful, and possibly in a prison cell. I collapse onto the couch, and as I doze off, imagine myself a lawyer's wife on a dairy farm in Iowa, milking cows, calling the children in for their supper.

I sleep deeply through the afternoon then wake in a panic. I see now that what happened between Steven Swanson and me was a colossal error of intention and judgment. The double date was a sham, a pretense, and I ended up betraying Esther. Poor Steve's bound to be hurt. In the clear light of day, I see things as they are, not how they're supposed to be.

31

I'm kneeling at the edge of the bed, lost in prayer, when Esther comes bounding up the stairs, surprising me. She's sorry she's so late, she's calling out, the traffic out of the city was terrible.

"What are you doing on the floor?" She's stopped in the doorway.

"What does it look like?"

"It looks like you're praying."

"I *was* praying," I say, and I fear what's coming. Esther tends to question things, and I have no energy to make up a story. The events of last night and this morning have exhausted me.

"For anything in particular?" she asks.

"No reason."

"There has to be a reason, doesn't there? I mean, I'm no expert."

"You don't need a reason, Esther," I tell her, which isn't exactly true. I've said my Hail Marys as penance and moved on to praying for Esther and me, that nothing pulls us asunder, Steve Swanson most of all. When you lead a secret life, one secret leads easily to another, I'm discovering. Secrets lead to lies and half-truths and confusions, even in your own heart and mind. I'm feeling lost, and when I'm lost, out of habit I speak to God.

"Anyway, prayer is private," I say.

"You and God have some secrets, do you?" she says, sitting down heavily on the bed.

"God is all-loving and all-knowing," I answer, alarmed.

Esther shrugs. "Well, carry on. I'll go take a bath."

She gets up and heads down the stairs. I should be relieved and quit while I'm ahead, but something's working in me, perhaps a need to self-destruct, to play with fire, to be punished. I find myself following her as far as the doorway.

"I can't *carry on*. Prayer invites no interruption."

"Now I've heard everything," she says, gripping the banister with both hands. "Do me the favor please of keeping your all-loving, all-knowing God to yourself." She turns and looks up at me with something like revulsion. "And your prayers, too."

"Forget it, Esther," I say, quietly, and close the bedroom door. She's hurt me to the core, but I won't let on, and that should be the end of it, but I find I'm not done. I open the door and call back down.

"For the record, you're the one who asked. And anyway, who are you to interrogate my soul? How dare you? Quite frankly Esther, I've had it with you and your *Weltschmerz*!"

Esther lets out a loud guffaw in answer. I slam the door and fall onto my bed, but I can hear her rummaging around in the cupboards and realize she's spending the night on the couch. It's the first time we've slept separately in the house, and I sleep very badly. I listen for her step on the stairs. Once I think I hear her creeping into the room, but it's only the old elm in the wind.

In the morning I wake up to find her standing in front of the bed. She appears to have something she wants to say. She looks determined. I watch her warily as she begins to speak.

"You were right to be angry. You're lucky to believe in something. I'm sorry." She looks down at the floor, then up at me, and waits.

No, I want to say. You've got it wrong. I'm the one who should be begging for forgiveness. But instead of answering, I just nod.

"I love you," she says, simply.

She's never said those words before. Well, in the heat of passion, yes, but not like this, direct, clear-headed. Her light nightgown is slipping off her shoulder, her hair is loose, disheveled. She hasn't slept at all, I can tell, because her eyes are red, the dark circles more pronounced than usual.

I want to tell her that I've cheapened those very words by using them with a perfect stranger and can't bring myself to utter them again, that I'm not worthy of her love, that I've betrayed her. But I don't say anything because I don't want to lose her. Only God is all-loving. Only God is all-forgiving.

I pull back the covers instead, and invite her in.

Word does get around that I've been on a date. June Harding, my neighbor, stops me at the Piggly Wiggly and lets me know she saw a handsome young man on my porch the other day. I shrug playfully and change the subject. Marilyn leans over at lunch and whispers in my ear. She's heard the news, she says. She's so excited for me she can hardly sleep. She's got her fingers crossed he's the man of my dreams. With Marilyn in on the secret, it's only a matter of time until the whole school knows, Esther included. I've no choice but to tell her myself. I catch her in the hallway at the end of the day, beg her to take a walk with me. But it's bitter cold, she protests, before giving in.

"By the way, I meant to tell you," I start in, "Louise tried to set me up with her fiancé's brother over the weekend."

"Oh," she says, and she looks surprised. "How did it go?"

"Disastrously."

"Did you sleep with him?"

Her directness startles me. "Of course not," I practically shout, and I look her in the eye. "How could you think such a thing?"

With my hands on my hips, I'm the very picture of indignation. I'm telling her a bold-faced lie for the very first time, an occasion of sorts, and for the last time too, I swear to God.

"Well, that's good," she says, and she smiles widely. She's convinced beyond a shadow of a doubt, by the look on her face.

"I'd like a hot chocolate," I announce. "How about you? My treat." I take her arm as we saunter downtown. I feel as light as air and as free as a bird, as if by denying a thing it never happened. Or better put, as if it happened to someone else, not me.

Hardly a week's gone by when Steve Swanson calls. I'm more surprised than I have any right to be. Steve exists and the world spins on its axis, free of my influence. Louise gave him my number, he tells me. He hopes I don't mind his calling. How am I? he asks, his deep voice trembling. He's nervous and excited at the same time. It's a feeling I know too well, and sadly for him I also know what's coming. He's crossing the tracks, head in the clouds, and doesn't see the train approaching. I tell him I'm fine and wait. He can't stop thinking about me, he says. Could he see me this weekend? He had the idea we might take a drive out to his family farm. Iowa's a winter wonderland at present.

I tell him I enjoyed our evening very much. I tell him he'll make someone very happy, which is true. I tell him I've never been to Iowa. The fields must be very beautiful under all that snow. But I'm not able to see him again. It was a mistake, I'm not available, and I hope he understands it would be best if he didn't call again. My voice is calm and steady, my purpose sure, like the hand of an executioner. And because he's a gentleman, he says he understands, and we say our good-byes and wish each other all the best. I put the phone down, find myself shivering. It's warm as toast in the house. It must be my cold heart.

I bundle up and practically march to Louise's rooming house. She's alone tonight, making dinner in the kitchen as it happens. She's thrilled to see me, she says. She was feeling lonely. The girls are away and Gary's working late. I sit her down and explain firmly but gently that though I like Steve very much, I am not looking for a husband at present and have enough on my plate with the teaching. I know teaching comes easily to her—she's a natural, as Esther would attest, but for me it's a bit of a struggle. Steve is much too honorable and too serious to be strung along, and anyway I have no intention of moving to Iowa anytime soon. All in all, it would be her job to help him and me both by pretending the whole thing never happened.

32

I'm starting in on the Western Expansion when Alan raises his hand. Lydie's sitting innocently in front of him studying her pencil with great concentration, but I can see she's put him up to it.

"Yes, Alan, what is it?"

"Miss Murphy, how does a girl get pregnant?"

Why me? goes through my head. But there's no time for self-pity. The children are staring wide-eyed, and I'm kicking myself that I didn't see it coming.

"That's a question for biology, Alan, and we're in history now."

Lydie has turned her back and is gesticulating something wildly to him.

"Lydie, turn around in your seat," I say. She does turn around and raises her hand.

"What is it, Lydie?"

I'm letting my exasperation show, but I'm not in the mood for pretense.

"But Miss Murphy, can best friends have a baby?"

So help me, Lydie, I'm thinking, and you could hear a pin drop.

"Well, if they are a boy and a girl, they can."

Lydie's not content with my answer. She looks crestfallen. She bites her lip and frowns. It occurs to me she might like to start a family with Janie, who's absent today. Perhaps that's why Lydie's taking the chance to broaden her knowledge on the subject.

"If they've reached sexual maturity, that is," I clarify for some ungodly reason.

"What's *sexual*, Miss Murphy?" Karl shouts out.

Change the subject at once, I tell myself. You're not trained for this. But I can't just change the subject. They'll be suspicious and even more curious. They're on the edge of their seats, mouths open, like hungry chicks in a nest.

"All right, class. That's it. I'm going to answer your interesting questions, and then we're moving on."

I take up my chalk, like a weapon of sorts, and proceed to enlighten them.

"Pregnancy, girls and boys, is part of something we call the *reproductive cycle*." I write it with brusque strokes on the board.

"It occurs in some form in all plants and animals and is the process by which we reproduce ourselves."

I don't recognize my own voice. The sound is clipped, almost harsh, and clinical, and I'm speaking very fast.

"Plants and animals and even insects are divided into male and female. There are a few notable exceptions, but that doesn't concern us now. Humans are animals, too, of course. We learned that already."

There's some laughter and grunting and ape-like gesturing. I sigh and wait it out with a smile. Though I'm attempting to make it sound very ordinary, like a point of grammar or a math equation, they know very well a taboo is being broken. Sparks are flying across the room.

"The mature male produces seeds, which are called sperm. And the females . . . and the females . . ."

186

I'm lost. I cough. I'm in way over my head. I should have paid more attention in biology class. I don't have the scientific words at hand. I want to go home. I want to go home and get into my soft bed and wake up and find I've been dreaming.

"And females produce eggs," I say finally.

A hand goes up. "Joanne?"

"I don't understand." There's nervous laughter in the room.

"Well, that's reproduction, Joanne. A sperm entering an egg."

"But how does a sperm get into the egg?" she wants to know.

And there's no turning back.

"Well, the male and female come together in a process known as human intercourse."

I wait. I know what's coming. I feel like Joan of Arc at the stake. It's Lydie. Who else would it be?

"What's *human intercourse?*" She draws the words out interminably.

I have two options as I see it. I can walk to the closet and get my coat. Or I can answer her.

"What is intercourse?" I'm stalling for time. "What is intercourse," I say again. I'm so hot suddenly that I tear at my collar. "I'll show you what human intercourse is."

I take up the chalk again, poking it in her direction.

"The male penis ejaculates sperm into the female vagina, Lydie."

I turn sharply to the board and illustrate my words with lines and circles and squiggles and arrows.

"At which point the sperm travel up into the uterus, or womb, as it is commonly known. They swim like little minnows— you've seen those, children, traveling up a stream—where the eggs are waiting. If a sperm enters an egg, the egg starts growing, receiving food and warmth from the mother. This process lasts nine months. And that is what we call pregnancy, children."

I've done it.

"At the end of the nine months out comes a baby."

I stop. I'm in shock.

187

"Any other questions?" slips off my tongue.

"Where does the baby come out?" asks Nancy.

"It takes the same route out as the sperm took in," I answer, pointing to my version of the vaginal canal.

"The baby swims down the stream?"

"In a manner of speaking," I say, running my chalk up the canal, then down again.

Their eyes are glued to the crude images on the board. I realize I've not mentioned love or marriage once. I've not mentioned desire, either. Perhaps I should. We are more than our biology, children, I'll tell them. There is more to life than reproduction. But if I do, I would need to mention the desire of boys for boys and girls for girls. I'll do just that, why not? They ought to know, it's part of life in all its facets. *Don't you dare*, I tell myself. *Hold your tongue. You're in enough hot water.* I seem to have willed them into silence, in any case, and take my chance.

"If there are no more questions, I'd like to move on. Please, open your history books."

I wipe the board clean with vigorous sweeps. Behind me I hear a scurry of activity, pencils dropping, desks slamming, books opening, pages turning, like music to my ears. But then out of the corner of my eye I notice Marty, who never asks a question, waving his hand from the back of the room.

"Well, Marty," I say, turning back to the class. "What is it?"

"What is the *feemale vaginal*, Miss Murphy?"

In a flash of insight, I understand I've made a very big mistake, a mistake for the ages.

"The word is *vagina*, Marty," I correct him, and I watch twenty children mouth vagina in unison.

"Or the *vaginal canal.* Take your pick. But you'll learn more about that in human anatomy, children."

The bell rings, too late, too late. It's over. I feel a flood of relief, even elation, like the moment before you drown, after the panic and the struggle.

"After lunch, it's on to the Gold Rush," I call out, over the scraping of chairs and desktops slamming.

I'm about to head downstairs to pick the children up from lunch when Will pokes his head into my room.

"May I bother you, Karen?"

"Sure," I say.

He comes in, closing the door behind him. I get up from my desk and wait.

"Karen, the children are talking about that most delicate subject."

"Do you mean sex, Will?"

"How did you guess?" he says, and he smiles regretfully. "I need to ask you for an explanation."

"I didn't bring it up, Will. The children asked me about pregnancy. What could I have done but answer honestly and factually?"

"Well, there will be some parents who are not amused. And quite frankly, Karen, it seems some pretty graphic language was used, unnecessarily, I might add."

"It's biology, Will. If I may say so, I feel we speak too little and too late on the subject."

"I take your point, Karen, but I've got the specter of irate parents in front of me."

Will wipes his brow with his handkerchief and shakes his head. He's right to be worried. Sex education is viewed as the end of civilization as we know it, and that's at the middle and high school levels. There's organized resistance across the country now, much of it coming from churches, my own included. The schools have taken God out of the classroom and put Sex in its place, so the slogan goes. In my mind's eye I see parents marching up the school steps, torches in hand, asking for my head. I've stolen their children's innocence and will be heading straight to hell with their assistance.

"Please refrain from any more sex education in the classroom," Will pleads. "And let's just hope it all quiets down.

189

My neck is on the line, here, Karen."

It's too late, Will, I think to myself. "I'll do my best," I promise him.

But if I've learned anything all year, it's that I can't control what the children say or do. They're governed by primal urges and self-preservation. The fact is, I don't have the slightest influence on them, but I don't tell Will this, of course. That should be it, I'm thinking, but Will has placed himself between my desk and the door, and now he's slicking back his hair and smiling.

"If you're free, I thought we might have a bite and discuss the issue further after work."

"I'm sorry, Will, but I'm meeting a friend."

I try to get past him but he's gripping my arm.

"I'm sure there are things you could teach me on the subject."

"The children, Will," I say, but he's not letting go.

"Over the weekend, Karen?"

"No, Will, I'm sorry," I say firmly.

He releases my arm and shrugs, straightening his tie.

"But I'd be happy to join a sexual education committee," I tell him, surprising myself and him, too, by the looks of it.

I push past him and make my way down the hall. I've held my own, but find I'm trembling. I may not have a job in the morning.

33

I'm not sure what to make of Henry Kaminski's paintings. The giant canvases are covered in slabs and swirls of thick red paint, which is daubed and slashed with black.

"This is Henry's *Red Series*," Alice tells me, her voice hushed as if it's something holy we're discussing.

"It's a very bright red," I say, for want of something clever. "What does it mean?"

"That's up to you, Karen," she says simply.

I'd received a letter on beautiful stationery inviting me to tea with Alice Kaminski, and making good on my promise, I'd accepted. Perhaps a glimpse into her home life would unlock the key to Lydie's behavior, particularly in light of recent classroom events.

But we haven't yet sat down to tea.

"You mentioned you also painted, Alice. I'd like to see *your* work, if I may."

"All right." My request seems to have startled her. She's looking at me in disbelief. "If you're sure you want to. But let's have tea first."

I follow her from the hallway into the dining room where there are fascinating objects to catch your eye everywhere you turn. On a table in the corner, wooden figures with breasts and male genitalia stand big with child. I'm riveted to the spot. Suddenly Lydie's confusion as to the nature of pregnancy makes perfect sense to me.

"Have you traveled widely, Alice?" I ask.

"Only through museums, I'm afraid. Henry collected these before we were married. He served in the North African campaign, barely survived, but that's another story. After the war he traveled down to Mali and the Western Sahara before coming home. He brought a trunk full of objects with him."

On the walls, carved masks from Henry's travels stare down with open mouths, snarls and fierce frowns. They look appalled by the indignity of hanging in this dining room. And then there are Henry's paintings—I can tell by the slabs and swirls—occupying every nook and cranny. Behind the paintings, I can't help noticing, the walls are stained and crumbling, the paint peeling.

But the table is set exquisitely. Tea with Alice is not a cup of tea, but a feast for the senses. There are tiny sandwiches and cream pastries, tangerines and sugared almonds and tea in pottery without handles. Alice explains the Japanese tea ceremony to me, and we laugh at my awkward attempts to grasp the small, hot object. She guides my hands around the bottom and the upper rim and shows me how to tilt my cup.

The tea is delicious, and it's going to my head like some kind of potion. I've arrived on the shore of an exotic new world, albeit from a dining room chair, and I'm enjoying it immensely.

"Lydie's not here?" I venture, taking a sip.

"Henry's taken her to her cousin's birthday party in the city. They'll be back tomorrow."

Somehow it makes me inordinately happy to hear that Lydie is doing something rather ordinary and possibly harmless, and I'm not unhappy to be alone with Alice. Now's a good moment to learn more about Lydie, I decide.

But before I can utter a word, she says, "You're exceptionally expressive. I wonder if I could ask you to sit for me."

I don't know what she's talking about, and I guess it shows. Alice is laughing.

"I'm a portrait painter," she explains. "I'd like you to sit for a portrait."

"My ignorance is astonishing when it comes to art," I say, and I feel myself blushing.

"How funny. I couldn't imagine life without it. Well, art is life, really."

"Not for me." It comes out before I can stop myself. I've offended her, no doubt, and am thinking how best to explain myself when I look up to find her smiling delightedly.

"And what is life for you, Karen?"

"Teaching," I answer without thinking. *Esther*, I add silently.

Alice is watching me attentively, studying me more like it. She's leaning this way and that to get a better view like a keen shopper at a market.

"I like history, too. Nature."

"Don't move! Stay exactly like you are!" she cries out, and she's bounding out of her chair and disappearing into the next room. I hear a drawer open and some rustling, and she's back in her chair in no time flat with a pencil and pad, and the next thing I know she's sketching me. It happens so quickly there's no time to protest.

It's an odd feeling being sketched, a bit like being at the dentist but without the pain, and it's making me self-conscious. I'll carry on as before, I decide, until further instruction.

"Life and art can be worlds apart, Alice." I feel a need to draw her out, to defend my own existence and ever so slightly to challenge hers.

"The cavemen were painting on walls tens of thousands of years ago," she answers, unperturbed. "What do you make of that?"

"Well, those were hieroglyphics."

"Some things can't be expressed in words," she says.

A lock of hair falls into my eyes, but I don't dare move. Alice sees and pushes it away. It's the rough gesture of a craftsman, solving a practical problem.

"You know what, Karen. I'm going to take you to the Art Institute."

"I'd like that very much, when the school year ends."

Something tells me it's best to keep a certain distance with Alice while Lydie's in my class, despite my pleasure in her company. Something's also telling me that if I know what's good for me, I'll keep my distance even after the school year's over despite the temptation of a schooling in art. Art is starting to feel a tad dangerous, though I can't put my finger on the reason why.

"So, we'll go in the summer," Alice decides. "If I'm still here by then."

"Why, Alice? What do you mean?"

"Oh, don't mind me."

Then out it comes, how she found Henry with a student in his studio a week ago, and was tempted to kill herself, but thought better of it because of Lydie. It's not easy living with an artistic genius. She drifts into silence. The only sound is the scratching of pencil on paper. To keep myself occupied I observe Alice sketching me. Her eyes fix on my face and on the paper by turns with great purpose; her tongue grips the side of her mouth. She is clearly in her element. I can't help noticing that her lovely neck is bare, and I can see her cleavage, which is ample, and my eyes stop there.

"Karen, can you lift your eyes, please," Alice asks amiably. "Look out the window if you don't mind."

I look out the window.

"Yes, yes, like that, just like that."

I look out the window across Franklin Street and up at the sky. I watch the clouds, I count the clouds, and then I imagine that I'm a bird flying above the town, looking down on Alice and me.

The sketch is startling. Alice has drawn a face with fierce,

194

probing eyes in a few fine strokes with a bird flying out of the top of its head, which is uncanny, to say the least.

"Is that me?"

She shrugs. "You don't recognize yourself? I think you may have been a bird in a past life. Perhaps a bird of prey."

I study my face on the paper, seeing myself through Alice's eyes.

"I have a feeling," and she is struggling for the right words, "you are observing us all from a great distance and arriving at your own unique conclusions. I believe you have an active imagination, Karen."

I'm not quite sure how Alice would know this. I've hardly revealed myself to her and she hasn't asked. It's true I imagine things, people mostly, like a photograph come to life or a moving picture, without a pen or brush or camera.

"Maybe you're an artist yourself without knowing it," she says.

I have to smile. Right now, I am willing to believe anything. I feel buoyed by intangible things, like art, beauty, her beauty.

She takes me upstairs to show me her work. She keeps her small portraits in a box in the cupboard in the bedroom and we sit on the edge of the bed to look at them.

"They're not very good," she warns me.

In her portraits, something is always exploding—out of the head, the eyes, ears, mouth. I don't have the artistic vocabulary to express their effect on me, to ask the right kind of questions so I say nothing. I study them, one by one. It's as if Alice has let a person's soul loose in drawing them. Her work is much better than Henry's if you ask me.

"I like them," I say, embarrassed at once by my inadequate response.

She shrugs. "They're just sketches." She's dismissing them with a wave of the hand. "I don't have the strength to finish anything."

I glance over at Alice, so full of vigor. She's brushing a tear away with her sleeve.

"No one's looked at my work in years."

"Well, they should," I tell her, forcefully.

She's wiping another tear. It would be my role to comfort her, offer her my shoulder. But her tears only serve to anger me. I want to tell her she should stand up for her work, that she's an artist herself, not a mere artist's wife. It's criminal to keep these portraits hidden in a box. They deserve to be seen. They deserve the light of day. Their souls may be haunting her, for all I know. I want to tell her that false modesty is the least attractive thing in a woman. It doesn't suit her. And while she's at it, she should stop making excuses for her inaction. She's much too strong in her own right. Anyone can see that. She's not helpless. She doesn't need pity. She's very capable. She could do anything she set her mind to. She should get out of the house more. But to tell her this I would need to face her and look her in the eye and make my case, and she's currently sitting so close to me I can feel her chest rising and the pounding of her heart against my arm.

"Karen," she says, and her sentence trails off. "Karen," she tries again, and there's a question in her voice. She's asking for something she has no words to describe. I realize too late that I've unleashed something inside her. She feels neglected by Henry. She feels needy. I hear a quick intake of breath against my ear as she clutches my hand in both of hers, brushing it gently across her lips. She uncrosses her legs and leans in toward me so that she's practically on top of me and I'm forced back on the bed.

The scene plays out in slow motion, and as it's happening I'm overcome by horror. She is Lydie's mother, and I'm her teacher. After such a lovely tea with Alice, the afternoon is ending in ruin, my ruin. But she's scared herself it seems. She jumps to her feet, and I do the same. At the door, she thanks me so much for coming with a light pat on the arm. Lydie has been all but forgotten. I've let her down again.

I practically run the length of Franklin Street, passing St. Mary's on the way. I'll stop in quickly, I decide. I take a seat in a pew at the back and catch my breath, asking myself how on earth I could have let things get so out of hand. But I have no answer. I'm not sure Freud would have one either.

It's calming in the church, near empty and silent. There's a kneeling woman, in mourning by the looks of it, praying for the soul of her beloved dead. She could be my mother, but there's something kindly in her face, and part of me is tempted to approach her and ask her to pray for me, too. A middle-aged man with a worried expression, his head bowed, sits alone on the pew across the asile. What sorrow or blunder brings him here, I wonder. Was it a sin of the flesh? I recite three Hail Marys and reflect on God's goodness. I thank Him for intervening, for saving me from disgrace and possibly worse.

34

A thick, late snow has surprised the town. It's the janitor's job to shovel the pathways free, but Cliff Johnson can't keep up, and we, the younger and fitter among the teachers, join in the shoveling. At recess, the children play King of the Hill on large snow piles. Needless to say, Lydie is king of her hill, or five-star general more like it. Janie stands shivering by her side while her deputy, Alan, receives his orders from a dugout below. But today the earth is a soft blanket and no one gets hurt. In the snowy air, nothing is distinct and the children in their colorful hats and scarfs tumble down the hill like color wheels, their bellows, laughs and screams muted in the softness. Snow angels carpet the playground. By the end of the school day the whole town is stilled by a blizzard and tomorrow has been declared a snow day. In the teachers' room, we're all agreed that Esther shouldn't drive on country roads, and I offer her my couch, which she gratefully accepts. The snowfall allows us a night together free of suspicion.

We walk home arm in arm, holding each other up, sinking in snow drifts. I eat fistfuls of fresh snow and Esther laughs so hard she's crying. I slip and fall, taking her down with me. The raging snow and winds release us from all constraints. We lie there, she on top of me, practically invisible. I want to stay here, frozen, cheek to cheek, forever, but Esther is pulling me up, and practically carrying me along in her arms. It feels miraculous to hold each other openly. We make it home and shovel a path from the street to the door. We recover from our hard labor by making love and devour our supper. We go back to bed, this time to read at leisure. Tomorrow is a snow day, and we've no lessons to prepare.

Esther is starting one of her beloved mysteries. I borrow them at the library and keep them in a little pile on the nightstand for when she spends the night. The books I choose are not always to her taste, but she reads them anyway. Her favorite author is Agatha Christie, and she loves Miss Marple best. The British countryside holds a special fascination for her.

"I find it soothing," she explains. "It's all so tranquil and harmless, until it isn't."

She reads voraciously and quickly, and I love to watch her face in total absorption with what can only be described as an innocent expression, not at all like the Esther I know.

I tell her our life would make a fine paperback novel. *The Secret Lives of Schoolteachers* would be the title. I might just write it one day, I warn her.

"We're a cheap romance. Is that what you want to say?"

"Our love story will be bought and sold on every corner, Esther."

"Well, I hope it's a mystery," she says.

"I haven't thought that far."

"Bear in mind, a good mystery needs a lively plot with a twist, two or three murders, and a surprise ending."

"Not ours. Our mystery goes on and on."

"A story has to end, darling."

"Well, happily ever after, then, till death do us part."

"So, it *is* a murder mystery!" she says, making us both laugh.

Esther sighs and picks up her book. She turns to the back and is studying the last pages.

"You can't have finished it already, Esther?"

"Uh-uh," she says, shaking her head. "I've just started."

"What are you doing then?"

"Reading, why?"

"Because you're at the back of the book."

"I'm reading the ending."

"You're reading the ending first?"

"I always start at the end. It's more interesting that way."

"But that spoils it. The surprise comes at the end. You said so yourself. What's the point of reading a mystery then? I don't get it."

"I read my way, you read yours."

"But that's not how to read a mystery."

"So, tell me, Karen," she says, closing her book, which means something. "How do you read a mystery?"

"Well, you start at the beginning."

"Who says?"

"Or else there's no mystery!"

"Mystery, Karen, is something else entirely," she says, as if she's stating the obvious. "May I get back to my book now, please?"

But I'm not finished. "You don't believe that. You can't. You wouldn't read mysteries if you thought like that." I should get off my high horse, but I can't stop myself. "There's got to be a reason."

"I don't know why I do it," she says finally. "Is that okay?" and she's looking at me with a wretched expression.

"Is something wrong, Esther?" The sudden blackness of her mood has startled me.

"I don't know. I don't know." She's fighting back tears. I've never seen her this upset. She's been angry, yes, and often, and pensive, even sad. But not helpless, which is how she now appears.

She lets her book fall to the floor and curls up on her side away from me. I hold her tightly until she falls asleep. Something wakes me in the middle of the night. Esther is restless by my side, and then I realize she is whimpering and mumbling in her sleep in what must be German.

"Marga," she cries out. I freeze where I am. I think I must be hearing things. "Marga," she cries again. She's convulsed by sobs and shivering. I shake her gently to wake her.

"Esther, Esther."

She opens her eyes, which are wet with tears. The room is lit by the moon and falling snow. It takes her some seconds to realize where she is.

"You were having a bad dream."

She sits up in the bed and holds her head in her hands.

"The snow," she says, looking out, as if she wants to change the subject.

"You called out a woman's name."

She looks quickly at me. Her lips close tightly.

"You called out *Marga*."

"Did I?" she says, dropping her head.

"Who is she?" I'm pressing her against her will, but I can't stop myself.

"Leave it, Karen."

"I want to know."

"Someone I knew once, that's all."

"Tell me about her."

"There's nothing to tell," she says, shrugging.

"Please."

Esther says nothing. I'm thinking that's the end of it, as it so often is, when she glances over at me.

"You remind me of her," she says, simply.

So she's the one, the woman from her past. I think back to Lee-Anne's words in the diner, tossed as lightly as a bomb from across the table.

"In what way?" I hear myself ask.

She studies me a while.

"In every way," she says quietly. "It's uncanny."

I sit up and wait. Every cell in my body is on high alert.

"It startled me when I first saw you."

I see her turn toward me in the teachers' room, taking me in for the very first time, that look of surprise. I feel her eyes on me continuously, her fascination, so that I often have to blush. Her eyes that watch me, even when we're making love.

"We look alike, you mean?"

"She had your black wavy hair. Your smile."

I try to smile, but find I can't.

"But her eyes were brown."

Well, that's something. I'll hold on to that.

"You couldn't put a thing past her. She was very observant, like you. And brave."

You've confused us, I want to say. *I'm not brave. I'm afraid of what you're telling me, afraid of words.*

"She made me laugh."

Esther is smiling at me in her loving, bemused way, but there's something else in her look, something I haven't seen before. Perhaps it's been there all along. I have the strangest feeling she's seeing Marga, not me. Or that I've become Marga. I check my hands and they're mine, all right, with their bitten nails, and I glance over into the mirror, and it's me, no question. But the feeling doesn't go away.

"People took her watchfulness for shyness, but she was anything but shy when she wanted something."

"She wanted you."

"Yes, we wanted each other."

And she still has you. The look in your eyes is longing for her. Is it any wonder I lose myself with you? I'm seized by panic, but Esther doesn't notice. Her hand reaches for the delicate Star of David on her neck, and she fingers it as she often does.

"She gave me this soon after we met. I promised her I'd never take it off. We swore we'd stay together no matter what."

And you have, I tell her silently.

"Then, as luck would have it," Esther goes on, and she's almost cheerful, "we were deported together and both of us survived the selection."

We stay where we are on the bed. There's nowhere else to

go. She doesn't say much more at first and what she says comes in the form of short staccato bursts, but then a floodgate opens, and she is telling me a story so strange and terrible that I can't take it in. I listen, but I want her to stop. I want the story to end.

"They marched us out of the camp. Snow covered every living thing. We ate snow as it fell from the sky. Anyone who couldn't keep up was shot. Half of us died on the road."

Esther looks at me from a distance neither she nor I can cross. She's numbered herself among the dead, but it must be a slip of the tongue. Outside, there are the first stirrings of morning.

"We lay down on the side of the road in a field to sleep." The faintest of smiles crosses her lips. "The cold and hunger disappeared. I felt myself leaving my body. Something, a force, was lifting and carrying me through a tunnel. It was very bright, and at the end of it I could make out my mother and father and my little sister, Leah, and brother, Sammy. They were seated for the Sabbath meal at a banquet table laden with the most delicious foods, my mouth was watering, and they were beckoning me."

She raises her hand and beckons, and I'm quite sure I will never forget that gesture as long as I live.

"And the next thing I knew, I was woken by barking dogs and the forced march continued toward the next camp."

"And Marga?" I ask her, hardly able to breathe.

"Marga was luckier than me. She didn't wake up."

She stops talking. She's done. She gets up, and as she does so the room disappears and all I see is snow. It's a blizzard. I can't see out or in, and Esther has vanished. But then I see her, clasped in a woman's arms in a field on the side of a road. I run to her, sink down next to her, kiss her cold face, her lashes that are covered in snow, beg her to wake up, but she won't move. I force myself to look at the woman in her arms, and it's my face I'm seeing, and I understand finally that Esther died in the war, on a road in Poland with Marga, and that I am Marga, and everything else has been a dream, someone else's dream.

When I come to, she's sitting on the chair by the window,

arranging her nightgown, her hair, as if she's finished a long, hard day at work and is waiting for a bus to take her home.

"You fell asleep," Esther says, smiling at me.

"Yes," I say and leave it at that.

She stays where she is, and time must be passing because the sun has risen and a new day is getting under way, a snow day. I kneel at the foot of her chair and start to pray, but stop. *Stay with Esther*, I tell myself. Anyway, I find I've nothing to say to God today. I've lost my faith. I lay my head in her lap.

The heavy late snow melts quickly with the sudden arrival of spring. The streets out near the Kish become one with the river, and mounds of slush transform into small lakes on every corner. For several days the sensation that I may be dreaming my current life stays with me, but the look in Esther's eyes has changed. Her gaze is direct, as if she's seeing me for the first time, unfiltered or through a new pair of glasses, as if I've caught her attention, and it's a little unnerving, I have to admit. I don't know if I can meet her expectations. But she's relaxed, and there's a lightness to her step. Perhaps the burden of carrying her terrible story has been eased in the telling. I won't let on that she's unwittingly passed it on to me. I find myself fighting off unspeakable images that appear unexpectedly when I'm thinking of something else entirely, preparing lessons for example, or getting dressed in the morning. I have to stop what I'm doing and close my eyes and wait for the image to pass. I understand her months of silence now. She wanted to spare me, to protect me, and I do everything I can to reassure her through my behavior that I'm perfectly fine and all is well. But she sees through it and does her best to comfort me. It is I who should be comforting her, and I'm embarrassed by this reversal.

She's taken to hugging me, something she's never done before and, even stranger, to asking me how I'm feeling.

"Not again, Esther," I tell her finally, pushing her gently away. "I've never felt better, honestly."

And generally speaking, it's true. We are inseparable. We have glorious days, delighting in simple pleasures, not only in each other's bodies, but in household chores. We attempt a soufflé and laugh at our failure. We read the local paper out loud to each other. Its crime and style reports, so harmless and out of date, amuse us no end. We listen to Esther's beloved classical music collection, to Bach's Concerto No. 5 in D major, in particular. *Musical science*, is what she calls it. We listen to the recording over and over until I'm humming it in my sleep. We dance around the house, blinds down, to the latest hits of Elvis. It turns out Esther is quite an Elvis fan. She knows all the words to his songs.

"Another thing I learned from the American GIs," she says, twisting up a storm.

"You sure know how to move those hips," I tell her.

She's even sleeping better.

35

"Our government's job is to write laws, children."

They're bored. They're studying their desks, shoes, fingernails, the points of their pencils. My lesson on the government is leaving them cold.

"Laws allow us to live together in peace and safety. Where would we be without them?"

No one's speaking up, but I won't be deterred.

"We'd be living in a lawless chaos, that's where." *A lawless chaos like this classroom*, I think to myself.

"What's chaos?" Karl shouts out.

"Chaos, Karl, is speaking out of turn. If we all called out at once, without raising our hands, we wouldn't hear anyone, would we, children?"

They're nodding, at least.

"Laws protect us from harm and stop us from harming others. No one has the right to take a life, for example, or a stop sign for that matter. If you steal a stop sign, someone might get in a very bad accident. That's why stealing a stop sign is *against the law*. It is a serious offense, a crime, in other words. If you break the law, you will be punished. This might be in the form of a fine, which can be quite a lot of money, or time spent locked behind bars in a prison."

"Can you go to prison for stealing a bike, Miss Murphy?" Matt, the bully, asks with a worried expression.

"Well, what do you think, Matt?"

He shrugs, looks down.

"Is stealing a bike against the law, children?"

They're all shrugging now and eyeing each other.

"Stealing a bike is *against the law*. You won't be sent to prison for it, but you will be expected to return the bike or pay for a new one to replace it. What does the law say about robbing a bank? What do you think?"

"It's against the law," the children shout.

"That's right. And you *will* go to prison for robbing a bank," I assure them.

Lydie raises her hand. The thing about Lydie is she raises her hand.

"Yes, Lydie?"

"If you burn down a school, is it against the law?"

"Well, class?" I ask.

"Against the law!" they shriek as one. The frenzy of the posse is in the air, the Wild West, the angry mob, but I don't care. It's going too well to stop.

"And there are more laws where those came from, hundreds, even thousands of them, enforced by police and judged by the courts. We'll be learning more about our justice system before the year is out. But let's name a few more laws while we're at it, now that you've got the hang of it."

"Littering is *against the law*," Nancy volunteers.

"Excellent!" I'm practically giddy. "The law says you must not throw garbage on the street. If you get caught, you will be *fined* quite a bit of money by the government. Until we had laws, people just tossed their garbage out the window. Imagine that. And where there is garbage there are rats. Rats caused the plague, a terrible disease also known as the Black Death. Half of

Europe's people died in the Black Death. They didn't understand that their garbage was behind it. They thought the world was coming to an end."

Their eyes grow big. They're sitting forward in their seats.

"Did the world come to an end, children?"

They don't seem to know. Some nod, others shrug.

"No, it did not. But it sure felt like it to them."

"Did the rats bite the people, Miss Murphy?" Karl calls out.

"No, Karl, and please raise your hand. Rats are actually quite gentle and fearful. The rats were bitten by fleas. And the fleas bit the people."

I'm feeling elated. The class is in my hands. I'm forming law-abiding, useful citizens. I'm doing my job. In this moment of triumph, Lydie jumps out of her chair, screaming bloody murder.

"What is it, Lydie?" I shout over the din.

"A flea," she cries out, "a flea just bit me."

The room erupts with hoots and giggles and expressions of disgust. She's scratching herself wildly, starting with her hair, disheveled as usual, which now stands on end like a banshee's. She's tugging at her clothes until she's ripped the buttons off her blouse. She's scratching her arms and legs, her knees, which are covered in cuts and scabs in any case.

"But it's true, look," she tells them, and you'd have to believe her. The children get up warily from their desks, unable to resist, willed on by Lydie, and gather around her to see the flea.

"I don't see any flea," someone says.

"Show it," another says.

"It's here, between my fingers," Lydie says, shuddering. "Look!" and she lets out another blood-curdling scream and flings the flea up into the air and now everyone is screaming, scattering to the four corners of the room.

"Back in your seats," I bark out like a drill sergeant, but the room belongs to Lydie. No one's listening to me, not Joanne, not Alan. They're all scratching and tearing at their hair, their arms and legs. I'm ready to tear my own hair out.

"QUIIIIEEEET," Lydie yells at the top of her lungs. The

children, who are strewn around the room, fall instantly silent. Lydie sits back down at her desk and waits. She looks at me and shrugs as if to say what's next. I take a deep breath to gather my defenses and in slow, steady motion make my way toward her like a tank rolling through a battlefield, pushing desks and chairs and children out of my way until I'm leaning over her desk, our faces almost touching.

"That's it, Lydie," I say, under my breath.

She looks up at me with a beatific expression. I've seen that look. It's the one she wore in the Christmas play. She's the angel Gabriel, messenger of God. And maybe she is. Maybe this is God's way of telling me I should give up teaching.

"Gather your things and go down to the principal's office."

The entire room lets out a gasp.

"You won't be coming back today."

The silence is deafening. The children slink back to their desks and slide down in their seats. I've never sent a child to the office before, never mind the school day's almost over. I return to the front of the room and write THE RULE OF LAW on the board in giant wobbly letters. My hands won't stop shaking.

"Our government was founded on the rule of law, but it has yet to fulfill its promise," I tell them, and my voice is shaky, too.

Lydie has whispered something urgently to Janie and is making her way to the door, her school bag dragging along the floor, but now she's stopped. All eyes are on her.

"The world is coming to an end," she tells the class, ignoring me. "The world is coming to an end," she wails, this time, like an itinerant preacher.

I'm ready to believe her.

I toss the chalk onto my desk and lean back against the board. I'm beyond fury now and I've come out the other side. I'm floating on a cirrus cloud above the room and looking down.

"Well, Lydie, it comes to an end for each of us." My voice sounds almost pleasant. "I'll grant you that. Everyone dies, but the world lives on. You can go down to the principal's office now."

She's out the door, slamming it shut.

"Why does everyone die, Miss Murphy?" It's Karl.

"To give other people a turn to live," I hear myself answering, "and please remember to raise your hand."

36

Dorothy is calling on St. Anthony to find Lydie. She finds
everything that goes missing with his help. Not only Will
Lindquist's reading glasses, children's hats, gloves and lunch
boxes, teachers' keys and purses, but living things as well. She
found a child locked in a cupboard by accident at the end of the
school day. She found a rabbit, a hamster, even a turtle who'd
managed through slow determination to escape the confines of
the school and head for the relative safety of Lincoln Highway.
No one knows how she does it, but if it's lost, Dorothy finds it.
She would dispute this. St. Anthony guides her every step, she
insists.

We discover Lydie's absence around supper time when
Henry Kaminski calls Dorothy because she hasn't come home
yet. I race back to school to help in the search of classroom
cupboards, the stairwells, and basement. Her disappearance
seems almost inevitable, the grand finale of a spellbinding
performance. There's very little I'd put past Lydie. I refuse to let
myself imagine the worst.

Henry Kaminski appears in the doorway to the office,

looking a little lost in his own right. I'm startled by him. Lydie is his spitting image, the same dark eyes and heavy brows, the sturdy frame, the reddish hair. Despite his daughter's claims to the contrary, there can be no doubt about his paternity. He's wearing a tweed jacket with a pipe protruding from its pocket and corduroy trousers. A navy beret is perched on his head. If I had to paint an artist, it would look like him.

Alice is at home waiting by the door for Lydie, he says. She's distraught and blaming herself. She's certain Lydie's run away.

It would be most convenient to lay the blame at her feet, but it wouldn't be fair. I'm the guilty party here. I'm thinking how best to confess to my crime when a policeman arrives and begins to question Henry. "Did your daughter say or do anything unusual this morning? Anything and everything out of the ordinary could mean something. Think back and take your time."

Henry sits blankly and shakes his head. Too busy painting, I can't help thinking. But I know only too well how Lydie's day unfolded. I'm the one who sent her to the office. It was I who humiliated her in front of the class.

"I'm to blame," I blurt out. All heads turn in my direction.

"I sent her to the office without accompaniment. I was going to ask Joanne or Alan to go with her, but the situation had gotten a little out of hand."

Out of the corner of my eye, I can't help noticing Will's brow furrowing. He's straightening his tie and clearing his throat. He seems about to speak.

"That's plain silly, hon. You're not to blame," Dorothy says, stepping in and stopping Will. "I told you specifically to send her down anytime. Sending children to the office is par for the course. Let's stay focused on the one goal that matters, bringing Lydie home."

That's Dorothy for you, smoothing what's rough.

"If anyone knows anything, it's Alan," I tell them.

"I'll phone his parents and ask to speak to him," Dorothy says. "They live right across the street."

Alan's parents send him back to the school to talk to me. I meet him on the stairs.

"I think Lydie's dead," Alan says, burying his face in his hands.

The world shudders to a halt.

"Why, Allen, why do you think that?"

He shrugs, whimpers, and tries to back away. I grab hold of him and I'm shaking him, too hard I know, but I can't stop myself.

"Why, why? Why do you think Lydie's dead? Why? Answer me. Tell me. Why, why?" I'm not in control, and I am shouting.

"I don't know," he wails, twisting to get away from me.

"There must be a reason."

"Because everyone dies, you said," he cries out finally as if his heart is breaking. Everyone dies, of course. That's what I told them in class today. They take it all in, take it to heart. The children are listening to what we say. The enormity hits me for the very first time.

"That's it? That's why you think so?" I say, laughing at the same time in pure relief.

He nods, and I hug him tightly to me.

"Oh. I'm sorry, Alan. Oh, God. That's it?"

He's nodding, but he doesn't think it's funny. I let him go. He eyes me strangely and straightens his clothes. My behavior has confused and upset him, and without another word he runs back home. I'm left there on the school steps, helpless. I know better. I know the golden rule. You keep your hands to yourself, as well as your emotions. They're children and we're adults.

A search party is formed to look for Lydie. I'm walking down side streets and alleyways, glimpsing into windows lit up by TVs. There's not a soul on the streets. I'm after Lydie, I tell myself, but the longer I walk, the less I look. As night deepens, I'm searching for the meaning of my existence. I've failed miserably in the classroom and a child has gone missing as a result. I'm no

213

guardian, that much is certain. My pedagogical objectives have been laid to waste. Not a single lesson has gone according to plan. If the children evolve into good and useful citizens, it will be in spite of my actions. Irene was right: nothing is accomplished without authority. I missed the boat on inspiring respect. I've let both her and Esther down. I'm an embarrassment to the profession, plain and simple. I'm left wondering what on earth I might do instead. I'm a sloppy typist. I'm terrible with figures. I couldn't sell a dress to save my life. It's too late to change course. I'm a schoolteacher. And because there's nothing else, hadn't I better go about the task in a completely new way? But not tonight, or even tomorrow, not while Lydie's missing.

Before long I'm talking out loud to myself, a forlorn figure in the drizzle and fog. All I ask is that Lydie be found. The days would be empty without her. I rely on her presence more than I can say. She keeps me on my toes, all right. By the time I've circled the radius of the school a dozen times or more, I realize it's a kind of passion I feel for the awful little girl, a passion that might even be construed as love. Or put another way, I know Lydie like I know myself. Which is to say, not at all. But it's a kind of recognition, nonetheless. Aren't we both lost, in the end? I stop where I am. The rain's coming down in sheets now and I'm quickly soaked to the bone. But I don't care and it's just as well. If someone were to happen along, they wouldn't see the tears streaming down my face, tears of despair and shame.

The phone rings near dawn, jolting me out of heavy sleep. It's Dorothy. She sounds cheerful. Lydie's back at home, unharmed.

"Where was she?" My heart is thumping wildly.

"With Janie."

"You're kidding."

"Kid you not, honey. She was hiding out in Janie's room. Janie's mother had no idea she was there."

"How'd you find out?"

"Alan confessed to his mother and she called the police. He

214

was in on Lydie's plan."

"Wait a minute," I say, and I'm forced to sit down. "Alan told me he thought Lydie was dead and scared me half to death."

"Sounds like something Lydie would cook up, doesn't it? It's like *The Lady Vanishes* or something."

Intrigue, accomplices, a *rendezvous*. If you ask me, it's more like a soap opera. Still, Alan's performance is worthy of an Oscar. If I've learned one lesson, it's never to underestimate the passion of children. I feel my body relax, though my head is spinning. I take a deep breath, but no breath comes, and I end up coughing.

"All's well that ends well," Dorothy says.

"I guess," I say with a sniffle.

"You sound like you might be coming down with something. You better take the day off," Dorothy says. "I'll call a sub in."

Reluctantly I agree, and the instant I do a strange exhaustion overtakes me, and my head begins to throb and my throat burns and I start sneezing violently.

"*Gesundheit!*" Dorothy exclaims. "Go back to sleep now and get yourself better, honey. Lydie's been found. And when you get up, give a little shout-out to St. Anthony."

37

Joan Smith drops by the house to discuss a few "delicate issues," as she calls them, which she feels might benefit from her psychological expertise. She's brought a bottle of red wine, which surprises me. She apparently feels there's much to discuss. She's sitting upright and forward on the couch, notes perched on her thighs.

"Lydie should be getting help," is how she begins.

Not from the likes of you, I tell her silently.

"There are some good child psychologists in the suburbs."

I know why she's here. Word has gotten out about Lydie's disappearance. The whole school knows, thanks to Marilyn, no doubt. It's not something I'm prepared to discuss with Joan of all people. Even Esther, who's been reassuring and most sympathetic, doesn't know the half of it. I'm too embarrassed by my insufficiencies. I fetch two glasses and open the wine. Something tells me I'm going to need it.

"I put her schoolyard antics down to childhood experimentation, but now I'm convinced there's something else behind it." Joan searches my face for confirmation.

"Lydie's willful," I say with a shrug.

Joan lets out a dark laugh. I pour us both a very full glass.

"She and Janie have to be split up."

"Not a chance. Janie is her best and only friend, apart from Alan."

Joan rolls her eyes. "Exactly," she says.

"I'm afraid I don't know what you're getting at, Joan." I stare her down as if I haven't a clue, but I know where she's heading.

"She clearly needs the influence of other girls in the class. Anyone can see that. You could encourage them to include her more, invite her over for example, for sleepovers, things girls do."

She thinks for a moment. "Or maybe that's not such a good idea."

"I think it's a very good idea. But I can't force them."

"The fact is she's developing in an unhealthy direction, Karen, and it would be your job as her teacher to help her adjust."

"Adjust in what way, Joan?" I'm drawing her out against my better judgment.

"Adjust to societal expectations. Come on, you know what I mean. So she doesn't end up an outcast. So she can lead a normal life."

"Normal, Joan?" I hear myself asking. "What on earth is that?" I feel a need to provoke her, come what may.

"So she can eventually find happiness in the way people do, get married and have a family, for example."

"If she so chooses."

"Of course," she says, with little conviction.

It's my turn to sit up and I do. "There's more to happiness, Joan. I happen to know some very unhappy wives and mothers, starting with my own."

"I'm sorry to hear that," she says, and I'm regretting I mentioned it. The last thing I need is to open up to this woman. "You must have suffered," she adds, with a look of pity.

"It's all right, Joan, really. I'm only pointing out that happiness is something else entirely."

"I know that," she says, finishing off her glass. "I'm not an

217

idiot. But we both know there's something wrong with the girl. You've said so yourself on more than one occasion. You don't know what to do with her. You send her to the office out of sheer desperation, and the next thing you know she's disappeared. Police are roaming up and down the halls. And suddenly you're making light of it, Karen; I don't get it."

"Are you suggesting I don't care enough about the well-being of my children, Joan?" My fierce indignation surprises even me. "Because if that's the case, you're seriously mistaken."

The wine is really going to my head. I've never challenged Joan before tonight.

"I'm sorry," she says, quickly, backing down. "I didn't mean to imply such a thing. I just thought I could be helpful. I've studied the subject, and I'm pretty sure Lydie's behavioral problems stem from the distortion of natural emotions. She's confused and doesn't know what to do with her feelings."

"Her feelings are natural to her. Why make her self-conscious?"

"That's irresponsible, Karen. I mean, would you say that if she were a criminal?"

"That's ridiculous, Joan."

"Is it? She's aggressive and secretive; you know that. She can't be feeling good about herself. She knows there's something wrong with her. It could be the start of a lifelong battle with mental illness. If she had cancer, you'd want her to be treated, wouldn't you?"

"Yes, of course. What am I saying? There's no cure for feelings."

"I believe there is, Karen. And the entire psychiatric profession agrees with me. We owe it to her to give it a try."

I decide to give in. There's no convincing Joan and I'm tired of arguing, besides which we are getting dangerously close to a topic I must avoid at all costs—the secret of my own nature.

"All right," I say, crossing my arms with a sigh. "What's your advice?"

Sensing victory, Joan smiles agreeably and her voice takes on a conciliatory tone.

"You've had Mrs. Kaminski in, I believe. Call her in again and give her this list." Joan shuffles through her notes and drops a neatly written list on the coffee table. "These are all child psychologists who come highly recommended."

She can keep her list. In any case, I won't touch Alice with a ten-foot pole. I've been making detours around the Kaminskis' house on my way downtown and intend to continue doing so.

"Anything else, Joan?" I ask, glancing demonstrably at my watch, hoping to draw the meeting to a close.

"Try engaging her in feminine activities. My girls love beading and potholder weaving."

"Lydie loves potholder weaving."

So does Alan, as it happens. But I don't tell her that; she'd have a field day. What feels like an eternity has passed. Joan is on her third glass, and I'm not far behind. She drains hers, and I'm thinking that's a good sign, and she'll get up and head for the door, when she leans back heavily against the couch.

"Karen," she says, and she's looking desperately my way. "I'm going to tell you something I've never told anybody."

I shift in my seat. I have the distinct feeling the evening has been leading up to this moment. The real reason for her visit is not Lydie, but something else entirely.

"From the day we met, remember, in the lunchroom? I said to myself, thank God I've got someone I can talk to now. I've found a friend."

"Was it the lunchroom, Joan?" is all I can muster.

I can see no earthly way to stop her now. She's kicked off her shoes and tucked her feet underneath her and all her inhibitions are flying out the window.

"Karen, I've been married for ten years. Ten years! Dave and I have two beautiful children. They're just beautiful."

"I'm sure they are, Joan."

"Dave is my best friend."

She raises crossed fingers with some difficulty. "We're like this. Like this, you understand? But he doesn't know what I'm about to tell you."

"Are you sure, Joan?"

She stops me. "No one living knows."

Oh, no, I'm thinking. *Oh, God.*

"My parents are both dead."

"I'm so sorry."

"*They* knew."

"Some things are better laid to rest," I say, but I'm clutching at straws.

We sit in silence. Mine is appalled. I am not sure what her silence means until I look up and see her face emptied of all expression. Her arms have fallen to her sides. She looks for all the world like Patsy, my childhood rag doll.

"I'm not sure I can even tell you," she says weakly.

I see my chance. "Maybe we should wait, Joan, for another day. We've had a lot to drink. It's getting late."

I struggle to get up from my chair, which is no easy feat. I'm officially drunk.

"But I have to tell someone," Joan cries out. She reaches over and grabs me by the shoulders, and for all intents and purposes Joan Smith is pinning me to my living room armchair. But I'm not having it. I stand my ground and get to my feet. She looks up at me with those big round button eyes of hers.

"You're the only one who'll understand."

No, I won't, I want to say. *I'll never understand you, Joan. I don't want to. We live in two very different worlds. Let's call it a day,* I want to say, before one or both us says something we regret.

"I gave up my baby, Karen," she practically screams. "My firstborn child. I let them take her away from me. It's her birthday today. She's eleven. She's in fifth grade! She could be in my class! Or yours!"

She stops and gasps for air. The secret's out.

"It could be Lydie, for all I know!" She lets out a loud and very dark laugh.

"No," I say, "that's not possible."

"How would you know? You think they'd tell you if she were adopted?"

I don't have an answer, but her state of mind has so alarmed me I move to the couch and sit down beside her.

"You live a lie and then one day it gets to you," she says, and she's covered her mouth with her hands.

"If it helps, I'm here to listen," I say.

She nods, sits up, catches her breath.

"Don was my high school sweetheart, Karen. I was only sixteen, but I didn't care. I loved him. I loved Don so much. I was in my third month by the time I found out. I'd have left school and married him immediately. I mean, we were planning to marry, anyway. My father went into a rage. He was a minister, Karen, *a Man of God*. I'd humiliate him before the entire congregation if word got out. Within days they'd pulled me out of school on the pretext of being ill and shipped me off to a maternity home. And the worst of it was ..." She stops.

A tiny moan escapes her throat.

"Go on," I say, gently.

"My father forced me to call Don and break up with him. I wasn't allowed to give him a reason. My father stood over me while I made the call."

I take her shaking hands and hold them tightly. It does feel like she's telling this story for the first time. For all Joan's faith in psychology, it appears she's never sought help for herself.

"Don was stunned and so hurt. I gave birth alone, Karen. Even my mother stayed away. The social workers, if you can call them that, advised me not to see the baby. They put the adoption papers in my hands to sign."

"No one asked you what you wanted to do, Joan?"

"No. They'd convinced me I was unfit to be a mother by then anyway. I'd have probably said yes if they'd bothered to ask."

Her eyes grow frightened, and I feel her shuddering.

"The home was terrible, Karen. They treated us like prisoners. Being pregnant was a sin. We were promiscuous and immoral. They shamed us every day. There was a girl there no older than

Lydie, who'd been raped, Karen, by her father."

If walls could talk. My small living room bears more secrets than it can hold. I need to open a window, let them out. My head's begun to pound and my mouth is dry. I need water desperately. But I don't dare leave Joan alone.

"Once I'd signed the papers, everyone was so friendly suddenly, telling me how I'd done the right thing for my baby, how they'd already found loving and deserving parents for *her*. That's how I knew it was a baby girl."

She's in anguish. "They had no right to take your baby," I tell her forcefully.

But she's not listening. She's pulled away, clenching her fists.

"They say things like that don't happen in 'good' families, Karen. Well, I'm here to tell you they do. I don't blame the childless couple. They were lied to. They were told the baby was unwanted. They never learned the truth. Well, my father succeeded. He'd kept it quiet. That's all he cared about. I hated him after that, and I always will. I was happy when he died."

"And Dave?"

"What about Dave? I couldn't tell him. I was afraid he wouldn't marry me if he knew. What would he have thought of me? And once we were married, well, he'd want to know why I hadn't told him before. I live in fear it'll all come out. I'll shout something out in my sleep or let it slip after a glass too many. You live in hiding," she says and stops.

"Maybe it's time to tell him the truth."

She looks at me, startled, and begins to laugh and cry at the same time. I'm not sure what's come over her, but she's seeking my arms and I hold her tightly. Soon my blouse is soaked with her tears. I'm not sure how to comfort her.

"I live in hiding, too, Joan," I hear myself saying.

"You do?" She sits up, wiping her nose on her sleeve, those large, wet eyes on mine. She takes my hands in hers. "You gave up a baby, too?"

"No," I say, shaking my head, "not that. But I know what it is to live a lie."

I tell her about my engagement to Larry, about my love affair with Adele. I'm telling someone for the very first time. The words feel strange on my lips, but they keep coming. I tell her about Esther, and in the very moment I'm telling her, I know I've done a terrible, stupid, and irredeemably wrong thing, but I've gone too far to stop. I feel Joan's body tense.

"I'm not sure it's quite the same," she says, releasing my hands, "as giving up a child."

"No," I manage to say, "not quite."

"But I see how you might think so." She looks at her watch and then to the door. She gets up, straightening her clothing, her hair.

"Anyway, it's late. I think I better get going."

At the door she stops, and her tight little smile is back.

"Thanks for listening," she says.

38

"Karen, I hate to be the bearer of bad news," Will says, closing the door to the principal's office behind him, "but I'd rather tell you myself than have you find out some other way. Please take a seat."

"It must be bad," I say to lighten the gravity. I don't want his news, but I do sit down, wondering what in the world Lydie's gotten up to now and how bad it can be.

"Esther Jonas will not be returning to the school after Easter vacation, Karen," he says, and he stops to gauge my reaction.

I'm entering a bad dream. I clear my throat and wait.

"The fact is there've been rumors circulating, well, going back for a number of years, regarding certain *proclivities*, for want of a better expression. We've been presented with some pretty damning evidence of late."

I remain perfectly still, betraying nothing. He could be sharing a report on next week's schedule or a room change.

"We've found a temporary replacement who'll be ready to take over after Easter. We can see no reason to prolong things any further."

"The children," I manage to say.

Will sighs, shakes his head. "Her teaching record is exemplary as is her dedication to this school, her many years of service. She's been teaching here since leaving training college. But, in fact the children are our overriding concern, as well as the school's reputation. It pains me to have to tell you this," he says, putting on a very pained expression.

I don't move. I don't say a word.

"I suspect this won't come as a complete surprise. I'm aware that you're friends as well as colleagues. What you may know about her private life is not for me to decide."

He looks at me, and I meet his eyes.

"Who . . ." I say, but can't finish the sentence.

"That's confidential, I'm afraid."

And it's over. He has nothing to add. I nod, get up, and make for the door.

"I'm sorry," he says quietly, glancing up at me.

My body moves out of the room, I don't know how. I'm not in charge. I'm carried down the hall to Esther's room, but she's not there. Dorothy is minding the children. I go through the motions of teaching my class. I give them free time, let them play and talk among themselves, take them out for an early recess. In the afternoon, I give them free time, let them play, take them out for a late recess, unable to imagine words, thoughts, lessons to be learned. The children sense something is wrong. Their little minds are busy piecing together the odd progression of their very free day. They're well-behaved, even the troublemakers, as if they understand I'm absent and unreachable no matter what they do. At the end of the day I wish them a happy weekend, and they file out almost silently. We'd been discovered, that was clear. Will has issued me a warning, an ultimatum. Why Esther and not me? Is it because I'm the new girl? Does he think I don't know what I'm doing, what I want? Why didn't I speak up? Defend her with my life? Dignity is everything, and I've shown none. And worse, I've let fear come to define me.

● ● ●

I've been sitting on the couch in my coat since getting home, motionless, waiting for some word from Esther.

She lets herself in, slides down next to me, so that we're both splayed on the couch, unable to move.

She's been promised a clean record if she resigns effective the end of the month and without complications. Discretion has been advised on her part, and she's been assured that no one on staff will be informed.

"Why did Will tell me then? He knows about us from someone at the school."

"It's possible."

"No, Esther, I'm certain. I know who betrayed us."

"What does it matter? It doesn't matter *who*, Karen. At least you've been spared. It's done." Esther sighs, and there's something like relief in her voice or at least resignation.

"It matters to me."

"It's never who you think it is."

"That's in your mysteries, Esther, not in real life."

I tell her about my drunken night with Joan. I've kept it to myself until now, too afraid of her reaction. It spills out of me in the form of distraught and bitter confession.

"That was foolhardy of you. But she shared her dark secret with you, remember. You've got something on her. Like I said, it doesn't bear thinking about. It's happened. It's over."

She may be right about Joan, but I won't be pacified. I'll get to the bottom of this if it's the last thing I do.

"Anyway, I need to get home and take care of a few things. I'll call you later." Esther looks at me with eyes devoid of feeling, almost blank. I reach for her hands but they flutter away like moth's wings. She pulls herself up from the couch, pats me lightly on the arm, and leaves.

I'm in my bed when she finally calls. She tells me she'd like some time alone, if that's all right; she's not feeling well, a headache. I call her in the morning, but she says she's sorry she can't talk right now and asks me please to understand. It has nothing to do with me, she assures me. As soon as she feels better, she'll come by, she promises. She needs to take a few days off from school next week.

I don't hear from her for the rest of the weekend. It occurs to me that life consists of vacant stretches of morning, afternoon, and evening that we struggle to fill. There's no real meaning or purpose to it. *The best thing of all is not to be born.*

I call Esther first thing Monday morning, but she's not picking up the phone. I find I can't get dressed for school and call in sick.

"If you need a doctor, honey, I've got a good one," Dorothy says.

By day's end, I'm going out of my mind with need for her and despair and also panic, because I'm certain she's hurt herself. It's only then that I think to call Bettie and Liz. Liz tells me I just missed her, Esther's been staying with them, but she's been gone about an hour. They'll let her know I called and make sure she gets in touch. I shouldn't worry, she's fine, Liz says to reassure me. I hang up the phone. I'm in a state of shock. She's abandoned me. I'll kill myself, why not? I step out into my backyard desperate for air, and there's Cliff Johnson repairing his lawn mower by the looks of it, getting ready for the spring. He waves and turns the motor off, calls out to ask me if anything needs fixing. *Everything's broken, Cliff,* I answer under my breath, *and nothing can fix it.* But I shrug and nod, and he's quickly crossing the alley, wiping his hands on his pants. Without further ado, he's following me into the house.

He's busy solving the riddle of a window that refuses to open and promises to look at my tepid shower next.

"Maybe I should just move in, Miss Karen. Save gas." He cocks his head and winks at me.

"Don't get any ideas," I hear myself saying. I'm feeling lightheaded, emptied of thought.

"Marry me," he sings, in answer, like a crooner.

Maybe I should. I'll do just that. I offer him coffee, which he cheerfully accepts. Over coffee he tells me how he's finally settling down, back in his hometown, enjoying the routine of being a school janitor. But he's been many things, a soldier, a horse whisperer, a lumberjack, and that's just for starters.

"The only thing I haven't done is give birth, Miss Karen. I would if I could."

He's had at least nine lives, it seems. He was shot up in Korea, left for dead breaking up a knife fight in Texas. I go in and out of concentration, but his voice is soothing. He shows me the scar on his chest and it occurs to me that I could reach over and touch it. He's too big for my kitchen chair, and I find myself laughing at how he's sitting there, hunched over his knees, his blue eyes wide open. His wife, Lizzie, skipped town with his best friend two years ago. It just so happens he has a photo of her and of his daughter, his pride and joy though he rarely sees her, in his wallet.

"They're both lovely," I say, pretending to study the snapshots in his large, rough hands.

"Why, thank you, Miss Karen. You're lovely, too."

I don't feel lovely. I feel desperate. I stand up. He does the same.

"Thanks for helping out, Cliff," I tell him, and I let out a sob.

"Are you all right, Miss Karen?" His voice is gentle, warm with concern, after all the playfulness.

I nod, putting on a brave face.

"I'm at your service, any time. You know my number."

He goes to shake my hand, but I pull him toward me and struggle to open his belt buckle until he takes over, grinning, hard put to believe his luck. I'm beyond reckless. Nothing matters. I could fly off a building just as easily.

The next thing I know his hard hot tongue is down my throat as he lowers me onto the kitchen floor, and we're having clumsy sex, my dress hitched up, his janitor's pants around his knees. From above us, I watch Cliff pounding his way into me and sucking my breasts. My hands are grasping his thick neck, fingers entangled in his curly blond hair. And then my hands let go and I drown. He's doing up his belt when Esther's car pulls up. I send him out the back door and wait by the window. It doesn't matter to me that she's shown up. If she'd caught me with Cliff, I wouldn't have cared. I'm officially dead inside. But then she steps out of the car, and it's all I can do to stop myself from running out to meet her. My fury and despair come roaring back, and I'm alive again.

"There's a position opening up at Bettie's school in the fall," she tells me.

We're sitting at the kitchen table where we first came together, but now we're torn apart. She looks exhausted, but I'm not in the mood for pity.

"Fourth grade, believe it or not."

"What a coincidence," is all I say.

"It looks like I have a good chance at getting the job. I drove out to see them this weekend as you know."

"I couldn't reach you. You didn't call."

"I'm sorry, Karen. It was the only thing I could think of doing. I just got in the car and went. *My back is up against the wall*, as you Americans say. Liz and Bettie are my best friends. We've been looking out for each other for what feels like forever. Lee-Anne will be helpful, too. She's going to make sure the news doesn't travel. I'm lucky, really. So many never work again. Think of poor Albert Sims. He had no friends in high places. He didn't stand a chance. But that won't happen to me, this time at least. We're never completely safe."

I find I'm too upset to speak. She hasn't mentioned my feelings once.

"There's nothing you can do, you know that, don't you? You're endangered yourself," she says, eyeing me.

"And us?" I ask.

Esther looks surprised by the question.

"What about us?" She gets up and stands at the window to

the backyard, looking out. For a moment I imagine Cliff out there, doing his boots up.

I join her at the window, lean heavily into her, kiss the back of her neck. My actions are helpless, clumsy. She flinches, but I won't let go. I feel her body's longing, but she breaks free from my grasp.

"You'll meet someone in the city. Maybe you already have." I'm frantic and nauseated at once.

"I've just lost my livelihood, Karen," she says sharply, stepping back the better to take me in. She's shaking her head, unable to believe what she's hearing. "Forgive me if I've got other things on my mind."

But she follows me slowly up the stairs to my bed. We travel someplace very frightening. I feel my body tearing open. She needs to punish me, to make me feel pain. I need to make her suffer, too. We are no longer making love, but fighting for our survival. A fly on the wall might be forgiven for thinking two prim small-town schoolteachers are trying to kill each other. Then it's over and our anger towards each other subsides. We're panting, bloodied, and furious at the world.

"All my life," she says, "someone or other has been intent on breaking me."

"They can't do this to us," I cry out to an indifferent universe.

We're emptied and spent. There's nothing left to do but fall back on the bed. We hold each other and drift off. I wake in bright sunshine with a plan. Esther is already up, to my surprise, and making coffee. I take the steps down two at a time, brimming with intention.

"I'm going to learn to drive this summer."

"Well, that's good. It's the first step on the road to independence as I've told you many times."

"Meanwhile, I'll let it be known that I've met a man who works in the city and start looking for a job immediately."

Esther turns to me, hands on her hips.

"You can't leave now. You're at the start of your teaching career. You have to learn your craft. And you're happy here."

"I'm happy with you," I say.

"With your children too, Karen."

"I can't stay here after what they've done to you." I'm shaking my head, wringing my hands. "The whole town has betrayed us." The prospect of life in town without Esther is unimaginable, and I refuse to give it a second thought.

"What happened to me happens everywhere," she says and she's practically shouting. "It happens in cities, too. There's no safe haven. You're respected in the school, Karen. That counts for something. It may not feel like that right now, but all the teachers have nothing but praise for you. This place suits you."

"No," I say, and suddenly all the energy has drained out of me. "I never liked it here. It's only you who've made it bearable."

Esther looks at me and sighs. "I won't be going far."

But we both know that's not true.

She's moving toward the door. If she walks out now my life is over.

"You can't leave me," I scream out.

"I have to go," she says, reaching for her jacket.

I grab her arm. "Stay with me. We'll leave together the day school's over."

But even as I say it I know how desperate I sound and that it's futile.

"What am I supposed to do here? Pack your lunch for school every day? Wave to my children as they walk by? No. As soon as I can catch my breath, I'll start packing my things."

She's going home. I follow her to the door and we stop there. I fall to my knees and swear to her that I am hers and will love her and her alone whatever happens and forever. She looks at me and has to laugh.

"Get up, Karen," she says, lifting me into her arms. "We'll be okay, darling. We'll simply carry on."

She opens the door and steps out into the sun. "One day all this will change."

"Too late for us," I say.

"That's how progress works. You can't take it personally."

231

I watch her walk the path to her car. She's hunched over, head down, clutching the collar of her jacket, body leaning to one side as if she's battered by the wind, but it's a windless day. The air is mild, harmless. A perfect day, in fact. She looks so small and frail, and it hits me for the first time that Esther has been broken by what has happened, her very existence called into question. She straightens herself with a deep breath, summoning her dignity, and seeing me watching at the door, she waves to me.

We carry on, like Esther says. She travels back and forth between town and the city. She slowly packs her things. She goes for an interview and gets the job at Bettie's school. I try to be happy for her and insist that we celebrate. We spend the night in a fancy hotel in the city. The room is elegant, just as I imagined a hotel room should be, with high ceilings and a chandelier, velvet curtains hanging from tall windows. The bed is soft, the sheets pure silk under our bodies. But the stress of keeping up good cheer has exhausted me and I can only think of sleep. Esther holds me tightly to her. She wants me, but I pull away.

"Why?" she moans. "Please."

"I can't," I tell her, and she holds me differently, almost like a child, and I fall asleep in her arms.

I discover that being held in her arms now transcends physical desire. She is my place of solace, my refuge. And something else, as she prepares to leave for her new life—Esther is more and more herself with me. I am a confessor, of sorts, for her doubts and misgivings. She's losing her will, she tells me. She doesn't want to start again. She's overwhelmed. The thought of a new school fills her with anxiety. It's all too fast. She hasn't had a chance to think it through, let alone to catch her breath, she's too impetuous. Don't I know it, I want to say, but I just listen and hold her close. Knowing her is another kind of mystery, I realize, different from the unknown.

On the train home from Chicago I take her hand, I don't stop myself. It doesn't matter who sees or what they think. Esther looks at me, surprised, but she doesn't pull her hand away. Above the screeching and chugging of the west-bound train I tell her very loudly that I love her. I don't care who hears. Esther hears and grips my hand very tightly, and in that moment I'm convinced that nothing can separate us, come what may. I look out the window at plowed fields shimmering in morning light, take in the scent of fresh manure wafting in on the spring breeze, and close my eyes. I won't let the stares of strangers enter my world. I hold her hand in my lap for as long as the train ride lasts, which is just over an hour.

39

Esther has officially departed from the school and officially left town. She's staying with Bettie and Liz in Evanston until she finds a place of her own. The farmhouse she shared with Lee-Anne for so many years is practically empty, and Lee-Anne, ensconced in her new job in Chicago, has volunteered to hold on to Esther's things.

We're packing her last possessions because the farmhouse has been rented. We work methodically, side by side in silence. Neither of us has anything to say as we wrap fine china, the silverware kept for special occasions, the remaining stockings, into boxes.

I've brought a lunch for us, and we sit on the floor with our backs to the wall and eat. Esther eats hungrily as if she is storing energy for a long winter, but it's spring outside the kitchen door with all spring's delicate glory. The blossoming apples and plums surrounding the farmhouse would take your breath away in happier times. I try to make light of things, like we're having a picnic, though I'm feeling sick to my stomach. The truth is I've been feeling ill without letup since her dismissal, though I keep it to myself.

Lee-Anne arrives in a pickup truck to transport the boxes, and we haul them onto the back. She seems friendly enough as if all's been forgotten between us. I suggest we go out for dinner, but Lee-Anne says she'd prefer to get back right away if it's okay with Esther. She's got an early appointment tomorrow. They drop me off at home, and I watch them drive away.

Without Esther, my old house is an echo chamber, jarring sounds bouncing off walls. The bed and kitchen perform their practical duties devoid of any passion but anger. I find that Esther has possessed me. She follows me everywhere or, put another way, she has replaced me. It's her voice I hear in my head almost constantly, and it's her feet that walk me through the small-town streets. Her strong arms carry my shopping, her hand grips the banister as I drag myself to bed. Our telephone calls preserve my sanity temporarily. I listen dutifully as she describes the tour of her new school and the concerts she's attending. She asks me how I'm holding up, about my lessons, interested in every detail. But it's like pulling teeth. I have nothing to tell her and only one question to ask, and it's a selfish one, I know.

"When can I see you?"

"Soon," she tells me, but it's never soon enough.

I don't tell her that it's only when she's in my arms that she's real and not a phantom.

Poor Louise is at sea without her mentor and feeling betrayed.

"I don't know what I'm going to do without Esther. She could have told us she was leaving. What do you think, Karen?"

I tell her the news came as a shock to me as well, but we shouldn't be angry.

"I'm sure there are reasons we don't understand for her departure."

"But so suddenly? No, she must have decided this some time ago, but didn't let on. She could have prepared us. I thought she was my friend. And *you*, Karen," she says with innocent outrage. "How could she do this to you? You're even closer. It's so cruel, so unlike her. Or at least the Esther I thought I knew."

The others tiptoe around Esther's sudden departure "for personal and professional reasons" and carry on with little outward fuss, and shamefully I do the same. I am not free like Louise to show my despair and fury. I'm next in line for the chopping block.

But I won't give up on discovering who betrayed us. I swoop in like a hawk when her name comes up, study the reactions on faces, dissect sentences for clues, determined to uncover evidence of criminal intent. But my efforts come up short. Everyone averts their eyes at the mention of her name. They take a step back. There's hesitation in all their voices. They all feel badly about her leaving and say as much, but feeling bad is not the same as guilt.

The O'Connor sisters express their surprise and regret discreetly and in unison.

"The school is not what it was, now," they say, shaking their heads as one.

Celia sighs and leans heavily on her cane. "I'm sorriest for her children. And all the children down the line who won't have her as their teacher. It's a terrible blow for this school and the town. Well, I wish her luck in her new position. Our loss is their gain."

Marilyn, who should be gloating, is oddly quiet and even odder, thoughtful. Now that Esther has left town to join Lee-Anne in Chicago, or so she thinks, she seems surprised to have gotten it right, even remorseful. She and Joan busy themselves with the substitute teacher who has taken Esther's class until the end of the school year. They present a forced, cheerful front of normalcy in the teachers' room, which I avoid now at all costs. The teachers' room was sacred territory. I first laid eyes on Esther there, and we'd rush there to find each other every day.

I hole up in my classroom to plan my lessons and eat my lunch alone, or with Louise and Irene who sometimes join me. I go to Mass on Saturday evenings, find comfort in rituals that are always there for me. I gently turn down Christine's invitation to join her and Adele for dinner or a night out. But Adele stops by the house, regardless, to offer sympathy and comfort, as she says, and that's how I discover she's suspected all along that Esther and I were *an item*, as she puts it. She knows I must be suffering with Esther leaving so abruptly. I must be feeling lonely, she says, putting her arms around me.

"Esther's a good person and a friend, but there's no excuse for breaking your heart."

I don't remind her that she did that very thing to me.

"How did you know about us?" I ask her.

"Some things go without saying," she says, shrugging. "Christine's in the dark, though. She has no idea about the two of you. No one at the school suspects a thing. I told you I could keep a secret."

Adele has stopped talking and her embrace is tightening. She buries her face in my neck, breathes me in, kisses me.

It dawns on me that generally speaking Esther and I have done a mighty fine job of keeping our love a secret, as well as her betrayal and dismissal from the school. Such a good job, in fact, that our story remains as unknown as if it never happened. The higher-ups have done the same. Not the slightest evidence has come to light of our days and nights together. Somewhere in a file at the Board of Ed Esther's *sexual proclivities* may have been recorded in the form of a report. But apart from whoever turned her in, the town's citizens, including its teachers, remain blissfully ignorant. Even Adele has no idea as to the circumstances of Esther's departure from the school. Her humiliating dismissal has been carried out with the utmost discretion.

I should be relieved that we've escaped exposure. I should be grateful. Instead, an odd sensation overwhelms me, the feeling of being invisible. We've been swept under the carpet. Our life together here in town never existed. We've been erased from history before it's been written. It's disconcerting to say the least and leaves me feeling emptied, hollowed out.

Adele's kisses have grown persistent, and her hands have found their way inside my bra and under my skirt at the same time, like some kind of Houdini. I lead her up to my bed, without forethought or hesitation, in the hope of feeling anything at all.

"Karen!" Nat says, beckoning me dramatically into her room, "if you see Esther, *please* remind her I'm counting on her coming to our production of *The Chalk Garden*. She's never missed a show."

"I think she has other things on her mind right now, Nat," I say, too sharply. "The world doesn't revolve around the theater, you know."

I feel bad as soon as I've said it, and Nat looks crushed. The theater *is* her life, and she's not to blame for anything.

"Oh, Nat. I'm sorry. I'll see what I can do, I promise. I know it means the world to you that we're all there. Be sure to reserve us front row seats, okay?"

"God, no!" she shrieks, "No friends allowed in the front row! I'd see you down there and lose my lines."

As for Irene, we're having coffee at her house, though these days we skip right to the sherry, when she leans forward in her chair and with her famous sternness looks me in the eye.

"Karen, follow her to Chicago," she says, startling me. "Leave this place. You only get one chance at happiness, and that's if you're lucky."

THREE

HOW TO READ A
MYSTERY

•

SPRING 1964

40

Esther's life is quickly becoming a whirlwind of activity. She keeps me abreast by telephone, but it's hard to keep up. She joins the synagogue she's been attending at holidays and the local chapter of Daughters of Bilitis. She'll take me to their next meeting, she promises. She plans a march for civil rights with Bettie and Liz and new political friends. She signs up for an evening class in Hebrew in preparation for a trip she hopes to make to Israel and takes up subscriptions for the Chicago Symphony Orchestra and the Chicago White Sox. There are discussions and potlucks, and she insists I'm always welcome to come along.

On a Friday I take the train into the city and accompany Esther to Temple Sholom. It's impressive, all right, with its white bricks piled in three tiers like a wedding cake, its high arched windows and doorways. But despite its elegance, the atmosphere is anything but formal. Men rush to greet one another with hugs and handshakes. Women huddle in animated conversation, ignoring the antics of children playing hide and seek along the carpeted aisles. There are stories galore, health updates and tips exchanged, jokes and teasing sending laughter up into the vaulted ceiling. Esther knows everyone, it seems, and introduces me to a squat, redheaded man in middle age with mischievous eyes, *our rabbi*, she says, and he shakes my hand heartily. She puts her arm around me like I'm a member of her family, a sister of sorts who she's proud to introduce, as we meet her younger single men and women friends, and they're welcoming and so happy to meet me, they say.

As we take our seats, Esther explains that this is a reform synagogue where men and women sit together to worship instead of separately like they are forced to do in orthodox temples, something she would never accept. There's a sanctuary with an altar, and she points out the Holy Ark with its mysterious curtain and later the Torah, wrapped in its cloth like the baby Jesus, I can't help thinking. The singer is called a cantor, and his voice is achingly moving, so raw and human that it makes me want to cry, but I don't want to embarrass Esther, and hold my tears in. Though welcoming of strangers, this temple is a place of belonging. I glance over at Esther, sitting straight-backed by my side in a kind of trance, and it's clear she feels at home here, and I can't help wondering if she believes in God now. She's happy, or at least she's at peace, and maybe she's transported elsewhere at the same time, back to her childhood before the world turned cruel and inexplicable.

She takes me to a public discussion organized by the Daughters of Bilitis. The small back room is full to bursting with elegant women in dress suits and high heels. We're late as usual, and the meeting is in full swing by the time we arrive. The animated speaker at the podium is Del Shearer, Esther whispers to me as we enter, founder of the group's Chicago chapter.

"I will not wear a mask," Del is shouting above the din. "I will be seen for who I am. It's time to come out of hiding, ladies."

She's modestly dressed compared to some, in a full skirt

and flowered blouse, her chin-length hair pulled back from her pleasant face by a hair band. She could be a housewife or the local librarian, but she's a fiery speaker. We manage to find two chairs together near the back. A heated debate on the pros and cons of today's topic, VISIBILITY, is underway, according to the program I find on the seat. A handsome woman in business attire stands up and turns to face the room. "I'm a lawyer, and I'd like to remind you that you are under no obligation to incriminate yourselves. It's dangerous out there. You have every right to protect your privacy. Get yourselves a copy of your legal rights. There are pamphlets on the stand at the back."

"So we should be content with our invisibility, is that what you're saying, Val?" Del answers sharply. "Well, I for one am sick and tired of being invisible."

I find myself agreeing with Del completely. I know what feeling invisible is like. I want to be seen for who I am. But one by one, women who've lost jobs or custody of their children, who've spent time on psychiatric wards, speak up, warning of the costs of discovery, and I quickly change my mind. I have the urge to join in and tell them about Esther and me, how we've lost everything, and I nudge Esther, but she just shakes her head. We're free to be open here, I want to say, but instead I hold my tongue. By now I know not to question Esther. There's always a good explanation for her behavior. Del is adamant, though. Only visibility will convince society to see the homosexual as a person worthy of acceptance, she tells us. Visibility in greater and greater numbers is our best protection, she insists. To that end, we need to keep our demands moderate and demonstrate through our demeanor that we are upstanding citizens, no different from our neighbors who must be brought around slowly. And, yes, that means staying out of the bars, which only exacerbates the negative impression society has formed of us, and conforming to the standard dress code for our sex: stockings and heels.

"It should be no one's business how I dress," shouts a very elegant woman in stockings and heels.

"It's *all* of our business," someone answers. "That's Del's point. Drawing the wrong kind of attention doesn't help our cause."

"And landing in prison is no help to anyone," somebody adds. "Dress code is the law, period."

"The point is we're women, not men," another voice calls out.

"Come off it," says the elegant woman, and now she's standing up. "Let's not mince words here. We're talking about butches. They offend your notion of what a woman should be. So what. Butch women will always exist. And they have every right. They're the bravest among us. It's your problem if you're embarrassed by them."

I find myself clapping vigorously in agreement. Esther glances at me, surprised, and shifts in her seat. Let her think what she likes, I tell myself. I agree with the elegant woman and want to show her my support.

"As for keeping our demands moderate, I'm sorry, Del, but I'm not buying it," she goes on, and I'm riveted. "I don't have time for society to *come around*. I don't have the patience. I'm not waiting for anyone's acceptance. I'm not beholden to the opinions of others. I don't care what they think of me, quite frankly. I want to see equality and justice in my lifetime. I'm angry and I have every right to be. We have to take to the streets! We have to make our voices heard!"

She sits down decisively to a mixture of cheers and boos. "Rome wasn't built in a day," someone calls out. "Some of us can't afford to lose our jobs," another shouts. "Then stay home," a third answers.

Del, meanwhile, is rallying for a last stand, it looks like, drawing herself up to her full height. "Do you honestly believe that marching around with a picket sign and shouting slogans is going to have the slightest effect? Apart from turning public opinion against us. It's plain ridiculous."

"You can't suppress a movement, Del," the elegant lady calls out in answer, and she turns to take in the women in the room. "Some of you can't afford the risk, and that's okay. We'll march for you! We're all in this together, aren't we, ladies? Aren't we in this together?" Some shout in affirmation, others hem and haw. Our eyes meet. I nod my approval, and she smiles and winks. I feel acknowledged by her and strengthened. Her rousing call to action has affected me greatly. I'm ready to take to the streets!

This month's guest speaker, a woman psychiatrist from the Institute for Sexual Research, joins Del on stage. Her demeanor surprises me, I have to admit. Everything about her from head to toe could best be described as mousy. In fact, with her beady, frightened eyes and gray-brown hair, her nondescript clothing in various shades of gray and beige, she looks for all the world like the field mice I observe along the cornfields on the outskirts of town. I can't imagine this sexual expert having sex with anyone until I remember that field mice have very active sex lives and you should never judge a book by its cover. Her name is Dr. Ruth Harrington and she's come here to inform us of mounting evidence that the female homophile is not, as Freud had claimed, arrested in adolescence. Homosexual neurosis is a response to social stigma, repressive conditions, and prejudice.

"Homosexual women have played major roles throughout history, leading the struggle for women's suffrage for example," she reminds us. "They hold positions of serious responsibility as teachers, nurses, doctors, and lawyers, and yes, even in the field of psychology. They are productive citizens."

"Thank you for your profound insight," a voice calls out sarcastically, and the room erupts in laughter.

"Please, let me finish," she begs us. "They are also, according to our studies, among the most sexually satisfied women in the country."

And now she's receiving a standing ovation. We're all on our feet.

"In conclusion," she goes on, quickly, and she's red and flustered, "one can be both well-adjusted and homosexual."

"Surprise, surprise," someone says, and laughter fills the room again.

I find myself feeling sorry for the well-meaning psychiatrist and think to tell her how much I enjoyed her lecture when she steps down from the podium, but she's not finished. She's urging us, please, to participate more actively in research studies, which can only benefit us. There's a study currently being conducted at the Institute, for example, into lesbians' sexual behavior. Absolute anonymity is assured.

"Why should we trust you?" someone calls out. "What's in it for us?" another shouts. "Psychiatrists have done us more damage than good," says a third, and the claps of approval are deafening.

Dr. Harrington seems lost for words. She clearly hadn't expected this line of attack. She turns in desperation to Del, who is standing off to one side. Del quickly joins her at the podium.

"Calm down everyone, please," Del practically screams. "Ten years ago, the publication of the Kinsey report on women's sexuality shook the nation. It was a giant step forward for women and also for lesbians. No one could deny the reality of our existence anymore. But the work is still in its infancy. We need your help."

Despite Del's pleas, the room is far from calm. The psychiatrist's presence has unleashed unrest, and Del's frustration is apparent. She throws up her hands and bows her head. She waits. The room slowly quiets.

"For those of you who aren't convinced," Del starts, her voice hardly above a whisper, "hear me out at least." Her new tactic has the hoped-for effect. You could hear a pin drop. "The research questionnaires provide the social scientists with proof that we exist. And in high numbers, I might add. The social scientists share their findings with the press, and the politicians are forced to take notice. That's how change happens."

A sizable number of the women in the room still aren't buying it and are murmuring their discontent, but I'll sign on, I decide, why not? I like the idea that my questionable behavior might prove useful to our cause when filled out in a questionnaire. I find myself thinking more positively about my own indiscretions for the first time. It's all been in the interest of science, it turns out.

As Dr. Harrington is ushered away from the podium and out the door, Esther leans over and quietly informs me that the timid psychiatrist is a lesbian herself. She knows a woman who dated her, a teacher, in fact. It's the first time I've heard Esther utter the word *lesbian* and I tell her as much. She doesn't like the word, she says; it sounds unflattering.

"I like the sound of it," I tell her, but she just rolls her eyes.

"Ruth Harrington is in hiding like everyone else in here, despite what Del says," Esther continues under her breath. "None of the members use their full names. Or they've got pseudonyms. Don't turn around right now, but the blonde behind you on the right is here from the police. They send informants to all our public gatherings. The police are always on the lookout for a chance to cite us on some violation or other and to gather information on women to be used against them at some future date."

I turn around in my seat as if I'm looking for someone and steal a glance at the blonde on my right. She looks like everyone else in here, well-dressed, professional. She blends right in except she's sitting alone, a little off to one side. I catch her eye and smile. She smiles back without missing a beat and blows a kiss. I think I can't be seeing straight. I start to blush and turn away. This certainly puts a new perspective on things. The women here are even more courageous than first appears. Their every move is monitored, but that doesn't stop them. They carry on and refuse to let themselves be intimidated.

The group gets down to the business at hand. There is unanimous agreement to work more actively to support women isolated in the countryside in suffocating marriages and as single mothers. To that end, the safest and most successful distribution method of the group's monthly newsletter, *The Ladder*, is debated.

I'm reeling by the end of it from all the new ideas and impressions, but full of energy at the same time. I'm proud to be numbered among these attractive and opinionated women, these *lesbians*, elated by their very existence. I could hug and kiss each and every one of them and take at least half of them to bed—metaphorically speaking, of course. Afterward there's wine and cheese. We stand with Bettie, Liz, and Lee-Anne, who startles me with a friendly hug. She seems in much better spirits than I've seen her before, energized by the women in the room no doubt. But then everyone's on fire with the buzz of chatter and continued debate, the laughter of flirtation and comradery. Other women quickly join us—social workers, nurses, doctors, other teachers. They address me as a peer, despite my newness.

The outspoken elegant woman joins us, too. She knows Esther apparently because she's kissing her on both cheeks. It's a small and very affectionate world I'm discovering. The elegant woman turns to me and offers her hand. She tells me she's happy to see a fresh new face and asks me what I do. I tell her I'm a teacher, and how grateful I am to her for speaking up and that I agree with everything she says. She thanks me, tells me it's a tough crowd, and it's only then that she releases her hand from mine long enough to take a business card out of her purse and slip it into my waiting hand. I should give her a call sometime, she says. I'll do that, I say. She's a doctor, it turns out, with her own practice in the city.

Del comes over to inform us they'll be discussing the role of the homophile teacher in the fall. I promise to attend and sign up for the newsletter. We say our good-byes and Lee-Anne asks Esther if she can catch a lift with her, and Esther and Lee-Anne drive me to the station.

Lee-Anne's name comes up quite frequently now, and Esther lets me know that she'll be moving to her place while the search for an apartment of her own goes on. Space is too tight at Liz and Bettie's, she says. It can't be that hard to find a place, I can't help thinking. Days go by, and weeks pass, and Esther hasn't left Lee-Anne's.

She's spending the night with me at home. She's not set foot in town since leaving the farmhouse. She enters hesitantly, almost shyly, stealing glances as if she's been invited in for the very first time. She pauses at the kitchen table as if it's a long-lost object in a room she can't quite put her finger on. I lead her up to my bed and she follows, stopping on the stairs to look around, like she's unsure where she's heading or what to expect. And it's not so different with my body. She's strangely tender and wants to make love in slow motion, as if she's discovering and remembering every part of me at the same time so she never forgets. While it's happening, I'm distinctly aware that this is the last time I'll have her in my arms. She's leaving me, and it's not fear I'm feeling, and it's not grief either. It's love. It's love for this beautiful, beautiful woman.

We lie on our sides and look at each other for a very long time. We wipe the tears from each other's eyes, but they keep coming.

"You don't have to say it, Esther," I tell her. "I know."

She holds me very tightly while I cry myself to sleep, and in the morning when I wake up, she's not there.

41

Noreen O'Connor doesn't make it to the end of the school year. I'm wiping the blackboard at the end of the day when I hear the ambulance arrive and footsteps on the stairs. Dorothy pops her head into my room.

"She's just sitting at her desk, staring into space. A couple of her children came to the office to get me. They're shaken, but luckily they're first graders, still babies, and can't really take it in. Oh, Karen, we all knew she was forgetting things and repeating lessons, but she seems to have disappeared completely. It's your worst nightmare. One minute you're a cognizant being with a past, present and future and the next thing you know, you're gone."

"I'll check on Margaret," I say.

I find Noreen's sister in her classroom, hunched over her desk, head in her arms. I try to help her up from her chair, but her legs collapse, and I half carry her down the stairs and out to the ambulance to join Noreen. I'm here to help in any way I can, Margaret, I tell her, and I promise to stop by later. She asks me, please, if it's no trouble, to bring her sister's coat and bag because she can't bear to enter her classroom.

She's waiting for me on the front steps. I hand her Noreen's coat and bag and she clutches them to her. She invites me in for some refreshment, as she calls it, which is laid out in preparation in the front room, but she's shaking so much she can't pour the tea and has to put the pot down. I take over, trying not to show my dismay at her current state of mind.

"Will you be all right here on your own, Margaret?" I ask. "Why don't you come to me and spend the night?"

She smiles but shakes her head. "No, Karen dear, but thank you all the same. I need to be here, in our home."

She strokes the embroidered cloth on her coffee table. "Noreen made this."

"It's lovely," I say. And it is lovely, stitched with cornflowers and lavender.

"I thought I'd go first, and here she's gone and left me and left her body behind. I'd care for her here if I could. But I can't lift her. I've tried."

"You're a wonderful sister."

She takes a sip of tea and wipes her mouth with her lace hanky. She folds it carefully.

"Karen, we're not sisters," Margaret says.

I'm startled. She notices and nods her head.

"We're not even cousins, if truth be known. Not that it matters now."

"No."

"I thought you'd understand." She glances up at me, then down at her clasped hands.

It all makes sense: their quiet, fiercely guarded, inseparable lives. Margaret gets up and takes a book down from the shelf. She removes a photo from between its pages and hands it to me. It's a picture of her and Noreen, handsome young women, their suitcases and one trunk packed, on the gangway of the ship that would bring them to America where they had devised a way to spend their lives together.

"Margaret, how lucky you were. Not many can say that," I tell her.

To start again from scratch, someplace unknown, to be reborn as sisters, with all the intimacy sisters enjoy. What an audacious plan these quiet women, barely more than schoolgirls, hatched. I can't help feeling a touch of envy.

"I guess you're right," she says, and smiles.

"It was a stroke of genius what you did. I mean, to live as sisters."

"We had no choice, did we now," she says, shrugging.

42

Marilyn's grown noticeably thinner. She accentuates her new svelte figure with slim skirts and proclaims her secret diet a miracle.

"Come on, Marilyn, share the secret with us, please," Louise begs her. "I need a miracle for my waistline."

"My lips are sealed," she answers. But as she passes me, she leans in and whispers, "The cancer's back, honey." I'm startled and turn to face her, but the playful mask is on. "As the Indians say, if you reveal the secret, its magic goes away," she's telling Louise.

But the sad news spreads through the school like wildfire, even without our resident gossip's help. Within days she's out on leave and Dorothy takes over her classes. At our weekly meeting, Will informs us that no treatment can save her and she won't be returning to the school. We teachers make a schedule and visit her at home, bringing her hot meals for as long as she can stomach them. I help her put her makeup on, a favorite ritual of hers, until the day she shakes her head and pushes the lipstick away. I read her beloved *True Confessions* out loud to her and we watch *To Tell the Truth* and *I've Got a Secret* until she no longer has the patience and gestures for me to turn it off. The TV never gets turned on again. She tells me stories instead, from her childhood. She likes especially the one about feeding the chickens on her grandparents' farm and gathering the eggs until the day her grandma chopped the head off one of her favorites and she never ate an egg again. I know it by heart and could recite it with her.

She tells me she's especially happy when she sees me, her *sweetheart* as she's taken to calling me, though she's grateful to every single one of us who are like family to her, perhaps better. Her sister, who lives outside of town, hardly visits; they were never close and you can't squeeze blood out of a turnip. She feels like she can be herself with me, she says, because I don't seem troubled by the state of her. "I scare myself when I look in the mirror," she says. "When I get my strength back, I'll take every last mirror down."

I don't tell her dying doesn't frighten me. I helped nurse my grandma, who'd moved in with us when she gave up the farm, and watched her die. It didn't seem a bad thing, death, in and of itself. Death puts an end to suffering and is peaceful.

On what will be her death bed, by the sun-infused window in her living room, Marilyn smiles widely when I appear in front of her (she's too weak now to turn her head) and takes my hand and strokes it purposefully, an effort that exhausts her.

"He's on his way to town." Her voice is raspy, breathless.

"Marilyn, not again," I say, wetting her lips.

"No, sweetheart, I've seen it. You watch. He'll be here any day."

"In shining armor, right?"

"To sweep Miss Murphy off her feet. I had a dream this morning, Karen," she says, suddenly serious. "It was so real."

"What did you dream?"

"That you named your first girl Marilyn."

I bow my head. Let her have her wish, I tell myself. It costs you nothing.

"I'll do that," I say. "I promise."

Maybe it's the late sun, but she is glowing, as if my promise has released her and she can go now, filled with light. Her eyes shut and I feel quite certain she is dying. She's loosened her grip of my hand. She looks at peace in the presence of death. Then she's gripping my hand so tightly it hurts—I don't know where she's found the strength—and opening her eyes, and looking directly into mine, she says, "I shouldn't have reported Esther, hon." And then her eyes close and she's asleep.

I release her hand and collapse back in the chair, strain to feel outrage, delight in her suffering, anything at all. But Esther's right, it doesn't matter who betrayed us. I feel nothing.

It's only later while I'm at the sink washing dishes that the enormity of her confession hits me. I see Marilyn at her kitchen table, banging out a note on her Smith Corona, a half-empty bottle of red wine by her side. She's touching up her makeup in the teacher's bathroom, puckering her lips and teasing her hair. She's setting off to Will's office on her mission, a short flirtatious meeting, small talk, nothing more, a last-minute reference to something troubling she's heard and more worrying, seen with her own eyes, something she can hardly bring herself to say, so she's written it down, and then a folded note slipped into his free hand while his other hand is sliding down her back, and out she goes, back down the hall and out of the building. Perhaps she does a little shopping on her way home, something sweet tossed in the cart, a little treat to calm her nerves. How easy it is to destroy a life or two, casually, in the course of an otherwise harmless conversation. A bit of gossip passed on becomes a missile aimed with deadly force at its target.

Marilyn dies peacefully in her sleep in the middle of the night, according to the night nurse who was by her side. Her funeral is attended by quite a crowd really, including the teachers and staff

255

at the school, but also her Avon customers, numerous in number it turns out and obviously fond of her, as well as her only sister, a niece, and a nephew. I find myself viewing her in a somewhat kinder light. Poor Marilyn, I can't help thinking, how completely mistaken you were, and I'm almost ready to forgive her.

A will is found in her drawer naming me as the sole beneficiary of her life insurance policy. It's not a fortune, but every little bit counts on a teacher's salary. I'll put it to good purpose one day, I promise myself.

43

Nat has taken Noreen O'Connor's first graders into her own first-grade class, God bless her and God help the children, with special dispensation from the school board until a suitable replacement can be found. There'll be more drama in that classroom than on Broadway, Christine says. Meanwhile, the search for a new kindergarten teacher continues. Dorothy can't keep up double duties as secretary *and* replacement for Marilyn, and Will takes the major step of hiring an office temp. This solves the problem, in theory, but reality is something else entirely. The school system is collapsing without Dorothy in the office. We all knew Will was totally dependent on her, but the extent of the chaos would have been hard to imagine: jumbled schedules, misplaced files, unpaid bills, supply closets empty of contents, unreturned calls. We teachers rally like troupers, marching back and forth from our rooms to the office to help out. I take it upon myself to comfort the temporary secretary who is on the verge of tears at all times.

Esther's replacement will become permanent. She's pleasant enough, a serious young woman just out of college. On the tall side if I had to describe her, dark hair pulled away from her face, alert blue eyes behind thick glasses. There's something intriguing about her, I have to admit, a feeling like we've met before, and I find myself drawn to her against my will. We take the same route home as it happens, and she tags along with me. She has many questions, which I answer dutifully: where the school supplies are kept, how to use the library. She needs support and is seeking my friendship, which is only understandable. She's curious to hear about my experience at the school, she says. Perhaps we could have a coffee? But I make excuses and keep my distance. I can't bring myself to accept her presence in Esther's room and look the other way when I walk past. She's innocent, I know, but the wound's too fresh. I find it painful to say her name out loud, but that doesn't stop me from thinking about her.

She shares a free period with Irene and me. "Why did Miss Jonas leave before the end of the school year?" she asks us.

Irene shrugs and defers to me.

"For personal and professional reasons, we were told," I say, as if that's any kind of answer.

She nods and frowns at the same time. I can tell she isn't satisfied. She's about to pursue the matter further, but stops herself. "What was she like?" she asks instead.

"She was the best teacher this school ever had," Irene answers, so forcefully she startles us both.

"How do you mean?" I can't help asking.

She pauses, chin high, to weigh her words. "Miss Jonas had, simply, the finest balance of freedom and control of any teacher I've ever known."

It seems their running battle over how to teach the children had buoyed and challenged them more than I understood.

Whatever else, our school will never be the same. Christine's of the mind the profession as a whole is undergoing a seismic shift, with more married women staying on in the field and having children. She may be right, but it's still up in the air as to whether Louise will be with us next year. Her upcoming marriage leads me to fear the worst. She and Gary want a large family, and as quickly as possible.

"The old guard are dying off," Christine says, with a shrug. "A few of us are still standing, but barely."

It occurs to me that I might be the last spinster schoolteacher left in the world.

Then word gets out that Greg Jordan is leaving us too! Our only male teacher has lasted one year. Will drops the bombshell at our Friday meeting. Greg's taking Lee-Anne's job as vice-principal at the junior high school.

"Told you so," Christine says when Will's out of hearing. "It's the same old story. Men always rise to the top."

"Perhaps no woman wanted the job. You wouldn't take it with a ten-foot pole, you told us," I remind her.

"I know a couple of gals who applied," Christine says. "Excellent candidates with long years of experience. But they didn't stand a chance. Administration is child's play compared to the work we do, and it pays double. They won't surrender those jobs without a fight."

"Well, our children will be better off without Greg Jordan," Irene says, putting an end to any further debate.

But I like Greg and wish him well. I'd tell him as much if I could catch him in the hall, but he's dashing in and out and seems to be avoiding me. When he finally pokes his head into my room to grab his lesson plans, he doesn't mention his promotion, and I decide to hold my tongue. If I'm honest, I can't help feeling like a stepping-stone. Then a dozen red roses show up on my front porch with an elaborate thank you card and a handwritten note from Greg telling me that he couldn't have gotten through the year without me, and I am welcome to come to the junior high and teach sixth grade any time.

44

I find myself designated chairwoman of our school's first Committee on Sexual Education, with tentative approval of the PTA, tasked with devising a unit in the context of Biology on the human reproductive organs and pregnancy. I admit I'm more than surprised to be entrusted with this task by Will. The fact is I'm astonished to be in the school at all, my relationship with Esther aside. I've broken all the rules of conduct, laid waste to educative norms and values, the teaching of taboo subjects included. Not to mention I've turned down Will's advances.

Will proposes Alice Kaminski as our parent representative, and I can hardly say no. I can't say no to Joan Smith's involvement, either. We both teach fifth grade and the new unit, if approved, will be taught in our classes next year. Joan, Alice, and I will be joined by Christine Olsen, assuring me a much-needed ally in the inevitable battle of wills with Joan.

We start our first meeting without Alice, who hasn't appeared and hasn't called, and we're on to our second point of business, parental involvement, as it happens, when she rushes in breathless to let us know she can't stay today as she hasn't been well and has fallen behind on just about everything. She knows she's neglecting her duty as far as the school's concerned but hopes we understand. She shakes my hand politely, without a trace of familiarity, and promises she'll do her very best to attend our next meeting, tentatively scheduled for the summer. Though her coolness is disconcerting to say the least, I'm eternally grateful and much relieved and relish our newfound formality. I've courted disaster and escaped.

But even disasters are relative.

I'd managed to convince myself that my missed period was a sign of stress, my nausea a reaction to Esther's dismissal, but as my small breasts swell and my period doesn't return, panic sets in. I don't dare go for a test in town, but the evidence is overwhelming. My tryst on the kitchen floor with Cliff Johnson has left me pregnant. I need help and as quickly as possible but I don't know where to turn. Louise thinks I'm on the pill. Besides which I've insisted that men are the last thing on my mind, that I'm married to my profession. There's no point asking Irene for advice, though I trust her with my life. She's never been kissed, for heaven's sake. I'm not sure she knows how babies are made. I'm too ashamed in any case.

I'll ask Dorothy what to do, I decide. She can solve anything. At the end of the school day, I head to the office at a determined pace, but as I near her door, I find myself walking right past and down the school's front steps. She's too devout a Catholic. She won't approve of my ending the pregnancy. It would be like asking my mother for advice. She'll pray to Saint Gerard to make a mother of me. The fact is, I'm utterly alone, and either I walk downtown to Sue's Yarn and Buttons and purchase a knitting needle, which I'm ready to do, or I call Esther the minute I get home. Among her circle of friends in the city is surely someone who can help me.

I'm barely in the door before I'm reaching for the phone, no time for second thoughts. *Esther, I'm pregnant.* I'll give it to her straight. But my hands are shaking so badly I dial the wrong number, not once but twice. And it's only then that I remember the elegant doctor from the Daughters of Bilitis. I've tossed her card in my kitchen drawer. I forage through sandwich bags and recipes and bits of string, and lo and behold it's there, stuck in a corner. I ease it out gently and study it, gripping it tightly with sweating hands. The name on the card is Dr. Lillian Schmidt.

"Of course, I remember you," Dr. Schmidt says, when I reach her on the phone. "The enthusiastic young teacher, am I right? A colleague of Esther's? That was quite a meeting! Tell me your name again?"

I tell her my name, and I tell her there's been a most unfortunate turn of events in my life, a one-night stand. I've made a stupid, careless mistake, one that I'll never make again.

"Haven't we all made those," she says with a laugh. And then her voice grows serious. "Let me guess. Are you pregnant, Karen?"

I tell her the truth, the whole truth, and nothing but the truth out of sheer desperation. It doesn't appear to shock her at all.

"We've got two options." Her voice is businesslike and reassuring. "The city's cracking down. Raids are taking place on a weekly basis. The only clinics open for business these days survive by making payoffs. It's risky, but it's an option. As for the legit route, the city's shaking up the hospital boards. Most of the doctors sympathetic to our cause have been replaced with political appointees who are downright hostile to women, poor excuses for doctors. But you've come to the right place."

I realize I've stopped breathing. I'm grabbing on to her words like a lifeline. "I'm so grateful you offered me your card, Dr. Schmidt. I didn't know where to turn."

"I had something else in mind when I handed you my card, sweetheart, and please call me Lillian." She stops, clears her throat. "But we need to get this problem of yours fixed *ASAP*."

She tells me she has a friend, *one of our tribe,* a psychiatrist, and he has connections with a few of the board members at Cook County Hospital. *The last of the good men* is how she describes them. "I'll try to arrange an appointment with my friend and call you back, how's that?"

"Forgive my ignorance, Lillian," I say, "but couldn't you take care of things yourself?"

"God, no," she practically shouts, "I'd lose my license. They're keeping special tabs on women doctors, just waiting for us to slip up. I'm pretty sure our office is bugged. It's like the McCarthy era all over again. It's a witch hunt."

She calls back quickly and tells me her friend the psychiatrist will see me. The plan is for him to provide me with a letter explaining to his friends on the board that I'm a single woman, a teacher, and suffering from suicidal thoughts brought on by the pregnancy. It's just a formality, but I have to meet him to go over my story. This should get me an interview with the board and, with luck, a board-approved medical abortion, a rare thing these days but doable, if you know the right people.

But as she reaches the bit about the interview in front of the board, I know I can't go through with it.

"Would I have to give my name, Lillian? Because if so, it won't be possible, I'm sorry."

But that's only half the story. The idea of a panel of men sitting in judgment as to the state of my mental health is like a monstrous confessional. I wouldn't make it through the door. I wonder what state of mind, what desperation, would bring a woman to her knees in such a fashion. I'll try anything else before I end up there.

There's a pause on the line. My decisiveness has rendered her speechless, it seems. I may have lost my only chance. I'm ready to take it back, give in. I'll meet the psychiatrist, tell him whatever he wants, sign my name, check any box. I'll face the hospital board, fall at their feet, beg for their mercy, sob, tear my hair out, whatever it takes.

Then I hear a sigh. "All right," Lillian says. She's been chewing the problem over. She doesn't sound the least put out. "Plan B. This one's illegal. And it'll cost you."

"I have the money," I tell her quickly, and I'm flooded with relief. "I've been saving for a rainy day."

It's Marilyn's money, in fact. It's true I had been saving for Esther and me, so we might take a trip together to the Holy Land or New York City. But with my teacher's pay I had little to show for it. That was in another life in any case, a life in which I had a future with Esther.

Lillian tells me a friend of a friend of hers has an acquaintance who performs abortions for unmarried women in need. It just so happens he's one of the most skillful in the business. She says she'll call me back.

She does call back, and like magic it will all work out.

"He'll need cash up front, that's just how it is these days. There's a lot of organization involved. But for you, it's simple. Someone will be there to pick you up at the station. They'll drive you to a kind of waiting room; the location is always changing. When it's your turn, you'll be picked up and driven to his office." She could be giving directions for a treasure hunt or a city tour. Her voice is upbeat, almost cheerful, but then she stops.

"Rocky times for us gals. There's no political will for change right now. But our day will come. I have to believe that. Anyway, someone will call you with the details tomorrow."

I tell her it's a fine plan. I'm more grateful than she can ever imagine. She'll never know how much. She tells me not to think twice about it. "Plenty of us have been there," she says.

I thank her again and again. I'll never be able to thank her enough. She's like an angel, I tell her. She's laughing softly.

By the way, she says, she knows someone who knows someone who runs a rooming house with nursing staff where I can stay over the weekend and recover. "That'll cost, too, of course."

"That's all right," I say.

"Bring a couple of nightgowns, a robe, toiletries, and a change of clothes. And call in sick for a couple days."

"All right."

"When you've gotten through this, Karen, and you *will* get through this, I promise, I'll take you out for dinner and a show. How's that?"

"Sure," I say, "I'd like that," and it's only then that a picture of the elegant woman at the Daughters of Bilitis comes into my mind, and I remember how it felt when we shook hands and the look in her eyes as she passed me her business card.

Dave Palmquist at the Trust and Savings counts out a thousand dollars in fifty-dollar bills, licking his thumb and finger as he goes along and smiling at me.

"Planning a nice vacation, Miss Murphy? Can you fit me in your suitcase?"

I laugh at his stupid joke. The money presently in his possession is all I care about. I want to reach over and snatch it out of his hands.

"I wish," I say, and sigh. "The washing machine's broken down and I'm looking into a television set." My voice is a mixture of yearning and regret.

"Blaine Coon over at Montgomery Ward is your man for all appliances." He's picking up his phone. "We'll get you the best deal, Miss Murphy. *The schoolteacher's special.* I'll give him a call."

"No," I practically shout. "I'll do it myself."

He looks at me, surprised, puts down the phone. "Suit yourself," he says with a wounded expression. I smile widely to reassure him he's the most important person in my life.

"Thanks for the offer though," I say as he hands me the money.

I have to stop myself from running out of the bank.

I pack a small suitcase with my robe, two nightgowns, a change of clothes, my toiletries, and on Friday, directly from school, I walk to the station in a kind of trance and take the bus into Chicago.

From the examination table in the small office above a beauty shop, flat on my back, legs in stirrups, in nothing but my dressing gown, I look up into the clear blue sky outside the window.

"Marilyn, wherever you are, this is the baby I'm naming after you," I call out, just above a whisper.

There won't be another.

To pass the time while I wait my turn, I try to imagine a girl named Marilyn or a boy named Marilyn, but no image comes. I try to imagine married life with Cliff Johnson. But I can't. It's impossible. Marriage with any man is unthinkable. I try to picture myself as an unwed mother forced to give up teaching, raising a child on my own, or barring that, a hushed-up pregnancy like Joan's and the grief of adoption, but not a single image comes. The act of giving birth is simply unimaginable.

A parade of mothers I've known appear before me, from this, my curbside seat. I'm not an expert in mothers, far from it, but I have made my observations all the same. Whatever their differences, from the young women barely more than children themselves to those raising the last of a large brood whose production and upkeep have taken decades of their lives, they share some essential quality that is as strange to me as if they were a separate species. It's as if they carry something cellular, some form of life attached to them, like an extra limb. That's the best I can describe it. It's neither good nor bad in itself, but motherhood strikes me as very peculiar. Most women may be born to play the role intended for them by nature, but a good portion, if you ask me, are forced into it by circumstance, the circumstance of their bodies from which there is almost no escape. Whatever else I am or may turn out to be, I'll never be a mother.

What I have become, in the eyes of the Church in which I was raised, is a mortal sinner. God knows I've been sinning for years, but today I'm committing the gravest sin of all, the taking of an unborn life, for which there is no absolution. There's nothing for it but to accept my excommunication.

"So long, my Church," I say out loud, "I'll miss you," and I make the sign of the cross. I'm leaving home with one small suitcase packed.

There's a light tap on the door, which opens slowly, and the specialist comes in. He's a small, balding man with friendly eyes. I tell him I'm very grateful for his help. He smiles, averts his gaze. He doesn't know my name or who I am. As he gently places a needle in my arm, I'm enveloped by a warm and calming breeze and drift into the void.

45

Celia James has invited me to dine with her at The Steakhouse downtown! As the school year draws to a close, I'll finally have a chance to get to know her better. I'm quite sure she has secrets to impart when it comes to the art of teaching, but something else as well. Her calm, focused and elegant approach to life, a life struck early by polio, seems to me to hold the key to happiness. I'm most urgently in need of inspiration as to how to live going forward. Despite the relief of my medical procedure, I'm anxious about the future, a future without Esther, and though it's painful to admit, I'm lonely.

"So, what do you think, Karen dear," Celia says, lighting a cigarette, "as your first year comes to an end? Are you going to stick it out?"

The directness of her question takes me aback.

"I don't mean to pry. But I sense it's not been an easy year for you."

"No," I manage to say. *Don't cry,* I tell myself, but the tears well up anyway. Celia observes me, but it doesn't feel intrusive. I feel oddly strengthened by her gaze.

"Can I be of help in any way?"

"I don't know," I say, wiping my eyes. "It's not the teaching, well, not only the teaching."

The teaching has in fact been going relatively smoothly of late. The children are settling down at last, and perhaps I'm settling, too. Lydie's passion for attention has been dampened by Janie's abrupt departure from the school. She spends the day ignoring me and saves her dramatics for Nat's drama club. Remarkably, the clique of three have exhibited real kindness and invite Lydie to join them at lunch and recess, and she's made friends with a couple of the other girls, including Susie the runner, her new best friend. I see them biking past the house, getting up to God knows what mischief.

"A teacher's life brings many challenges. A good deal of them outside the classroom," Celia says.

She's looking into my soul, I can't help thinking.

"I could tell you a story."

"Yes, please," I say, nodding briskly.

"Okay." She takes a long drag of her cigarette, blows a smoke ring.

"It begins at a bus stop on Chicago's North Side in 1929. I was twenty-one at the time and already training to be a teacher here in town. Richard and I were both heading to the beach but we ended up ditching our friends and spending the day together. And the night, too. He'd moved up North to Chicago from Mississippi as a boy. I should mention he was a Black man and I a white girl. That's how the world saw us, anyway."

The waiter comes over. Celia orders us scotch on the rocks and steak dinner.

"He was already spokesman for his union at the plant and studying law at night. He dreamed of a political career. I was so impressed. He was a fiery speaker, very charismatic, and his laughter filled the room. But he had a temper on him, too. He was full of rage, understandably. The main thing is, we were head over heels in love and defiant. We were readying to marry. Marriage between the races was legal in Illinois, but still we faced hateful looks and comments. We weren't always safe walking down the street together, not on the South Side or the North, so we'd walk separately and meet up later. We were fearless but we feared for our lives if you know what I mean."

She stops and studies me, and I have the distinct sensation that she knows about Esther and me, but that's not possible.

"What happened?" I ask.

Celia doesn't answer at first. She's thinking back, reliving some inner battle it looks like.

"I chose teaching, Karen."

She crushes her cigarette in the tray. "I chose teaching," she says again quietly.

"And Richard?"

"He went back down South to join the struggle. Lawyers were needed to fight the Jim Crow laws. My God, it's over thirty years ago. He married a Black girl, a teacher as it happens."

"What made you choose teaching over your heart, Celia?"

She looks up at me. Her answer comes slowly. "Richard had a calling. That was clear to me. But I did too, Karen. That's the best I can explain it."

"Have you ever felt regret?"

She shrugs and sighs. "I'd be lying if I said I didn't. And yet I know it was the right thing."

Celia sits forward in her seat, places her elbows on the table.

"I was pregnant on top of everything," she says, startling me.

She takes me in, and from what I read in her eyes I'm convinced beyond a doubt that she knows a great deal more than she's letting on about me. Perhaps more than I know myself. She nods and sighs as if to confirm my suspicion.

"We all have stories, we teachers. But in the end, what matters is the teaching."

"You've never been tempted again?" I can't help asking.

"There were a couple of fellas who caught my eye. I had a fling or two." Celia laughs, perhaps because my jaw has dropped. "That surprises you, huh? But those days are long behind me. At this point, I can barely make it from here to the doorway."

She's humoring me. This woman is capable of anything; she's unbeatable. She lights another cigarette, casts her eyes down.

"I spent much of my childhood on my back, Karen, in splints and casts and the worst of those years in an iron lung."

It hits me that the joy emanating from Celia's classroom is no accident. I look up and discover her watching me.

"I get a kick out of happy children," she says, shrugging. "Today we've got the polio vaccine in a sugar cube. How amazing is that? Children grow into scientists and change the world, Karen. With our help."

We've hardly touched our food. We toss off our scotch and order more, and when the restaurant closes we move to Andy's bar next door. We discuss teaching into the wee hours.

46

It's finally happening. *The Chalk Garden*, which has preoccupied Nat for weeks on end, at the expense of her first graders and all else, is opening with Nat as director and in the leading role. Tonight's performance is the event of the season by the looks of it, and the country barn is filled to the rafters. Dave Palmquist from the Trust and Savings is waving and winking in my direction, and there's June Harding with her grumpy dieting husband. Even my neighbor, Bill Soros, has made an appearance, missing his night shift for the occasion. Our school has come out in full force to cheer Nat on. Cliff's turned up, looking nothing like himself in a suit and tie, accompanied by what appears to be a new lady friend. He's avoiding me, as he has been dutifully since I informed him no further repairs were necessary. But I make it a point to go up to him, and he introduces me to Annette, who looks a lot like his ex-wife, Lizzy, very pretty indeed. We shake hands warmly and Cliff seems relieved. He doesn't know the half of it. He's blissfully ignorant of the pregnancy and its near calamitous outcome and will be from here to eternity.

Louise, in her first public appearance with Gary, rushes over to tell me she's changed her mind regarding the color scheme for the late June wedding at which I'm to be maid of honor and Steve the best man. Mauve is out, pale rose is in! By the way, she says, she saw Steve last week, and he's still pining for me. "It's not too late for a double ceremony," she tells me, more serious than joking. I know, I know, she says, when I roll my eyes. One day I'll tell Louise the truth if it's the last thing I do. If it's a death bed confession, so be it. I will not wear a mask forever.

Greg Jordan sneaks in late with his wife just before the curtain rises. The poor woman looks set to give birth to a new planet any minute. Only Esther's seat is empty, and we all move over a seat.

The story of Miss Madrigal, the spinster governess with a dark and secret past, and the disturbed and rebellious pupil in her care, Laurel, certainly holds my attention. In fact, I'm on high alert thoughout, heart racing at each encounter and revelation. Laurel and Miss Madrigal are playing quite a game with each other. The girl knows Miss Madrigal is not who she appears to be. Why does Lydie come to mind? The judge who comes for lunch ruined Miss Madrigal's life with his reckless indifference all those years ago. Just as Will Lindquist has done with Esther and me. My mouth drops as Miss Madrigal, her fate outside her control, grows so careless when all seems lost and discovery is inevitable. I can't help thinking of Esther.

I can hardly breathe with the tension of it, and my thoughts are racing back and forth between the play and life and back again. Those fifteen years behind bars have hardened her, but life can be a kind of prison, too, and poor Miss Madrigal is not free despite her release from prison. She is still in hiding. If she's found out, she will never work as a governess again. Her livelihood will be over, like Esther's here in town. How different is my own fate? I'm devastated by Miss Madrigal's loneliness and her suffering at the hands of the court, but find myself excited at the same time. By the end of it, I'm spent with emotion and elated at once and sink back in my seat. I now understand what had eluded me before. Art is life, after all, like Alice Kaminski says.

We're lifted onto our feet to give them all a standing ovation, and there's joy and relief on Nat's face in equal measure. Irene leans over and whispers that I should have played Miss Madrigal, making me laugh.

"I'll take that as a compliment," I whisper back, "but I found Nat convincing."

"Well, certainly not in years," she says, and I have to admit she's right.

But the English accents, all of us agree, sounded most authentic, and Margaret can't get over the elegance of the costumes.

Christine and Adele drop me off at home, and Adele says when I need a ride, I should just call her. She'll teach me to drive if I like, and I accept her offer.

The evening has concluded in a blaze of glory for the Barb Town Players, but *The Chalk Garden* stays with me. Miss Madrigal is spared in the end and will live out her days in peace, tending the garden. The true circumstances of her existence will never be known. Perhaps that's the most we can expect of life, the price of freedom.

47

Louise and I are invited to join the teachers for coffee and pie at the Hillside. We're part of the club now, *the inner circle*, I tell her as we make our way downtown, arm in arm.

No sooner are we all seated than Louise announces she has big news to share, something she hasn't even told me yet, her best friend. My heart sinks and I brace myself for the announcement that she's leaving the school.

"Gary and I have decided to wait to start a family until his promotion comes through."

She'll be staying on for at least another year or two! Our table erupts in claps and cheers.

"You don't have to give up teaching at all, Louise," I say, buoyed on by the good news. "You love your job and the children need you. You can be both a mother and a teacher. No one can stop you."

Christine says I'm right. We all have to read Betty Friedan's new book. It's taking the country by storm. I'm embarrassed to admit I haven't read it yet. I don't tell them Esther left a copy on the nightstand on her side of the bed.

"It's at the top of my summer reading list," I assure Christine.

"Mine, too," Irene says, nudging me and winking.

"Housewives will be abandoning the kitchen in droves," Christine says, her booming voice filling the coffee shop. Several startled housewives turn around to look. "Women want out of the house. Friedan has put into words what they've been feeling all along."

We nod, impressed. Even Louise looks thoughtful.

"That's all very well," Celia says, lighting a cigarette, "but until men share in the care of children and housework equally, nothing substantial will change. That won't happen until women are running things."

This gives us food for thought, but we promise to read Betty Friedan's book. Even Louise writes down the name. "You can borrow my copy when I'm done," I tell her. We'll discuss it at our next meeting, we decide. Our key lime pie arrives and we put revolution aside. Margaret swears it's almost as good as Noreen's, and her eyes well up with tears. We make a fuss over her, but she insists she's fine.

"You should all hurry up now and finish your pie before the waitress takes it," she tells us, dabbing her eyes with a lace hanky. She smiles up at me, and I squeeze her hand gently under the table.

There are expressions of delight and the scraping of plates. Christine taps her glass with a knife to get our attention.

"Where's your whistle, Christine?" I ask, and we all laugh.

"Ladies," she says, looking us over, "I'm starting a karate course this fall."

We look at her a little skeptically, mouths full.

"Well, who's signing up?"

There's not a sound at our table, for once.

"Come on. Women's self-defense is all the rage," she assures us, winking at me.

Out of the silence, Louise speaks up. She'll join if I do, she says, and I say sure, why not, I'm determined to present a stronger front to the world, and this makes everyone roar with laughter for some reason, including me. Irene says she'd consider joining too if it wasn't for her accursed knee, and the way she says it sets us off again.

Christine volunteers to give us a first lesson right now if we like. And before we can mount a protest, she's getting up from the table and demonstrating the *forward stance*. This consists of one very long leg bent forward bearing her weight, the other placed behind her, like a giant scissor, her huge feet straight ahead, her arms positioned in front of her face.

"Who wants to try?"

"Sit down, Christine, you'll get us all thrown out," Irene orders her in a loud whisper as other diners turn to face us. The townsfolk look nothing if not astonished by our antics.

"Thanks be to God, we've got a corner table," Margaret says, rolling her eyes.

"It's like this every time we get together," Celia explains to Louise and me.

Christine shakes her head good-naturedly and joins us back at the table, and then Irene gets the giggles and gives them to Louise and none of us are immune for long. It occurs to me that our easy banter is sustaining me. I feel peaceful and at one with my surroundings. I feel contentment. I say a prayer of thanks to the fire goddess for releasing me from passion and join in the laughter again.

When we've recovered and dried our eyes and blown our noses, the group decides on a date for our next get-together, and Christine insists on paying against everyone's protests.

"Oh, by the way," she says, as we're getting up to go, "Adele bumped into Lee-Anne the other day. She told her Esther's moving to Israel."

"Israel?" Louise cries out and gasps. "That's across the world, isn't it? We'll never see her again!"

"But she was to start in the new school in Chicago," Margaret says, perplexed, her voice trailing off.

"She met someone with contacts there, I guess, and changed her mind. Lee-Anne said it was all pretty sudden. I'll find out more next weekend. We're going in to see them."

"Did you know about this?" Louise asks me.

I shake my head, unable to speak.

"This is a surprise for all of us, I think," Celia says, and gripping my arm she steers me gently to the door. "Would you mind walking me to the car, Karen dear?"

"I'll walk with you," Irene says, taking my other arm.

We say our good-byes, and we're off, out into the sunshine, down Lincoln Highway, and it takes three of the street's main shopping blocks before I've broken down completely, and two aging teachers, one with cane, are holding me up for dear life.

48

I'm in bed when the phone rings. I find I'm not surprised to hear her voice. It feels inevitable. She's going abroad, she says, and would like to see me before she leaves, the sooner the better, tomorrow if it's at all possible. She has something to tell me. She suggests we take a walk along Lake Michigan, *for old time's sake*. She'll pick me up at the station.

I'm sleeping like the dead when the alarm clock wakes me. I take a bath and wash my hair. I eat a piece of toast with butter and jam, dress carefully, and throw my jacket on. In the hall I check my purse for my keys and wallet, take my umbrella because rain is threatening, and I'm about to step out the door and walk to the station when I turn around and walk to the phone instead.

"Hello," Esther says. Her voice is warm with sleep.

"I can't make it, Esther."

I don't pretend I've come down with the flu. I don't make any kind of story up. The truth is I cannot make it out the door, and there's no other explanation.

"I'm sorry to hear that," she says and waits.

"Good-bye, my love," I tell her, putting down the phone.

I place the umbrella back in its corner, throw my purse on the couch. I remove my jacket, hang it on its hook, and climb the stairs to my bed. Without undressing, I slip under the covers and drift off wondering what it was Esther wanted to tell me. I'll ask myself for the rest of my life most likely.

Esther is racing ahead. Either she is late as usual or escaping from something, it's not clear which. Slow down, I beg her, I can't keep up. She stops in her tracks, laughs, and takes my arm. Lake Michigan is as gray as the sky, just like the first time we walked along its shore. There's no telling where the horizon begins or ends. The uncertainty reflects my state of mind. I don't know how I've gotten here.

And it's then, holding me tightly as we walk, that she tells me she's moving to Israel. She's met someone in her Hebrew study group, someone like her. They lived through the same thing, the same camps. It's uncanny, she says. The woman's a teacher, too. They have in mind to start a school together.

"Are you in love?" I ask.

Her pace slows—she glances at me, then looks away. "I don't know yet," she says. She's never felt at home in this country, never felt understood. Until now. Is that love? she asks and shrugs.

She looks at her watch and sighs. She's late, she says, gazing out across the lake. She embraces me quickly, her body like a gust of wind. She takes my hands in hers. Her eyes have become stars. Her breath has become waves. She'll write me when they're settled, she says. She hopes I'll visit.

She lets go of my hands and backs away, her eyes trained on me, and then she turns and starts to run. Up ahead an ocean liner comes into view.

"Your luggage!" I cry out.

"I have nothing!" she shouts back and laughs. And that's when I wake up.

• • •

I find a letter in my mailbox two days later in her distinctive hand. She's moving to Israel, she writes. She's met someone in her Hebrew study group, someone like her. They've lived through the same thing. She's a teacher and they have in mind to open a school together. She'll write and let me know when they are settled. She hopes I'll visit her. She knows it's sudden, she writes as a postscript, but she never felt at home here, never felt understood. Until now.

I read the short letter again. Her script is barely legible, but the words are carefully chosen. She doesn't want to cause me pain.

Esther, I know I'll never see you again. But I'll imagine your life as it is happening in my dreams and waking hours as well. And that, a whole life long.

49

We've had a little party with cupcakes and ice cream to celebrate the last day of school, and the children are cleaning out their desks. Suddenly there's loud whispering and a rustle of activity, and Alan is leading a small committee up to the front of the room where he announces that the class has something for me. There's pushing and pulling, and then several sets of grubby little hands present me with a beautifully wrapped package. At Alan's frantic signaling, the whole class gathers at the front of the room to watch me open it.

"We hope you like it," Nancy says.

I open the flowery card and read it out loud. *Dear Miss Murphy, Thank you for being our teacher. We are going to miss you. Love, your fifth-grade class,* and underneath, they've signed their names in handwriting I've come to know so well. I unwrap the present, taking my time, savoring the moment, the ribbons and neat tape, the crisp folds of tissue paper. I hear the breathing and wheezing of little chests surrounding me. The present is revealed, a set of Yardley's English Lavender soap and talcum powder.

"Do you like it?" Karl asks.

"I love it!" I answer, and I can't help thinking Alice Kaminski is behind it. It smells just like her.

"We wanted to get you a diamond ring, but we didn't have enough money," Joanne says.

"Oh, I prefer this any day."

"Well, we're just glad you like it, Miss Murphy," Alan says, and I squeeze him so tightly I can feel his pounding heart.

At the door I give each child a hug in turn; no one is spared my affection. I thank them for being the best class a teacher could possibly have. It's a white lie at best, but so be it. While it's happening, the years collapse like dominoes, and I'm standing in the doorway sending children off for the summer into infinity.

The children are gone, except for Lydie. She's been hanging back from the rest of the group and busying herself at her desk until the others have left. I'm cleaning the chalkboard when she comes up and stands behind me.

"Miss Murphy?" she mumbles.

"Yes, Lydie?"

"Can I tell you something?"

"Sure," I say, turning to face her. This is quite an occasion. It's the first time all year Lydie's approached me of her own volition.

"Shall we sit down?" I ask her.

She shakes her head briskly and looks down at her feet.

"Well, then?"

"You're a good teacher," she says.

You could knock me down with a feather, but I try not to let my astonishment show.

"That's quite a compliment coming from you."

She glances quickly up at me. "And you're pretty." She's turned bright red and her breath is short.

"Thank you, Lydie," I say, and I may well be blushing, too.

We share a look, and it's all there in those fiery eyes of hers. *I understand you, Lydie,* I want to say. The road ahead won't be easy—there will be unsated longing, a life in hiding, shame, fury, possible betrayal, but instead I wish her a very happy summer. I want to take her strong little body in my arms and reassure her that one day things will be different, but I don't do that, either. I'm not a soothsayer.

And anyway she's flying out the door.

"Lydie!" I call out.

But she is gone.

Author's Note

Even a progressive and fiercely well-meaning white school teacher in the year 1963 is a product of her time. Karen Murphy could be taken to task for lessons that are inaccurate and culturally insensitive when viewed from today's standpoint. For these missteps and omissions, I beg the reader to forgive her and her creator. There is hardly a prejudice or stereotype that was not pervasive at the time and these are reflected in the book; to paint them over would be to whitewash history. I thought long and hard about how to convey the way things *were* while causing as little hurt to my readers as possible, but it is hurtful, nonetheless.

Lydia Stryk
Berlin, Germany
October 2021

Acknowledgments

The transition from writing plays to writing fiction is neither natural nor inevitable. It takes a leap of faith and something like a miracle. I found these during a residency at the Wurlitzer Foundation in Taos, New Mexico. My friend, writer Anna Steegmann, read several drafts and gently guided me through the basics of this very different form of storytelling. I am profoundly grateful to her. Several others took the time to read a draft and offer their honest thoughts, needed encouragement, and reservations, including pointed critiques. Thank you to Nell Stryk, Suzanne Stryk, Peter Hagan, Lisa Krimen, Dan Stryk, Kika Markham, Kathy Chalfant, Nancy Barnicle, Linda Faigao Hall and Catherine Filloux. Thanks, too, to Kia Corthron, for our many sustaining discussions about the art and business of fiction.

The story is inspired by the lives of teachers described in the revered historian Lillian Faderman's ground-breaking *Odd Girls and Twilight Lovers: A History of Lesbian Life in Twentieth-Century America* and also by Sheila Cavanagh's eye-opening and provocative paper, "Spinsters, Schoolmarms, and

Queers: Female teacher gender and sexuality in medicine and psychoanalytic theory and history." Two other sources were important to aspects of the story: Marcia M. Gallo's *Different Daughters: A History of The Daughters of Bilitis and the Rise of the Lesbian Rights Movement* and Leslie J. Reagan's *When Abortion Was a Crime: Women, Medicine, and Law in the United States, 1867-1973.* I must confess to never having read Enid Bagnold's play, *The Chalk Garden*, written in 1953, until very near the end of the process of writing this novel. I was aware that it was a staple of amateur theatres across the country and had a vague idea of the storyline. In one of the mysteries of artistic practice, when I finally picked it up and gave it a read, I discovered some uncanny connections. It's a wonderful play.

My thanks also to Joanne Seitzinger-Motley and Dolores Davison-Schroeder who provided me with essential memories, facts, and visual images.

At different points in the writing of the novel, I reached out to Lillian Faderman and Katherine V. Forrest who saw a story they felt was worthy of telling and encouraged me to tell it better. These two women have defined the course of lesbian history and literature while contributing to the transformation of the culture at large, and my association with them means more to me than I can express here. Thank you to Salem West for her generosity, openness, and good humor and to everyone at Bywater Books for taking a chance on this first novel. Special thanks to Fay Jacobs for her kind but razor-sharp editorial comments and to Elizabeth Andersen for her gently precise and sensitive copy edit of the manuscript. Ann McMan's inspired cover design was a thrilling gift. Finally, thank you to Halina Bendkowski, for accompanying me on life's (and this book's) journey.

About the Author

Lydia Stryk was born in DeKalb, Illinois. She grew up between DeKalb and London, England, and as a child also lived in the holy city of Mashhad, Iran and in Yamaguchi, Japan where she studied Kabuki and performed on the stage. After high school, she trained at the Drama Centre, London, and pursued an acting career in New York for exactly one year before returning to school to study History, Education and later Journalism.

She substitute-taught in New York City public schools, observing the social lives of children and the inner workings of the education system with fascination, and she completed a doctorate in Theatre at the CUNY Graduate Center. Her dissertation, "Acting Hysteria: An Analysis of the Actress and Her Part," was an attempt to understand why her own short-lived experience acting the woman's part felt pathological.

Her plays, including *Monte Carlo, The House of Lily, The Glamour House* (After Dark Award), *Safe House, American Tet, An Accident* (Rella Lossy Playwriting Award), and *Lady Lay* (Berrilla Kerr Foundation Playwright Award) have been produced across the United States and internationally. Actors have received awards for their work in her plays, most recently, the 2019 NAACP Theatre Award for Best Actress, for which she was also nominated for Best Playwright, for *An Accident*.

Her work has been part of festivals and playwrighting conferences and brought her to residency programs, including the William Inge Center, Hedgebrook, and the Wurlitzer Foundation in Taos, NM, where she began writing *The Teachers' Room*, a process she describes in her essay, *A Playwright Crosses the Border into Fiction*.

At Bywater, we love good books, just like you do. And we're committed to bringing the best of contemporary literature to an expanding community of readers. Our editorial team is dedicated to finding and developing outstanding writers who create books you won't want to put down.

For more information about Bywater Books, our authors, and our titles, please visit our website.

www.bywaterbooks.com

CPSIA information can be obtained
at www.ICGtesting.com
Printed in the USA
JSHW041916040422
24481JS00004B/8